Black
Lab Press

Seaside Manor Bed & Breakfast

AN *Emerald Cove* NOVEL

LILLY MIRREN

WELCOME TO EMERALD COVE

Read the duet in order...

Cottage on Oceanview Lane
Seaside Manor Bed & Breakfast

CHAPTER 1

EMILY

A seagull landed on a half-empty plate abandoned with chips on one side and eyed the remains of a milkshake in a tall glass cup. The bird flapped its wings as it lost its balance, knocking the milkshake over. The glass fell to the concrete tiles below and smashed even as Emily Jones leapt to catch it. She grimaced as milkshake sprayed across her feet and up her black leggings.

Customers glanced up, attentions attracted by the noise, then looked away again, engaging in conversation over coffee and brunch. Emily wiped the sweat from her brow with the back of her sleeve, then squatted to retrieve the pieces of glass with careful fingers, piling each shard onto the black serving tray she'd set on the ground beside the spill.

More seagulls hovered close by, landing on the fence, empty tables, wherever they could find a perch. She waved a hand in their direction.

"Shoo!"

They scattered for a few moments, but quickly returned. She'd have to clear up this mess before they'd leave. She hurried the broken shards of glass to the rubbish bin, then returned for the plates of half-eaten food. Birds were fighting over the scraps and she had to flap her hands at them a few times before they moved.

By the time she'd mopped up the spilled milkshake and wiped the tables clean, there were more customers anxious to be seated. With only two of them waiting tables, she had more than enough to do without having to clean up after a bunch of birds.

She led the customers to their seats and took orders, then disappeared into the bathroom for a few minutes of peace. She locked the stall door and sat fully clothed on the toilet lid, her face in her hands. How had she gotten here? She'd spent three years in culinary school, had worked in countless kitchens to pay her way, and yet still had thousands of dollars of debt from tuition. She'd landed a job as a sous chef in one of Sydney's up and coming restaurants and thought finally everything was about to change. Then, she'd met Callum.

Everything did change after that. And not in the way she'd hoped.

He was charming, handsome, and swept her away with his declarations of love and commitment. He'd had weekly gigs at the restaurant where she worked. A singer and guitarist in a small band, his tight jeans and messy hair had women swooning every time he looked their way—and he'd chosen her.

After losing Mum, and having never known her father, he came along at exactly the right moment. She was lonely, vulnerable, and afraid of a future on her own—Callum offered her everything she was looking for. He promised her forever, he was there for her and he loved her in a way she had never known before. He partied more than she liked. She was never one to drink much, didn't touch drugs, liked to go to bed as soon as her shift at the restaurant was done. But he stayed up for hours, drinking, experimenting, joking with his friends. She was sure he'd change if she gave him a chance. He couldn't live that way forever—he was young and in a band, so it was part of the lifestyle and she could accept it, for a while.

When his band landed a job in the tourist beach town of Coffs Harbour, it hadn't taken much convincing for him to get her to leave her restaurant job to follow him there.

There'll be plenty of cooking jobs, he'd assured her. She hadn't bothered to correct him—she wasn't a cook; she was a chef. There was a big difference. Still, she imagined there must be plenty of opportunities for someone with her skills in a place filled with hotels, resorts, and restaurants.

"You okay in there?" asked a voice. It was Helen, the other waitress working the same shift. She was no doubt feeling the push with Emily hiding away in the bathroom.

"Yeah, fine. I'll be right there."

She left the stall, washed her hands, splashed water on her face and stared at her reflection in the mirror. She'd never felt so lonely in all her life before. When Callum left for a new gig in Airlie Beach two months earlier, he hadn't seemed to feel the need to ask her to go with him. She wouldn't have gone anyway. Not after what she'd found. Not after everything that'd happened between them. They'd dated for a year, and he didn't even talk to her about his plans to move to another state. Irritation stirred in her chest.

Still, she missed having someone around who cared whether she came home from her shift at the cafe. Tonight, she'd walk down the boardwalk, up the street, and over the hill to a single bedroom apartment where she lived — it'd be

CHAPTER 2

REBECCA

*H*er eyes peeled open, shut, then blinked opened again. It was difficult, the opening part. And when they were open her vision was blurred. She couldn't figure out where she was. Not at home. Not at the station. Why was she lying on her back? Rebecca Mair squeezed her eyes shut for a few moments, then flung aching eyelids open again, widening her eyes in an attempt to focus.

Where was she?

Moving. She was moving. But on her back. The ground beneath her lurched, then turned. She was in a vehicle. Her eyes focused on a face—a paramedic. She'd worked with them often enough to know each of them by name.

"Steven?" she croaked, then coughed to clear her throat. "What…?"

He nodded, a smile brightening his tanned face. "Welcome back, Constable. Now stay with me, all right?"

"What happened? Where am I?"

"You were stabbed, that's all I know. You're on your way to Tweed Hospital. Okay? Do you understand?" His brown eyes fixed on hers, studying her, monitoring her responses. She knew that look on his face. He was worried about her, checking her vitals even as he spoke.

She attempted a nod but found that her head was secured in place by tight straps. With both hands she reached up and tried to pluck them away.

Steven gently lifted her hands away and put them at her sides. "Leave it alone, Bec. We have to make sure you don't have a neck injury."

"I don't," she replied.

He chuckled. "Let us be the judge of that."

"Where's Franklin... I mean the Sarge?"

"He's fine, he's got to take the fella into the station, from what I understand. He said he'd meet us at the hospital when he could."

She inhaled a slow breath, let her eyes drift shut. He was fine. She hadn't let him down, not this time. Memories lurched into her mind, one by one. Not a complete picture, but like a stop-motion animation—one moment at a time that her mind had to piece together to make a scene.

They'd gotten an anonymous tip about Thad Borseth, the creep who'd been stealing money from the Emerald Cafe for months. He was staying in a run-down cabin outside of town, near the beach. The sarge went in the front, Thad came out the back where she was waiting, and they'd fought. She flinched inwardly, remembering the feel of his fist connecting with her cheek, then the pummelling of her torso.

With tender fingers she reached for the place, and again Steven redirected her hands.

"Like I said, you've been stabbed. You'll be sore there for a while. I've patched you up as best I could for the ride to the hospital, but you'll need surgery. We'll have to wait and see what the doc says."

The hits to her chest must've been the knife connecting with her vest, but he'd found the tender place beneath the vest and connected with flesh.

She inhaled a sharp breath as a flutter of nerves flashed through her. What if he hit an organ? Her head felt light, her vision fading in and out. She could die.

She didn't want to die, not yet. Not this way. She wanted a chance to live first, not to spend her only days of freedom in hiding then have her life snatched away from her by a thug, a thief. That wasn't how things would end for her. Not if she could do anything about it.

With a defiant grunt, she forced her eyes open and met Steven's gaze.

He grinned. "There's my fighter. Good to see that spark in your eyes again, Constable. You're gonna be just fine."

* * *

THEY WERE TAKING her in for surgery. She lay on her back in the sterile hospital room, prepped, ready to go, but with tears in her eyes.

"Are you sure I can't call someone for you?" asked a nurse, pausing beside Rebecca's bed.

She shook her head, not wanting to make eye contact with the nurse in case the tears showed. She never wanted anyone to see her weakness, her vulnerability. She was strong, confident, private. That was all they needed to know.

The nurse gave a brief nod of the head, then wheeled a silver cart lined with medical supplies out into the hall, leaving Rebecca on her own.

There was no one to call. No one to tell. She was heading

into surgery, might not make it through, and not a single soul in the world cared. How had her life come to this?

She'd been raised in a loving family home, had plenty of friends, a good life. And now she was all alone, without anyone to say goodbye as they wheeled her into surgery. Loneliness swamped her like plunging into frigid waters that closed over her head. She couldn't breathe, couldn't speak, couldn't see a way ahead.

If she died in surgery, whose life would be impacted? Apart from the fact that she wouldn't show up to work tomorrow, how would anyone even be inconvenienced by the loss? Would there be a funeral, or would she be lowered into the ground by strangers?

Self-pity formed a lump in her throat and tears blurred her vision.

"There you are, Proby," said Franklin as he burst into the room, relief tinging his voice.

Startled, she wiped the tears from her eyes with the back of her hand. "Sarge?"

He stopped beside the bed, clenched his hands into fists, then relaxed them again. Finally, he reached for one of hers and held it. "I've been looking for you. They said you were in emergency, then I looked in the cardiac wing...anyway, I found you. That's all that matters. How're you feeling?"

Relief overwhelmed her and she couldn't speak. She shook her head slowly, desperately trying to keep the tears at bay. She knew Franklin well enough to understand that her crying would send him running from the room and she wanted him there. More than she'd thought possible. Having someone with her, even a boss who clearly disliked her, was better than no one at all.

His eyes found hers, softened and he pulled a chair up close to the bed to sit down, without releasing his grip on her hand. "Don't worry, Proby, you're gonna be okay. The doc wouldn't say much since I'm not family, but I can tell. I've seen enough people on death's door to know it when I see it, and you don't have that look. You'll pull through, I guarantee it."

She nodded, pushing down a sob. "Thanks for coming."

"Of course, where else would I be but with my partner?"

"I know I'm a disappointment, but I try..." Her voice broke.

He shook his head. "No, it's not you, I'm just an ass. Don't listen to me. I'm old and grumpy, and sometimes I say things I shouldn't."

She chuckled, then winced as pain shot through her gut. "Old? Really, boss? You're only a few years older than I am."

"I feel as old as time," he replied with a wink.

"Anyway, I appreciate you being here."

"Anyone I can call for you? Someone on their way?" he asked.

She looked at the ceiling, shook her head, lips clenched into a straight line.

He sighed. "Okay, but you let me know if you change your mind. Because there's one thing I know about you, Constable, and it's that out there somewhere are people who care about you. I don't know why you've walked away from them, why you don't want them here by your side right now, but I know they're out there."

She met his gaze, her throat aching. "How do you know that?"

He smiled. "Because as much as it pains me to admit, you're pretty darned likeable, Proby. It's inevitable that there'd be people who care."

CHAPTER 3

DIANA

TWO WEEKS LATER

*T*he caw of a crow outside her bedroom window woke Diana Jones at five a.m. The bird continued its monotone call like a metronome that couldn't be silenced; it grated on her nerves. Usually crows stayed away, since she had a large number of kookaburras who liked to perch in the gum tree at the end of the garden overnight. Still, it was there, and it had woken her before her alarm. She rubbed her eyes and swung her feet to the floor with a grunt, then pressed the button on her old clock radio to switch off the alarm. She'd let Rupert sleep this morning. Lately he'd looked more tired than ever, dark smudges beneath each eye. The doctor had told them he had to take things easy, but no one had talked about what that really meant—either she had to bear the load of running the business all alone or they'd have to sell up and move.

One glance revealed Rupert was still sound asleep and her movements hadn't roused him. He snored softly beside her. Her husband had never been a morning person, unlike her. She was grateful for her preference for the early hours, since as the owner and manager of the *Seaside Manor Bed and Breakfast* for the past twenty-five years she'd barely had a chance to sleep late more than a dozen times

Her morning was filled with routines. Shower, dress, hair, makeup. She took an envelope from the drawer where her makeup lived, stared at it a moment, ran a finger over the handwriting that spelled out her name and address, and shoved it into her cardigan pocket with a quick glance over her shoulder. Rupert hadn't moved; he lay on his side, the covers rising and falling gently with his breath. Then, she donned a pair of comfortable walking shoes and headed downstairs to begin making breakfast.

It was the only meal of the day they served at the Seaside Manor and she took pride in making sure guests would not only enjoy it but hopefully talk about it with their friends. Word of mouth had been her best marketing tool for more than two decades, and her breakfasts were a big part of that. Of course, the pristine beaches and azure waters of Emerald Cove helped as well. They'd never had a problem booking guests, but lately she'd begun turning some away, saying the rooms were fully booked even when they weren't. She knew she couldn't manage more than two rooms at a time anymore, especially now that Rupert wasn't as much help with any of the things he used to do around the place.

The kitchen was her happy place, and Seaside Manor had a spacious, if somewhat old-fashioned kitchen that let in light through a set of large windows that looked out over the back garden. Dark timber cupboards, a large kitchen island with pots and pans hanging above, and every surface gleaming. She was a stickler for cleanliness.

Diana flicked the switch on the kettle and stood waiting for it to boil while she gazed out over the lovingly maintained rows of shrubbery, flowers and climbing vines. She spent most afternoons in her garden once the guests had been taken care of and everything was done inside. At that time of day, shade from the large gum tree, a macadamia tree, and a sprawling poinciana drew long, cool shadows across the garden and gave it a pleasant, cozy feel. But now the entire garden hung in darkness, the sun wouldn't rise for hours yet and a sleepy stillness clung to the landscape. She shivered, tugged her cardigan more tightly around her plump frame, and poured herself the first cup of tea of the day from the steaming kettle.

By the time the sun had begun to warm the roof of the Manor, the four guests who'd spent the night there had eaten breakfast and retreated to their rooms. Both couples would be checked out before nine a.m., and while she waited, Diana stayed busy cleaning up in the kitchen and planning her menu for the following day. There were a few things she needed from the shops, and she also wanted to visit the Cove's new police officer. The poor woman was in hospital after she'd been stabbed by one of Cindy's cafe workers — the scandal was the talk of the town. Now he was in prison, awaiting a trial, and the officer was in the local hospital recovering from her wounds.

It had all been very dramatic, when two weeks earlier, the police had chased him down after a tip and video evidence from Cindy that Thad was stealing money from her and charging tourists for room keys from Diana's very own bed and breakfast to get them cheap food and drinks from the Emerald Cafe. It had been very vexing for Diana to discover that the Manor was involved in some sort of scam, and then for the poor police officer, a young woman who'd only been in the Cove for a few months, to be stabbed because of it—well, Diana felt the responsibility to visit, at the very least, since she wasn't sure Constable Mair had any friends or family in the area and she hated to think of her lying there, all alone, on those scratchy sheets.

Done with her cleaning, she carried a tray with a cup of tea and an English muffin with jam to the master suite on the ground floor. Anyone unfamiliar with the layout of the Manor would never guess that such a spacious suite was hidden beyond the grand staircase at the back of the structure. It was her refuge, the place she and Rupert had called home since the early years of their marriage. They had a large bedroom with sitting area, a small kitchenette that could be used for making the basics and a spacious bathroom. She set the tray on the small round table in the kitchenette, then strode to tug open the heavy, slate grey curtains that hung from the low ceiling to the thick charcoal carpeting. Once they were pulled back, a set of tall glass doors were revealed that opened onto a private verandah, hidden from the rest of the garden by large, manicured lilly pillies.

"Good morning, my love," she chimed.

Rupert struggled into a sitting position, rubbing his reddened eyes. "Good morning. It looks like I overslept. I'm sorry about that, my dear. I hope you didn't have any trouble with the guests."

She shushed him with a wave of her hand. "Never mind that, you needed your sleep. Besides, there were only four of them, and they're about to check out. I brought you some breakfast, then I'm heading into town for a few supplies. I thought I might visit the injured policewoman at the hospital as well."

He nodded as she set the tray over his lap. He reached for

the pot of tea and poured some into the empty china cup with a grimace. "Ah yes, poor woman. I hope she'll be okay."

"Cindy tells me she'll be just fine. Only it seems no one has visited her, so I'm going to do it. Cindy visited yesterday. We're trying to keep her spirits up between the two of us."

"Well, if you and Cindy can't bring a smile to her face, no one can." Rupert beamed at her then took a sip of tea.

She leaned down to kiss his lips. "I'll see you when I get back."

He nodded. "Thanks for the breakfast."

Once her guests had checked out, Diana said her good-byes to Olga, the local lady who cleaned for her and did a wonderful job of it, then shrugged on a jacket, and stopped in the small greenhouse at the bottom of the garden to cut some flowers to take with her—daisies, baby's breath, and lavender. It was a bit of a mishmash, but in the middle of winter she had no choice but to work with whatever was blooming in the greenhouse. She added some greenery from the garden, then tied it all with a ribbon from her gift-wrapping shelf in the large linen closet beside her office.

Downtown Emerald Cove was quiet at this time of year. There were a few tourists around, but not as many as buzzed along its streets in the summer months. The air was crisp, and the sky overhead looked as though it'd been freshly laundered then hung above in a blaze of blue that seemed to deepen the longer she looked at it.

She stopped at the local Foodstore, bought shaved ham from Marg Cook, the deli attendant, her frizzy blue hair stuffed into a hair net. Then, some apples, oranges, and bananas. She needed flour as well, and bacon. Finally, she checked out her purchases, carried them back to her car, and drove to the hospital. The nearest hospital to Emerald Cove was in Tweed Heads, so by the time she'd pulled into the parking lot her stomach growled.

She stuck to a routine in her life, it had helped to keep things in check when the Manor was bursting at the seams with holiday makers, but even now that her life had slowed to a more manageable pace in recent years, she'd stuck with the routine and her stomach alerted her to the fact that it was time for morning tea. Never mind, she had no intention of eating hospital food if she could avoid it, she'd simply have to wait until she got back to the Manor—there was a batch of fresh scones cooling on the kitchen bench that would be divine with some of the strawberry jam she'd made last week using fresh strawberries from the garden.

She found Rebecca Mair's room with help from a few different members of the hospital staff and after turning the wrong way twice. She knocked on the door, slightly out of breath after climbing a set of stairs to the wrong floor, then back down again. There was no response, so she tiptoed into the room, hoping the patient wasn't asleep.

"Hello?" she called.

Two large brown eyes focused on her with one eyebrow arched at the sight of the flowers.

"Hi."

"Are you Constable Rebecca Mair?" asked Diana.

The officer offered a brief nod in response.

Diana walked to the bed where she lay and offered the flowers. "How are you my dear? I brought some flowers to brighten up the room a little, they're from my greenhouse and I'm afraid that at this time of year they're not my most impressive offering but I hope you'll enjoy them all the same."

The policewoman offered a hesitant smile. "Thank you, they're beautiful..."

"You're probably wondering who I am."

Rebecca cocked her head to one side. "The thought had crossed my mind."

Diana laughed, a melodic titter that she'd caught from her mother and never thought she'd replicate but found herself utilising more and more whenever she felt a little off kilter as the years passed. One of the surprising things about getting older, she mused as she arranged the flowers in a small vase she found on a table beside the constable's bed, was that every year she grew more like her own mother, and in ways she'd never expected.

She turned to face Rebecca, then lowered herself into the armchair beside the bed. "I'm Diana Jones, I own the *Seaside Manor Bed and Breakfast.*"

"Oh, of course, I've heard of that place—seen it too. It's beautiful, lovely gardens."

Diana's heart swelled. "Thank you so much. Anyway, it was our room keys Thad was selling to tourists on the beach, so in a small way I feel responsible..." She waved a hand at the bed, unable to keep speaking as an unexpected wave of emotion rushed over her at the vision of Rebecca's slight frame tucked beneath the white sheets.

Rebecca reached for her hand, squeezed it then let go as suddenly. "It's not your fault. He was a criminal, I'm a cop. These things happen."

Diana shook off the emotion, breathed deep. "Still, I'm sorry it happened to you. I hope it doesn't sour your feelings for the Cove. This type of thing never happens in our little beach village."

Rebecca shook her head. "No, I like it just as much as I did before."

Diana thought it was a strange response; it certainly didn't reveal anything much.

"Do you think you'll stay a while?" she asked, linking her hands together in her lap.

Rebecca shrugged. "Hard to say."

"And your family...what do they think of your line of work?"

Rebecca's smile seemed forced, almost as though she didn't want to talk about her family. Diana's interest was piqued.

"I suppose they have to deal with it."

"Do they live close by?"

Rebecca looked away, staring out the window. "Not really."

It was very intriguing and yet frustrating at the same time, the way the policewoman batted away each of her questions with vague, brief answers that didn't unmask much of anything. Diana scanned the room: no other flowers, no cards, nothing to show that anyone had visited, that anyone cared.

The woman in front of her was young, most likely still in her twenties, although these days Diana found it difficult to guess anyone's age under forty. They all looked like babies to her. Regardless, why was it that a beautiful, young woman, one who seemed pleasant—kind even, if Diana's instinct was anything to go by—was all alone? Why didn't she want to talk about her family? Where were the suitors, the friends, the loved ones? It was all very interesting and confusing, and if Diana didn't have enough going on in her life, she'd have made it her mission to find out. Unfortunately, she didn't currently have the space for additional intrigue in her life.

A little deflated at not having discovered anything about Rebecca that she could pass on to Cindy next time the two of them met for tea, Diana said her goodbyes and headed back to her car. Even before she made it to the parking lot her mind had released its fixation on Rebecca and wandered back to the most pressing topic that had dominated her thoughts for months now.

What should they do with the Manor?

Rupert's doctor had told them at the last visit that with his diabetes progressing the way it was, it was time for him to slow down, take it easy. Couldn't they retire, he'd asked?

She inhaled a sharp breath as she climbed into her car and gripped the steering wheel with both hands until her knuckles whitened. What would that look like, retirement? They owned a bed and breakfast, and every day for the past twenty-five years had involved some level of work. Even when they'd taken their annual holiday, they'd always checked in on the Manor to see how things were going; managed staff, dealt with emergencies over the phone—the work never stopped.

They'd slowed things down by limiting the number of guests, and it'd helped. Only now they weren't making a profit and hadn't been for six months.

How much slower could they manage to take things? They couldn't keep going the way they had been, or before long they wouldn't be able to maintain the place and keep the high standard they'd always held. Not if they used their nest egg to pay for upkeep and repairs. They'd talked about selling, many times over the years, but neither of them had been able to bear the idea of parting with it.

She'd always hoped they'd have children and that one of their brood would take on the management of the place, but that'd never happened. She'd shed many a tear over the years, but now the memory of years of infertility didn't bring the familiar stab of pain, only a faint ache of regret. There were so many people in her life she was grateful for—Cindy, Cindy's children whom she'd always loved as her own family, her niece.

Emily lived in Coffs Harbour now, but she'd spent summers at the Manor during her teen years. Diana's younger sister, Mary, had died of breast cancer three years earlier and the memory of it still flooded her with a grief that covered her skin with a clammy sweat. She hadn't seen much of Emily since the loss of her sister, and she missed her. If she was to keep the Manor in the family, Emily was all she had. The only member of her extended family who'd loved the place at some time and whom she trusted to do a good job running it. Although Emily had a life of her own now and a serious boyfriend too, if Diana recalled correctly.

Diana turned the key and pulled out of the parking lot, careful to check both ways before accelerating onto the main road. She'd had an accident on that road, a minor fender bender Rupert had called it, a year earlier because of the crick in her neck. She hadn't been able to look all the way to the right, she'd told the officer, and because of that incident their insurance had gone up. Still, Rupert hadn't blamed her, only made her go to the physiotherapist to get the crick worked out of her neck so it wouldn't happen again.

She was so grateful for her husband. He'd stuck by her through all their years of marriage—always kind, always faithful, never holding it against her that she couldn't bear the children they'd planned, whispered over, and anticipated with hearts full of hope early in their marriage. He hadn't treated her the way Cindy's husband, Andy, had treated her friend. She shook her head as she changed lanes, her lips pursing at the thought. No, Rupert had been a good husband, and now he needed to slow down. They'd have to find a way and if that meant selling their beloved Manor, then that was what they'd do. But the thought brought her no comfort.

CHAPTER 4

ETHAN

*T*he blue sky overhead reminded Ethan Flannigan of home, though the Brisbane air was tainted by the scent of petrol fumes. He missed Emerald Cove and hadn't been back since Christmas. Still, it wasn't quite the same, what with his family splintered into pieces. Ethan lowered his gaze to the empty seat across from him. The cafe hummed with activity, people clustered in pairs and threes around small, black tables cradling mugs of steaming coffee or eating lazily from plates of toasted banana bread or hard, round protein balls.

A man slid into the chair opposite with a grin. "Sorry about that, another phone call I had to take. The building site is crazy at the moment."

"No worries, Sam," replied Ethan. "I think we're almost finished here. So, if you choose us for your next engineering job, I can guarantee that you'll be working with me, and that

I'll do the best I can to achieve the vision you've expressed today."

Sam scratched his chin with a sigh. "I believe you, Ethan. I'd work with you any day of the week, but Mammoth Engineering...well, I'm not so sure. There've been rumours."

Ethan frowned. He hadn't heard any rumours, at least not lately, but it wasn't unusual for there to be chatter. There'd been some talk a year ago, but he'd brushed it off as jealousy. Brisbane was a small city, everyone in construction knew each other to some degree, and everyone in the industry knew Mammoth Engineering. They'd come into focus five years earlier when the company seemed to emerge out of nowhere to take the lead in most of the large engineering projects across the state, and soon after that in surrounding states as well.

Ethan had been headhunted by them almost two years ago to join their engineering team. The company had grown so quickly there was plenty of opportunity for partners and one of the things Ethan had asked for when he joined the team was that they consider a fast track to partnership in the firm. He'd taken a pay cut for the opportunity and the board had met only last month to discuss it. According to his boss, it wouldn't be long before he'd receive the offer. Still, if clients were hesitant because of these rumours, whatever they were, he'd have to deal with them sooner or later, even if they were only the grumblings of envious rivals.

"Rumours?" he asked, taking a sip of his espresso.

Sam shrugged. "You know how it goes—Mammoth has grown so fast, no one can believe it could've happened organically."

"What does that mean?" Ethan's brow furrowed.

"I don't know... I heard the murmurs; I didn't say I started them." He shifted uncomfortably in his chair, his cheeks pinking. "But there are questions, people have questions, about how Mammoth managed to land those state government contracts in its first year of operation when others have tried for years... I'm sure it's nothing. Look, if you send me through the contract, I'll sign it. I trust you, Ethan. If you say it's all above board, then I believe you."

"It is... I've been with Mammoth for almost two years and all I can say is the team works hard, and we've had some good luck."

Sam's lips pursed. "Okay then." He reached out a hand and shook Ethan's. "Looking forward to it, mate. Give me a call and we'll get things moving." He downed the last of his coffee and stood to his feet. "See you soon."

* * *

THE STEEL DOORS dinged shut behind Ethan and he found himself in the lift alone. That never happened in a building with thirty floors. Well, rarely anyway. He enjoyed the solitude, momentary as it might be. Soft music floated around him as the lift rose through the building and his thoughts drifted to home. He'd lived in the city ever since he moved away from home, from Emerald Cove and the only life he'd known, to study at university when he was eighteen. Ten years later, he missed the relaxed coastal lifestyle, the surf, the golden sand, and his family.

The doors swung open and he stepped into the office. Hard, polished concrete floors, cubicles decorated in slate grey and black, and industrial light fixtures gave the place a half finished, trendy look that didn't lend itself to ease or comfort, but Ethan had grown used to the place. He strode along a wide concrete aisle, vaguely aware that the buzz of conversation was more hushed than usual. He glanced over a row of cubicles. One woman stood at her desk, a hand pressed to her forehead as she stared out of a floor to ceiling plate glass window, a phone against her ear. In the printer room, a man shuffled papers into a shredder, its churning momentarily blocking all other noise. Another woman ran into the room behind him, waiting in line for the shredder, one foot tapping with impatience.

He frowned. This wasn't the usual scene. Generally, he walked into the office to find casual conversation, meetings being held over egg shaped desks, laughter, coffee...what was going on?

His own desk was located in a cubicle up against one of the many windows that made up one long wall of the office. He slid into his chair and flicked on his computer. The flashing light of the message button on his phone caught his attention and he pressed the receiver to his ear, holding it there with his shoulder, while he logged on.

"Ethan, this is Sam, after I left the cafe, I got a call from my boss. Unfortunately, I'm going to have to back out of the deal we made, mate. I'm sure you'll hear why soon enough. Good luck to you. Call me when you're out of this mess." The sound of the dial tone buzzed in his ear.

What mess? What was he talking about?

The next message was from his own boss, Chester Vancroft. The man's thick British accent always sounded vaguely odd over the telephone, as though he was putting it on.

"Ethan, this is Chester. Give me a call when you get into the office. I'm on my mobile. It's important."

Ethan's lips drew into a tight line. He hardly ever heard from Chester. His boss took a hands-off approach when it came to his staff. A weekly status meeting was about all the attention he gave them unless something went wrong. If something wasn't going according to plan, he was on them every single moment of the day.

Something was clearly wrong.

Ethan dialled Chester's number. It rang so long he thought Chester wouldn't answer. Finally, his boss's voice filled his ear. "Ethan, thanks for calling. Just wanted to let you know that the company, I'm afraid, has had its day. I appreciate your loyal service, but it's time for us all to move onto something new."

Ethan's brows pulled low over his hazel eyes. "What do you mean? What's going on Chester?"

Chester sighed. "I'm afraid a few things have caught up with us. I can't say more than that, solicitors you know, anyway. I'll be at the office in a few minutes, we can talk more then."

Before he could say another word, Chester had hung up the phone. Ethan set the hand piece in its cradle and leaned back in his chair. Then he leapt to his feet, paced down the length of the hallway and found a man standing in the reception area, a messenger, dressed for cycling, his helmet still on his head and hands full of manila envelopes.

"Are you Max Woods?" asked the man.

Ethan shook his head.

"Lee Nguyen?"

Another shake.

"Ethan Flannigan?"

Ethan's stepped forward. "Yes, that's me."

The man pushed an envelope into his hands. "This is for you." He spun on his heel and click clacked down the concrete hallway in his clip-in cycling shoes.

Ethan slid a finger beneath the end of the envelope and ripped it open, his heart thudding against his ribcage. What was this about? He felt as though he'd walked into the middle of a play at intermission.

He scanned the single sheet of paper in the envelope. It was a letter from the CEO expressing sorrow at the dissolution of the company, thanks for the work Ethan had done, and luck for the future. There was a veiled reminder that they'd all be in this together and anything that befell one would have an impact on them all.

Ethan folded the page and shoved it into his suit pocket then hurried back to his desk. He spoke to a few colleagues along the way, but no one seemed to know anything more than he did, although many of them didn't seem as surprised. Had he missed something that was obvious to everyone around him?

Even as he packed up his desk, staff streamed from the office, boxes and bags tucked under their arms. The whir of the paper shredder continued and someone from the IT department went from workstation to workstation wiping computers. He emailed himself some key contacts, emails, and client details. Unsure of what else to do, he shut down his computer, picked up the briefcase he'd packed his few personal items into and walked away.

At the lifts, he waited patiently with a group of staff. They made idle chitchat, and one woman sniffled into a tissue. Most looked glum. When the lift doors opened, his boss, Chester stepped out, a harried expression on his usually cheerful face.

"Chester, we need to talk." Ethan fell into step beside his boss who marched along the hall towards the fishbowl he called an office.

"Right-o, Ethan, what can I do for you?"

Ethan frowned. "I want to know what's going on. Why is the company going under? We've got more business than we've ever had, I landed a big contract this morning. I don't understand."

Chester stopped, facing him with a sigh. "The owner's being charged with fraud, I'm afraid."

"Hank Mammoth?"

"That's right."

"Fraud, what did he do?"

Chester cocked his head to one side. "I can't really talk about the specifics. He's under investigation. I'd suggest you make sure all your paperwork is in order...these things tend to spread once they get started."

Chester spun around and strode away.

"What do you mean by that?" Ethan called after him.

Chester didn't respond. Ethan stood in the hallway for several moments, hands clenched at his sides. Now what would he do? He'd spent years getting to this point in his career. He'd worked hard to build a name for himself as a Mammoth engineer and now that name might tarnish everything he'd done. He wandered back to the lifts, now almost entirely alone in the empty office. Suddenly he felt very tired. All he could think about was going home. He adjusted his hold on the heavy briefcase and stepped onto the lift.

* * *

EMILY

"You seem a bit down today. Are you feeling all right?" asked Helen as she wiped the last of the tables down with a damp cloth.

The cafe doors had shut thirty minutes earlier and Emily was helping clean up before she left for the dark walk home.

"I'm okay."

"Have you heard from Callum?"

Emily shrugged. "He's called a couple of times, but I haven't answered. I don't really want to talk to him."

"That's probably for the best..." Helen's cheeks flushed pink and her gaze dropped. "I mean, I'm sorry... You're probably hurting. It's a difficult thing...going through a break-up." She busied herself stacking chairs on top of the small, round tables.

"What did you mean by that?" asked Emily, one hand pressed to her hip.

"What?" Helen's face flamed.

"That it's for the best?"

"I don't know...just the stuff he was involved in. You know..."

"Actually, I don't...well, not officially. Drugs? Is that what you're talking about?"

Helen dipped her head. "Yeah that, and other stuff. Look, I'm not sure of any of it...not my scene you know. But I've heard talk."

Emily couldn't believe it. Everyone in town seemed to know about Callum's vices except for her. How could she have been so naive? So blind to what was going on right under her nose? She'd never moved in with him. He'd wanted her to, but she liked having her freedom. If he wanted to live with her, she'd taunted him with a flirtatious smile, he'd have to marry her. He'd laughed at that and kissed the tip of her nose, vowing that he'd get around to it one day. But he had never asked, and she'd stayed in her single bedroom unit alone while he...she wasn't sure what he did. But right before he left town, she'd found drugs in one of his guitar cases.

She hadn't been looking for anything, wasn't nosy by nature. But he'd promised to meet her at his place and was running late, so for a lark she'd decided to have a go at strumming one of his guitars. Maybe she had an undiscovered natural talent for it. She'd never know if she never tried. So, she pulled it out then searched the lining of the case for a pick. When she found the small bags of white powder, at first she'd been confused. Was it something to do with guitar playing? But then it'd all come into sharp focus in a matter of moments—memories dripped like water from a leaky tap into her conscious mind. Callum with white powder on his sniffling nose. His mood swings, highs and lows that surprised her with their depth and intensity. The way he carried a guilty look on his face when she surprised him by walking into the room.

"I didn't know…but I guessed right before he left." Her vision blurred as tears swam in her eyes.

Helen patted her arm. "I'm sorry. I didn't know if I should say anything. I figured you knew, though I never understood…"

"Thanks." Emily sniffled and wiped her tears away with her sleeve. "I thought I knew *him*… but obviously I was wrong."

"Do we ever really know anyone?" Helen offered a half smile.

"I suppose not." Emily sniffled again. "What a sad thought."

Helen shrugged. "I guess, but I've come to terms with it. I've been hurt often enough to know that expectations are a killer. So now I don't have any." She chuckled and continued stacking chairs.

Emily shook her head. She didn't want to live that way.

She should've known something was up. But she hadn't. She wondered if the drugs were the only thing he was hiding from her or if there was more. So, when he left without notice for Queensland, she'd been hurt, heartbroken in fact, but she hadn't followed. And now, she avoided his phone calls. She missed him. His laughter, his dimpled smile, the way he embraced life and loved her with a passion she'd never experienced before. But she didn't want to be part of the lifestyle he'd fallen into.

When they were finished cleaning and setting up the cafe for the next day, Emily waved goodbye to the other staff and set off on the short walk to her unit. She tugged her jacket tighter around her body and shoved her hands into the pockets, hunching her entire body against the frigid wind that whistled up the beach and through the loose wisps of her hair.

Her mobile hummed in her pocket and she pulled it out, squinted at the screen in the dark.

"Hello? Aunty Di? Is that you?"

Her aunt's voice brought more tears to her eyes. A lump swelled in her throat. "Yes, dear it's me. How are you?"

She could hardly speak. It was so good to hear her aunt's voice. She wished they were face to face so she could give her a hug. "I'm fine."

"Good to hear, my dear. There's something I want to talk to you about."

"Oh?"

"Yes, you know, Uncle Rupert and I are getting older…"

"You're not that old," objected Emily, finding her voice again as the lump faded from her throat.

"That's kind of you sweetheart, but entirely untrue. We're getting older and the Manor is too hard for us to maintain on our own. We're going to have to sell the place, make way for someone younger to have a go at running it I'm afraid."

"I'm sorry to hear that, I always loved it there." Emily's heart sank. Another change, another memory from her childhood lost.

"Yes, well that's why I called dear. Rupert and I hate to sell it to a stranger. It means so much to us, after all the years we've put into it. It's part of our family, really. So, we wanted to offer you the position of manager before we do anything else."

Emily swallowed, her heart racing. "Really?"

"Yes, you're our only family and we know you'd do a great job running it. Of course, we understand that you have your own career and life down in Coffs Harbour, but we wanted you to think about it. We've decided to offer half of the business to a buyer, because we need the money for our retirement." Diana chuckled. "You'll manage the place and he'll be more like a silent investor. Rupert and I will look for a little house by the beach, somewhere we can relax and put our feet up… finally. You have no idea how much we're looking forward to that!" Diana chuckled. "And you don't have to give us an answer right away. Think about it and give me a call back when you've got questions or have made a decision."

Emily shook her head slowly as disbelief flooded through her. She could manage the *Seaside Manor Bed and Breakfast* - no more waiting tables. It was a job she could sink her teeth into, use the skills and experience she knew she had but that she'd given up for the move to Coffs Harbour to be with Callum. It didn't seem real. She'd stayed with her aunt and uncle during the summer holidays many times when she was a kid, and she loved it there. The atmosphere, the freedom, the beach…they were some of the happiest memories of her life.

"I don't have to think about it," she replied suddenly. "I want to do it. I'd love to accept. You have no idea how much this means to me." Her voice thickened with tears.

"That's wonderful!" Diana replied. "I'm so glad to hear it. When do you think you could come?"

"I'll be there on Monday."

"That soon?"

"Yes, that soon."

"I thought you'd have things to finish…you don't have to rush my dear, not if you don't want to." Diana's voice was warm, kind—it only made the decision easier.

"There's nothing here for me anymore. I'll give my notice tomorrow at work and tell my landlord, the weekend should be enough time for me to pack up."

"Well, what a surprise! Rupert will be delighted. We'll see you on Monday."

She hung up the phone and stood in the darkness, shivering as the cold seeped through her thin jacket. Her teeth chattered and she pressed the phone back into her pocket, her mind racing.

The Manor.

Diana had offered her a job that could take her away from the emptiness of her life. It was a lifeline, reaching out through the loneliness, the darkness of her days, and she would cling to it. Her only concern was the investor who would buy into the business. She should've asked more questions—would they want to participate in managing the Manor? Could she have a say in who they offered it to? Whatever the situation, she'd deal with it. This was a gift, an opportunity she couldn't pass up. The chance to have a family close by again, something to invest her life into that had meaning and purpose. With a smile she squeezed her eyes shut and jumped up and down on the spot. She laughed out loud, then buried her hands in her jacket pockets and trudged home.

CHAPTER 5

ETHAN

Their feet slapped the pavement in a steady rhythm. Ethan found his breathing matched the rhythm, almost like a musical piece. Beside him, Tim's pace matched his own, long legs striding, arms pumping.

"So, what are you going to do?" puffed Tim, Ethan's former room mate and friend from his university days. "The lease on the unit is up, I thought you'd be looking for a new place since I moved out. But now…"

Ethan grimaced. "Yeah, I'm definitely moving out. But as for my career, I have no idea."

"I asked around at work," replied Tim. "They said they wouldn't consider hiring anyone from Mammoth."

Ethan grunted. "I know. I've made a few phone calls myself. No one will touch me, it seems. Tainted by the same brush as my bosses, even though I had no idea what they'd been up to. I still don't understand what's going on. I'm hoping when I meet with a solicitor, I'll be about to find out more."

"I guess you'll have to take some time off then."

Ethan punched Tim in the arm. "Thanks, Captain Obvious."

Tim chuckled. "I wouldn't mind a break myself. Things are crazy since Mammoth went under. I think we've landed half of your contracts. We can't keep up."

"Which is exactly why your company should hire some Mammoth engineers, to help with the workload."

"But the clients wouldn't want that...they're all talking about it." Tim shook his head. "You really landed in it this time."

"Yeah, I did. Anyway, I think I'll go home to the Cove for a while. Take some time off to do some surfing, maybe build something with my hands. I miss it. I'm not sure I'm really cut out for the office life, doesn't really suit me. I get restless."

"I know what you mean." Tim stopped, pressed his hands to his hips breathing hard. "But there's no out for me. We put a deposit on a house."

"Hey congratulations, mate! That's great news." Ethan smiled and slapped Tim on the shoulder.

"Yeah, I know. I feel panicked thinking about it though."

Ethan laughed. "You'll be fine. Marrying Lisa is the best thing you've ever done."

"So, Emerald Cove huh? Will you stay with your mum?"

Ethan nodded, walking forward. Tim fell into step beside him. "Yeah, it'll be great to be home. I haven't been back much in recent years, always working. But now I can actually relax."

They said their goodbyes. Tim wished him luck. Ethan set off at a jog in the direction of his unit. Just as he found a rhythm again, his mobile phone rang.

"Hi, Mum, how are you?"

His mother's voice always brought a smile to his face. He pictured her sitting in her kitchen looking out over the backyard, the salty scent of the ocean in the air. "Hello darling, I'm well, thank you. And you? Anything new in your life?"

Ethan inhaled a sharp breath. "Yeah, lost my job."

"What? What happened? You were doing so well there." Cindy's cheerful tone quickly changed to one of concern.

"The owner has been charged with fraud, and the whole company has gone under."

"I'm so sorry, darling. I'm sure you'll come through this better than ever—any company would be lucky to have you."

He didn't have the heart to correct her. "I thought I might come home for a while, have a holiday before I look for work."

"That's a great idea. Come home, I'd love to see you."

"Thanks, Mum. I'm out jogging but I'll finish packing when I'm done. The unit was already almost completely packed up ready for me to move out after Tim's wedding. I should be able to make it to the Cove this afternoon. I'll put the rest of my things into storage before I leave. Most of the furniture was Tim's anyway, so it's already gone. The place is pretty bare. Seems like a good time to start over."

"What a wonderful treat. You've made my day."

Ethan laughed. "I'm glad. I'm looking forward to seeing you as well."

"It seems like everyone is going through big life changes at the moment," mused Cindy.

"Oh yeah?"

"Yes, well there's me—of course. And now Diana and Rupert are going to sell the Manor and move into a retirement home or something—can you believe it?"

Ethan's brow furrowed. "Really? I never thought I'd see the day they'd let go of that place. Wow, things really are changing."

"I know, it's hard to imagine us having different neighbours. Well, not entirely—Diana has asked her niece, Emily, to take over running the Manor, and she's going to sell half of the business to an investor to fund their retirement."

Ethan's heart skipped a beat. He'd always admired the Manor, looked at it over their shared fence many a time, dreamed of owning it, of living in the Cove.

"I wonder how much they'd want for it?" he mused.

"I don't really know...I could ask if you like."

He smiled to himself. "No, that's okay. I'll give her a call when I get home."

He hung up the phone and stared out over the Brisbane River as it snaked wide and brown through the city. The footpath shadowed the riverbank, the cool breeze blowing over its waters and mussing his hair.

The Seaside Manor would be a good investment. A solid place to put the money he'd saved over the past few years. There were always tourists visiting Emerald Cove, and the Manor was one of the premier bed and breakfasts in the area. In recent years, Diana and Rupert had let the business slip as Rupert's health declined, that much he knew. But whether they could build the business back up again was something he wasn't sure of—but he'd like to try. With a grin, he jogged away from the river towards the unit. He was going home to Emerald Cove.

CHAPTER 6

EMILY

*T*he road curved ahead, snaking around a sloping hillside covered in brown grass. The winter weather in Emerald Cove was milder than it'd been in Coffs Harbour. Emily scanned the town as it came into view. It hadn't changed a bit since she was a teenager.

Small, quaint, and picturesque, the town squatted on the edge of a golden beach, with small, clapboard and brick houses clustered around a series of rolling hills and stretching out against the shore.

She realised she'd been holding her breath and released it in one quick puff. She was nervous—she hadn't seen her aunt and uncle since the funeral years ago and didn't know what to expect. How would it all work? Would she fail and let them down? She'd never run anything like the Manor before, and she wasn't entirely certain she could do it. She knew how to cook and serve food, but every other part of the bed and breakfast experience was a mystery to her.

The directions to the Manor seemed to float out of grasp of her conscious mind, so she relied on her subconscious instead, turning left at the roundabout, then over the hill, left again, and then right along a long, straight road with large structures set back from the street behind impossibly green lawns and lavish gardens.

There it was.

A beautiful, three-story structure, painted all in white with forest green highlights on the architraves and shutters. The sight of it brought back a flood of memories—days lived in swimsuits, riding bikes with the crusted salt in her hair, sunburn so bad it pushed blisters to the surface of her back, and the boy next door.

The gravel on the long drive crackled beneath the crawling tyres. She pulled her car into a lot, hidden from the road by a manicured green hedgerow. Then she climbed out, and with a glance at her suitcase in the back seat, decided to leave it there for now and headed for the front door.

She stopped at the door, stared at it a moment, then turned the handle and stepped inside. There was a reception counter close by with a small, silver bell on it. She rang the bell, then waited with her hands linked together, heart thudding. A sweeping glance took in the majestic staircase, the dark hardwood timber floors, and wood panelling on the walls with chandeliers overhead. The room she stood in took up half of the ground floor, a wide living area stretched out on either side of the entrance, one area a formal sitting room, the other a lounge with a large fireplace, bric-a-brac on tables, soft, floral print armchairs, and cozy book shelves stacked with books.

"There you are! Welcome home." Auntie Di swept into the room in a navy-blue dress dotted with small red flowers, her dark-brown bob brushing her shoulders and brown eyes twinkling.

Her words brought a lump to Emily's throat. *Home*. It was a word she hadn't spoken out loud in a long time.

She embraced Diana. "Auntie Di, it's so good to see you. It's been far too long."

"Yes, it has." Diana wiped her eyes with a fingertip. "How beautiful you are, look at you—you've become a young woman. And so much like your mother." Diana regarded her with a wide smile and reddened eyes for a moment, then reached for her arm. "Come on, let's have a cup of tea. You must be tired after that drive."

* * *

"What do you mean you've found an investor? We only spoke on Friday, now it's Monday...how is that possible?" Emily's stomach did a flip-flop.

She'd known her aunt and uncle were selling half of the business, but she'd hoped she might have a role to play in choosing the person she'd be working alongside. It could be a disaster if they picked the wrong person. Besides, she had ideas for the Manor, things she wanted to do to help bring the business back to profitability. She'd been thinking about it all weekend long and was excited about the possibilities. What if the new investor didn't see things her way, or worse yet, what if they wanted to keep everything exactly the way it was now?

Diana beamed. "I know, can you believe it? Rupert and I are delighted. We thought it would take months, maybe even years, to locate the right person. We're picky, you know. We wanted it to be someone we could trust, someone we believed would take the Manor and treat it with love. Of course, we thought about you as well, and wanted to find you a business partner you'll be able to work closely with, and we've found just the man."

39

A man? Great. No doubt he'd want to take over completely, and she'd have no voice in any of the decisions about the business.

She sighed, rubbed her hands over her face. "I know, I'm really happy for you guys. And honestly, I'm so honoured and thrilled that you'd consider letting me manage the Manor for you. It's got a special place in my heart, and I know how much it means to the two of you."

Diana's eyes glinted, she leaned forward and reached for Emily's hand. "Rupert wanted to be here when we talked to you about this, but unfortunately he's not feeling well after we spent the morning scrubbing and cleaning in preparation for your arrival..." Diana shook her head. "Never mind, I'm sure he'll be down for dinner and you can catch up then. What we wanted to tell you is this—we're not asking you to manage the Manor."

Emily's heart fell. She knew it was too good to be true. All weekend she'd wondered why they'd chosen her to run the place. It was a first-class bed and breakfast, or at least it had been in its prime. And she knew nothing about how to manage it.

"We don't want you to be the manager, well not only the manager, I wanted to tell you in person that we're bequeathing half of the business to you. Giving it to you. It's yours."

Emily gaped. "What?"

Diana chuckled, squeezed Emily's hand. "We could've waited until we dropped off the perch, of course. But then, who knows how long that would be. We wanted to see you thriving here long before that, it'll bring us so much pleasure. Of course, you don't have to accept—I understand that it means a long-term commitment and if you don't want that—"

"I do," interrupted Emily. A cold sweat broke out across

her forehead. They were giving her half of the Manor? Things like that didn't happen to her.

"Well, then that's wonderful. Half of the business will be yours. You'll be a partner with an equal share in the business, and you and Ethan will take the Manor to amazing heights, I know it."

"Ethan?" Emily's heart fell into her gut as fast as it'd leapt for joy only moments earlier. "Do you mean Ethan Flannigan, the boy next door?"

Ethan Flannigan.

At the sound of his name the image of his face drifted across her mind's eye. He'd been a few years older than her, tall, skinny, and mischievous. Always pulling pranks on the rest of the gang of kids from the surrounding streets who'd travelled to the beach and back together, even to the occasional movie in the old cinema on the main street set on the second floor above the Foodstore.

She'd had a crush on him then. The kind of crush that had her mooning about the manor, crying when no one was looking, and staring at her reflection in the mirror as she mourned the fact that he'd never see her the way she saw him, never love her as she did him.

She smiled now, remembering how desperate and deep those feelings had run. That was before she'd lost her mother, back when the world had seemed like a warm and friendly place where anything was possible. She didn't feel that way anymore, didn't love that way either.

Even as Ethan's face filled her thoughts, her cheeks flushed with warmth and the familiar stab of shame punctured her chest. There'd been a time when he'd laughed at her, humiliated her, changed her entire perspective of her adolescent self. She'd hidden away from the world after that, then left to return home to Sydney to go back to school, where her mother, who was working shifts at the local hospital, was waiting for her at the airport, still dressed in her nursing scrubs. She hadn't seen Ethan since.

Diana's eyes widened. "Well, yes but of course he's not a boy anymore. I forgot that you two were friends until he brought it up when we signed the paperwork yesterday."

"You've signed the paperwork?" This was getting worse and worse. There was no way to reverse it then, if they'd completed the documentation. She'd hoped maybe she could talk them out of it, find a silent investor that none of them knew. Someone who'd stay out of the day to day running of the business.

"You'll manage the guest services and the kitchen, and Ethan would like to take on maintenance and grounds. Says he's looking forward to getting his hands dirty again after working in an office for so long."

Emily nodded, her face burning. She'd hoped Ethan Flannigan had moved away from the Cove and she wouldn't have to see him again after what'd happened the last time they were together as teenagers. But it seemed she'd not only see him but would be sharing a business with him and would likely run into him on a daily basis.

With a sigh, she ran fingers through her long, sandy-blonde hair, pushing it back behind her shoulders. "I'm sure it'll work out well."

"And Rupert and I have a few retirement communities to look at this week. We've decided to get out of your hair as soon as I've trained you in the basics, so probably in two weeks."

"There's no rush," said Emily, her brow furrowed. "This is your home…"

"No dear, we want to go. Rupert can't keep traipsing up and down these stairs, and honestly, I need a break as well. We want to move. It's time, and we're so happy with how everything's turned out we could jump for joy—if it wouldn't break a hip." She slapped one hip and winked.

Emily couldn't help laughing. "Okay, if that's what you want."

"It is. I'm thrilled, and I'm so glad you're back in Emerald Cove. I've missed having you around."

"Me too," replied Emily, and she meant it.

CHAPTER 7

ETHAN

*R*unning in the Cove was different to running along the bikeways in the city. Ethan pulled to a stop at the front gate and looked in the letterbox as sweat trickled down the sides of his face. There were a few bills, but not much mail came to his childhood home these days. Not like when he was a kid. He recalled running up the driveway with envelopes pressed to his chest — a big pile that threatened to break free and fall to the ground if he relaxed his grip. Now, it was one or two envelopes, if that, and only delivered every second day.

He flicked through the mail, realised that none of it was for him and carried it, still puffing, up to the house. He left it on the front step, then jogged into the backyard. He'd been working on building a new dining table for Mum, as a thank you gift for everything she'd done in letting him stay at the house indefinitely and telling him about the Seaside Manor investment.

The paperwork had gone through a few days ago, and the solicitor called today to tell him it was official: he was now the part-owner of the bed and breakfast next door. He could hardly believe it. The decision had been an impetuous one, but with each day that passed he grew more and more excited about the project. He'd work on the place, update it a bit and make sure it was in good hands before he returned to Brisbane. In the meantime, he could relax, surf, enjoy a break away from the office. He could feel the ever-present knot of muscles in his shoulders releasing from all the sleep, exercise, and fresh air he'd gotten since he arrived less than a week ago.

The table was sheltered in the garden shed, an open structure that was so old the timber walls had faded to a pale grey. He'd lined the floor with loose hay to keep out the mud, and the tabletop sat legless on a pair of sawhorses. He ran a hand lovingly over the smooth timber surface. The red gum timber fairly glowed in the fading twilight.

The sound of footsteps over the nearby fence thudded in the quiet. His eyes narrowed and he tip-toed to the fence. There was a gate that'd been built into the timber palings, Rupert had crafted it twenty years earlier so that the children could go back and forth between the two properties without having to go out onto the street. He slipped the rusted chain up over the top of the fence post and pushed open the gate. It creaked, then stuck in place, half open, against a stout green bush. He slipped through it and walked to the back of the garden where he'd heard the noise—if it was Diana, he wanted to talk to her about the Manor.

A young woman crouched over a climbing vine; her eyes fixed on one of the leaves. With a sigh, she stood to her feet. He saw she carried a basket under one arm, strands of clipped greenery filling it. When he saw it wasn't Diana,

Ethan decided it must be a guest, so he might as well say hello and make her feel welcome.

"Hi there," he said, waving a hand. "Enjoying the garden?"

She startled, then faced him with wide smoky grey eyes. Something about her was strangely familiar, yet a name eluded him. Where did he know her from? Her long, blonde hair swayed down her back like a waterfall, then she crossed her tanned arms over her chest as her grey eyes narrowed on him.

"Ethan Flannigan?"

He chuckled. "Uh, yeah—that's me. And you are…?"

"I'm Emily Jones, your new business partner."

With a hand outstretched he stepped forward. "Emily, wonderful to meet you. I'm so glad we'll be running the Manor together. It's such a beautiful property, I'm excited about what we can do with it."

She shook his hand but seemed hesitant to do so with her lips pulled into a tight line. He wondered if he'd offended her in some way.

"Is everything okay?" he asked.

She faced him with a smile he couldn't decipher. "We've met before Ethan…many years ago. I'm surprised you don't remember."

It all came back to him then, the little girl with the blonde pigtails had become the feisty teenager who'd followed him and his sisters around all summer long a few times during their childhood. She'd stayed at the Manor and had been part of the neighbourhood gang, as Mum always called them—kids who spent the entire summer running wild all over the Cove until the sun set each evening. Emily was one of them. She'd been there, but he'd barely noticed. She'd played mostly with Adele, his younger sister, while his attention had been focused on surfing, fishing, and skateboarding.

"Oh yeah," he said. "I remember you now... With the pigtails."

She cocked her head to one side. "I suppose I wore pigtails at one time. Although not for years..."

"Welcome back to the Cove," he said.

Her lips pursed. "Thank you. I'm looking forward to our partnership as well. My aunt and uncle tell me you'll be working in the garden and doing maintenance while I run the place..."

"Well, not exactly," he countered, brow furrowed. "I mean, yes, but of course I'll be involved in running the Manor as well. We'll be doing it together." He ended the statement with the kind of smile that usually broke through the female reserve in his experience, but it didn't make a dent on her pucker.

"Ah...I see," she said. "Well, I guess we have some things to work out."

"I guess so."

She turned away, walking back towards the Manor. The sun winked below the roof, casting a long, dark shadow over the garden and them standing in it. The cold came too, and Ethan felt it seep through his sweat-soaked running clothes. He shivered.

"Okay, good night."

She nodded. "Good night, Ethan. Glad we could catch up. Let's talk soon."

Then she was gone, striding for the back door and slipping through it. An internal light flickered on, and he was left standing in the darkening garden alone, a half smile fading from his face. Emily Jones, of course—he should've recognised the name the moment Diana told him about giving her niece the other half of the business. From what he recalled of Emily, she'd been a quiet child with big, stormy eyes. She'd certainly grown into a beautiful woman, even if she did appear to have a chip on her shoulder.

He shook his head at the back door, then left through the side gate and ran to the house. If he was out much longer, Mum would wonder what'd happened to him.

* * *

INSIDE, there were no lights on in the house. He listened for a moment. Petal, his mom's fluffy, white, and very spoiled dog, trotted over to greet him, her toenails scritch-scratching the hardwood floors.

He bent to rub behind her ears. "Good girl," he said.

Mum's voice wafted down the hall to him. He followed the sound and found her in her office. He walked to the kitchen, switched on a light, then ducked into the office to wave. She waved back keeping the phone pressed to her ear.

"Yes, I understand. Thank you so much for calling," she said.

In front of her, an accounts book lay open with paperwork scattered all around, covering every square inch of her desk. She hung up the phone and offered him a tired smile.

"There you are, I was about to send out a search party."

He grinned. "I was introducing myself to my new business partner."

One of her perfectly plucked eyebrows arched high. "Oh? And?"

"Why didn't you tell me Emily Jones was the little girl with pigtails who trailed after Adele every summer?" He shook his head. "And I get the feeling she doesn't have the warm fuzzies for me."

"Really?" Mum stood and stretched both arms over her head with a wide yawn. "Sorry, I thought you knew who she was. I doubt it really matters...She seems like a lovely young woman, I'm sure you'll get along great once she gets to know you better."

He shrugged. "I suppose we'll see. Want a cuppa?"

She nodded. "Yes please, in a vat."

He chuckled. "Hard day?" He wandered into the kitchen and flicked on the kettle before rummaging through the cupboard for the biscuit tin. He pulled out three chocolate biscuits and handed one to Mum, the other two he set down on the bench for himself.

"Get a plate, please," she reminded him with a head tilt.

He laughed. "Yes, Mum." Some things never changed.

"You know, you get more handsome with each passing day," she said, cupping his cheek with one hand.

He sighed. "You have to say that, you're my mother."

"Still, it's true." She stood on tiptoe to kiss his cheek.

They filled cups with hot tea, then carried them and the plates with biscuits to the back porch. They sat in comfortable wicker chairs side by side and set the drinks and plates on a glass table.

Ethan took a bite of biscuit and then studied his mother. "So, what's going on? Why did you have such a hard day?"

She shrugged. "I've been working on the accounts for the cafe. My solicitor called…" She eyed him, her cheeks pinking. "He's taken Dad's name from the business registration."

Ethan's throat ached. He hated how their family was being torn apart. He knew now it wasn't likely his parents would reconcile, but it still hurt to think of the separation as permanent. Removing his father from the cafe's ownership was another one of those steps that signalled an end to what they'd shared as a family.

"I'm sorry, Mum, but I think it's for the best."

"Yes, I know it is. Still, it's hard… I'm so angry with him for the way he risked my cafe; I could've lost it thanks to him.

But that doesn't mean I'm glad to have him out of my life entirely. I suppose this was the last step before the divorce."

"And no second thoughts?" he asked.

She sighed. "No...I'm sure about it. I can only imagine that Keisha wants to marry him, though heaven knows why she'd want to marry a broke man twice her age. Still, I'm not going to stand in their way."

"What will it mean for the debts?" he asked.

She shook her head. "Not much. I've paid off a good chunk of the loans he took out against the cafe, so I'll continue with that until they're gone. I don't want to have it hanging over my head; I want it done with and out of the way. Sarah's been helping me figure it all out. But having his name taken off the cafe means he can't do it again."

He studied the dark backyard, the outline of bushes black against the pink sky. A muscle in his jaw clenched. He hated what his father had done, but he still loved the man. Family relationships were complicated—a lesson he was learning more with each passing month. How could he love and respect a man who'd treat his own wife that way? And yet, he did, and in time he knew he'd forgive him. His father had a way of making even his harshest critic smile at his charm, and Ethan knew he was no exception. He couldn't stay angry at his dad even if he'd wanted to.

"That's good. What about the house?"

"He's still on the title. Although I've been thinking about downsizing...don't tell your sisters yet. I'm not sure, and I don't want them to be upset."

He squeezed her shoulder. "Don't worry, Mum. I won't say anything."

"Thanks, honey. The solicitor said I could sue him for the rest of the debt..." She glanced at Ethan, a pained expression on her face.

"Uh huh," he replied, not wanting to get in the middle of things.

"But he also said that since Andrew doesn't have any assets, I probably wouldn't get anything from him, and the court costs and legal fees would be more than the debt itself…so it's not really worth it."

Ethan breathed a sigh of relief. The last thing he wanted was for his parents to go to court as enemies. If their family wasn't already in pieces, that would be enough to tear it completely to shreds. His younger sister Adele always took his father's side, the eldest, Sarah, stood by their mother, and he'd be caught in the middle with nowhere to go.

"Seems like it wouldn't be a good idea, then," he said.

She nodded. "No, just easier to pay back the debt I suppose. And I thought that if I sold this place and got a small house by the beach, I could probably retire before I'm ninety." She chuckled. "If I'm lucky."

"I'm so sorry, Mum. Maybe I can—"

"I'm not taking your hard-earned money so don't even try to convince me," she replied, her chin jutting forward. "You've got your whole life ahead of you, hopefully with a wife and children. You'll need to save for all of the wonderful things you're going to do. I'll take care of my own problems; don't you worry about me."

He smiled, patted her arm. "Well, remember I'm always here and happy to do what I can."

"I know," she said, her eyes glimmering in the dull evening light.

CHAPTER 8

DIANA

*T*he quiet of her office was always a balm to her soul. Diana gazed around the small space, marvelling at the way it hadn't changed in so many years. She'd redone the decor about ten years earlier, but since then it looked essentially the same. The small, reading light on her desk gave off an amber glow that fitted the room with a nostalgic feel that suited the moment.

It was her last cup of tea in her office alone. She'd trained Emily on how to run the Manor and would give her the key to the office that afternoon. From then on, it'd be Emily's office. Diana's chest ached as a lump grew in her throat. She was ready for the next season of her life, ready to move on and let Emily take her place, but it still hurt to say goodbye to the familiar rhythms of her life.

The office had been a quiet refuge, away from the chaos of everything going on in the bed and breakfast in the early years, and then from the demands of an ailing husband more recently. Although she shouldn't complain, Rupert had been a hard-working and considerate husband to her, and she looked forward to the quieter days ahead the two of them would share.

The old-fashioned landline with long, looping cord on her desk rang and she picked up the receiver. "Hello, Seaside Manor. This is Diana."

"Di, it's Rupert. I've found our new home!" His voice spilled over with a joy that was infectious.

She smiled. "Really? That's wonderful. Where is it?"

"It's in the Emerald Cove Mews that we were talking about yesterday. It has a golf course, swimming pool, sauna, games room as well as the independent living units we like. They've got nursing staff on a twenty-four hour roster for the folks who need a higher level of care…and we might get there one day, I suppose. But the gardens are lovely, and you get your own small space to grow whatever you like. I think you'll love it. When can you come and see it?"

Tears filled her eyes as she studied the photographs hanging on the wall of her at the Manor with guests, dignitaries, and friends. "I can come later, after I've served the guests tea and biscuits if you like."

"Perfect," he replied. "I've got a tour booked with the office here at five, do you think you could be here?"

"I'll be there. Thanks Rupert, it sounds amazing. I'm so glad you went out today. We're running out of time to find somewhere if we're going to meet that two-week deadline I promised Emily."

He huffed. "Don't you worry about that. We don't have to stick to any time frame, but I think we'll make it anyway, if you like it here."

She hung up the phone and leaned back in her chair. Time to set out afternoon tea for the few guests they had staying that night. Emily was busy meeting with suppliers in nearby Tweed Heads. It was important, Diana had told her, for her to make a personal connection with everyone they worked with. After introducing her niece to each vendor over the phone, she'd set up in-person meetings for Emily to attend. Which meant that she'd be managing the Manor on her own for a few hours, perhaps for the last time.

She pushed the chair back a few inches and pulled open the desk's bottom drawer. From beneath a neat pile of notebooks and personalised stationery, she tugged free an envelope. The flap hung open, jagged edges of the envelope hiding what she knew to be three sheets of paper with handwriting covering each. She stared at the handwriting on the front of the envelope: her name and the address of the bed and breakfast, in stilted, black ink.

The first time she'd seen the letter, she'd been seated in that exact same place going through a pile of bills and junk mail. She hadn't expected it. It'd given her a jolt of panic and shock that'd lasted for days. Rupert had threatened to take her to the doctor in case she'd had a small stroke. But no, she assured him she hadn't. Perhaps it was a virus, was all she'd said. She couldn't tell him about the letter, hadn't expected the past to show up now. Not after so many years. If only she'd done things differently, it wouldn't be happening. It wouldn't threaten everything that mattered in her carefully constructed life. But it was too late for regrets now.

In the kitchen, she placed freshly baked Anzac biscuits on a tray, alongside slices of banana cake. She carried the tray to the living room and set it on a table. Then returned for the pots of steaming hot tea and matching china cups and saucers. When everything was laid out, she rang a small bell and stood to one side as three children rushed up and piled plates high with food, soon followed by their parents at a more relaxed pace.

"This looks delicious, thank you!" declared their mother.

Diana smiled and nodded as Cindy popped her head around the corner and winked. Diana made her excuses, fixed a small tray with tea and cake, and hurried to meet her friend. They kissed cheeks and walked side by side back to the office. Diana set up the tea and cake between them and they settled into chairs on either side.

"I can't believe you won't be living here soon," mused Cindy with a sad smile. "Times are changing."

"Yes, it'll be very different. I'm still trying to wrap my head around it as well. We'll simply have to make more of an effort to see one another, since we can't pop through the gate in the fence."

Cindy's eyes glistened. "That's right, we'll have to use the phone more and you can come down to the cafe to see me— we'll have our tea and treats there."

"Sounds perfect. You know I love you like a sister." Diana swallowed around the lump in her throat.

Cindy's brow furrowed. "You too, Di dear. What's brought this on? You're not sick, are you?"

Diana shook her head. "No, it's nothing. I only wanted to say it...important to tell people every now and then I think." She sniffled, reached for a tissue, and blotted her nose.

"Yes, of course it is. On another subject, before you make me cry, what do you think about Ethan and Emily working so closely together?"

Diana wiped her nose again, dropped the tissue in the bin beneath her desk. "I think it'll be great."

"Not too volatile?" Cindy arched an eyebrow.

Diana had thought of that. And from what she'd seen between the two of them, she knew Cindy had a point. "I think there's a bit of a connection there, a spark maybe."

"Do you think so?" Cindy's eyes narrowed. "Hmm, interesting. Is it a spark or antagonism?"

Diana chuckled. "And besides, if it becomes too much of a

problem, I've worked a clause into the contract that allows either of them to buy out the other. I didn't want the Manor to leave the family, but even if Ethan buys it, I feel like he's part of my family, so I'd be fine with that."

"Well then, it sounds like you've thought of everything."

Diana beamed. "I do my best."

There was a knock on the office door, a brisk tap of knuckles. Cindy hurried to open it and the new constable, Rebecca Mair, stepped inside, dressed in her uniform and with her hands clenched into fists at her side.

"Good morning," said Rebecca.

"Well, good morning to you Constable Mair. What a pleasant surprise." Diana hurried around the desk to shake her hand and ushered her into a chair beside Cindy, who'd resumed her seat. "Can I get you a cup of tea and a piece of cake?"

Rebecca eyed the cake. "No, I can't stay — I came to say thank you."

Diana tried to think of some reason the young woman in front of her would be thanking her but drew a blank. She didn't remember doing anything for Rebecca. Hadn't seen her since her visit to the hospital, and she'd been thanked for the flowers then.

"Well, it's lovely to see you," replied Diana, masking her confusion.

"Thank you both for visiting me in the hospital." Rebecca linked her hands together in her lap, fingers squeezing tight. "I don't have family or friends in the area, so I really appreciated that…"

Diana's heart squeezed and she exchanged a pitying look with Cindy. "Yes, of course, we were happy to do it. I hope you're feeling better."

"Much better, thanks." Rebecca stood. "Anyway, that's all I wanted to say. I'm sure I'll see you around town. Bye." She nodded to Cindy, then Diana and left, pulling the door shut behind her.

"Well, she's a quiet one," remarked Cindy, still staring after her.

"She certainly is."

"I wonder what her story is?"

Diana shook her head. "I don't know...but she seems strong, you know, beneath the surface. Tough even."

Cindy nodded. "True. I wonder where she's from."

Diana shrugged. "I have no idea. I did ask Franklin the last time I saw him. I took him a casserole and pried a little."

"Of course you did," chuckled Cindy.

Diana grinned. "But he wouldn't tell me a single thing. It was a complete waste of grass-fed beef."

* * *

REBECCA

The red brick building loomed in front of her and Rebecca squinted at it through the brilliant winter sunshine. Overhead, a blue sky sparkled crystal clean after a morning shower of rain. Droplets were still scattered on blades of grass and leaves around the nearby park, and over the bonnets of cars parked in the police station parking lot.

It was her first day back at work. Her injury was almost entirely healed, at least on the outside. The doctor told her she'd need to take it easy for a few more weeks, since she still had some internal healing to do after the surgery that'd stitched her spleen back together. But she felt good, great in fact. She wished she could get back into her boxing and running routine, but the only exercise she'd been allowed to do was slow walks along the beach and lifting light hand weights. She could feel her muscle mass disappearing with each passing day, and it frustrated her to no end after all the hard work she'd done to build it up.

She reached into her car and pulled out her lunch bag. Another car careened into the lot and she watched as Franklin lurched out, carrying a tray of disposable coffee cups in one hand and a stack of files in the other. He didn't see her standing there and rushed at the building in a flurry of footsteps and juggling. Halfway there, his phone rang. He shoved the files under one arm, reached for the phone and answered it, head down as he trotted up the few steps that led to the double automatic glass doors.

They began to open with a swish, then shut again as quickly. Franklin plunged into the doors headfirst, slapped a hand to his forehead and cursed loudly. Coffee cups threatened to fly in every direction and he deftly caught each one, setting them straight again. Then he slapped the doors, and they swung open, then he strode through, still cursing.

Rebecca laughed out loud, then pressed a hand over her mouth to keep him from hearing. Sometimes her boss seemed like an uncoordinated, unruly child. Other times, he was a strong, focused cop running down the bad guys without a moment's thought for his own safety. He was an enigma, there was no doubt about it. And the more she got to know him, the more she realised how much she didn't know.

With a shake of her head that set her long, brown ponytail bobbing, she slipped her blue cap on and walked into the station.

Once she'd buzzed through into the office, she wondered for a moment why Steph wasn't sitting in reception, then dismissed the thought as the scent of smoke greeted her. What was going on? Was there a fire? Why weren't the alarms sounding?

She hurried towards the kitchen, breaking into a run the closer she got when she noticed the entire office was empty of staff. They were in here somewhere, but where? What'd happened?

She plunged through the kitchen door and was met with a shout of "Surprise!"

Her heart stopped beating for a moment before her lips widened into a grin. "What on earth?"

"Welcome back, love," said Steph, embracing Rebecca.

Rebecca shook her head. "I can't believe you did all of this for me..." She scanned the group. Everyone was there, all smiling. She swallowed around a growing lump in her throat.

"Of course, we did," replied Franklin, waving his arms in a wide gesture. "We're all glad you're back. The level of testosterone in this place was getting a bit rich. We're grateful you're here. Maybe this lot will stop acting like a bunch of untrained dogs now." He laughed and the rest of the group shouted their approval.

One by one, they greeted her with handshakes, welcoming her back to the office, glad she was okay, hoped was she feeling better... She responded with soft reassurances that she was fine, happy to be working again, sick and tired of daytime television, ready to arrest some bad guys.

There was cake on the kitchen bench, with icing in an impressive shade of blue to form a police cap, and white on the top and sides. Sparklers as candles were the source of the smoke she'd smelled, and she watched them burn with a smile, then soaked in the warmth of the round of applause that followed. And as Franklin regaled the group with a lively and humorous tale of what'd happened the day she was stabbed, she couldn't help laughing along with the rest of the group as the dread she'd felt about returning to work and facing everyone again faded away, and was replaced by a feeling of belonging she hadn't experienced in years. She inhaled a slow breath, her heart swelling. So this was what it felt like to have a home—she'd almost forgotten.

years, but in the past two weeks she'd seen every single one. After the first few days in her new routine, she hadn't been able to sleep late. Regardless of that fact, it still felt like a punch to the gut every time her alarm woke her.

With a grimace she pushed down the covers, swung her feet to the floor, and padded to the bathroom, pulling her dressing gown over her arms, and cinching it at her waist. By the time she'd sat on the toilet, her teeth were chattering, and her body filled with a dull ache. She rubbed her eyes, still bleary with sleep and yawned.

Would she ever get used to waking before dawn?

There was so much to do before the guests came down to breakfast. And this morning was her first time doing it alone. Diana and Rupert had moved out of the Manor the day before, leaving her and Ethan to run the place. She'd helped transfer their things to their new home and found it to be quaint, well-equipped, and cheerful. The retirement community was set on the side of a gently sloping hill that looked down over Emerald Beach. They could walk there and to the main street for croissants, coffee, or anything else they needed. It was the perfect set up for them, and Emily found her throat tightened when she waved goodbye, as a swell of emotion surprised her.

She'd grown used to having them in the Manor with her, a family—smiling faces to cheer her on as she learned the ropes. Now, they were gone, and she was on her own. They hadn't moved far though, as Diana kept reminding her. Still, she was alone again—a state she was accustomed to, but which left an empty feeling in her gut that ached a little.

She'd hardly seen Ethan over the past two weeks; he'd spent most of his time out in the garden or fixing things around the Manor. And that suited her fine. Every time she saw him her tongue stuck to the roof of her mouth and irritation buzzed in her chest, along with a pang of shame. She couldn't shake the memory of the last time they'd seen each other as teenagers.

After showering and dressing, she got to work in the kitchen making breakfast for their two guests. It seemed bizarre to put so much effort into making a meal for only two people. And with many bedrooms in the Manor unoccupied, one the first things she wanted to work on was improving the occupancy rates. If she didn't do that soon, she and Ethan wouldn't be able to pay the bills, let alone draw an income to live on.

The first thing she did was flick on the overhead fluorescent lights. The kitchen sprang into sharp relief against the darkness that hovered outside its windows and in the living areas. She went throughout the ground floor, flicking on lamps to give some light in case her guests were early risers. There were always a few night lights on, but she preferred to have the place well lit in time for breakfast. Then, she set a fire going in the hearth, piling logs on top of a starter, and lighting it with a piece of rumpled newspaper. When the flames crackled and rose, she straightened with a satisfied smile then returned to the kitchen.

She pulled a carton of eggs from the fridge, along with bacon, fresh baby spinach and butter. She was making eggs benedict, one of her favourite breakfasts—it was always a crowd pleaser. The joy of putting together dishes of her choosing washed over her as she got to work. No matter how difficult the days ahead would be, she was filled with a sense of hope and gratitude that she got to work at the Manor, a place that'd always held a bit of romantic mystique to her. And she was able to cook for people again, which was her favourite thing to do.

Before she cooked the eggs, she pulled two pans of bread

dough that'd risen the previous day from the fridge, set them on top of the stove and preheated the oven. Fresh sourdough bread with eggs—her stomach grumbled in anticipation.

She boiled the kettle and made herself a cup of tea, took a sip even as her stiff fingers warmed around the mug. The steam tickled her nose and with another sip she set it down and pushed the bread into the oven.

Just as she was about to get started on the hollandaise sauce, the back door opened, and Ethan strode in. He trekked past her, wearing board shorts and a hoodie, along with a pair of work boots with mud covered soles, and sat at the kitchen table with a grunt.

"Morning," he said, smiling so that the dimple in his cheek flashed.

Her eyes narrowed, and she pressed her hands to her hips. "Good morning, Ethan. Could I trouble you to leave your boots at the door? You've scattered mud and dirt across the entire floor."

His eyes widened and he scanned the path he'd taken through the kitchen. "Ah...sorry. Don't worry about it, I'll clean it up."

She turned her back and searched for a whisk in one of the drawers. Finding her way around the kitchen, discovering where everything was, would take some time. She located it, then went looking for a bowl. It'd been so much simpler with Diana there to help.

When she glanced his way again, she saw him sweeping up the trail of dirt he'd left behind in stockinged feet. She inhaled a slow breath. She could do this.

The bowl located, she cracked and separated eggs, her thoughts wandering to the list of things she had to do that morning. She was doing her best to ignore the man helping himself to a cup of coffee in her kitchen, getting in her way when she had a breakfast to prepare. His very presence was irritating enough, his silence maddening.

"So, first day on your own, huh?" he said, leaning against the bench to sip his coffee.

She glanced at him, a tight smile on her lips. "Yep. That's right."

She needed the butter, which was on the bench behind him. With a deep breath, she stepped close, leaned around him, and closed her hand over it. When she glanced up, he was watching her with laughter dancing in his hazel eyes. Was he mocking her? She could feel the heat from his body. A tingle ran up her spine.

She snatched the butter away and carried it to the stove. "Is there something I can help you with?" She hadn't meant to sound rude, abrupt, but somehow, he brought that out in her. He'd always been so perfect, the suave, handsome surfer who everyone adored, and she'd been the awkward, quiet outsider no one noticed. It irritated her to think that he might still see her that way, that he knew what she'd been like all those years ago. She'd worked hard to bury that part of her in the past, to move on and become confident, outgoing, successful—although it felt more and more like she was failing in every regard. Especially when she saw Ethan.

He pushed away from the bench and returned to the table where he promptly sat and put his feet up on a chair. She swallowed the urge to say something.

"Sorry, I hope I'm not getting in your way."

She couldn't tell if he was being genuine or sarcastic. Either way, regret for her brusque words washed over her. He was her business partner, so she'd have to make more of an effort to get along with him. After all, he hadn't done anything wrong and seemed to be trying his best. It wasn't his fault he rubbed her the wrong way. "It's fine."

"Not a morning person, huh?"

She pressed her lips together, swallowing the retort that rose to her lips. Then she faced him with a shake of her head. "No, not really. I'll get used to it, I suppose."

"I love mornings, I've been for a surf down at the point. Ah…it's a beautiful day."

"You surfed in the dark?" She glanced outside, surprised to see the sky was orange with pink accents around the edges.

He chuckled. "It wasn't completely dark. There was a bit of light. And anyway, it's the best part of the day. Got to see the sunrise from the beach before I went in…spectacular. I've missed seeing it for a while. Glad to be back home again." His sigh was filled with a contentment Emily envied.

"Yes…well some of us were working." Her words sounded cold, harsh, even to her own ears. She shuddered inside. What was wrong with her? This wasn't how she spoke to people?

He downed the rest of his coffee, then carried his cup to the sink to rinse in silence. When he was done, he stepped close to where she was melting butter in the pan on the stove. "Is everything okay?"

He leaned in, sending a flush of warmth across her cheeks. Why did he have to stand so close?

She swallowed. "Yep. Fine. Why do you ask?"

"You seem tense. Is there anything I can do to help?"

Her brow furrowed. "No…thank you."

He chuckled, a deep resonant sound that irritated her more than anything else he'd done that morning. He was laughing at her. Again.

"I hope your day improves," he whispered close to her ear. Then louder. "See you later."

He strode away, picking up his boots on his way to the

back door. The door swung shut behind him, and he was gone.

She squeezed her eyes closed and sighed, a deep sigh that filled her lungs and let go of the tension in her shoulders and neck. She worked her head from one side to the other, stretching her neck, the pain radiating through the muscles on either side.

When was the last time she'd been this tense, this stressed? It was a lot of responsibility, taking on the Manor, along with all of its bills, its grounds, the guests, or lack of them. What had her aunt and uncle been thinking?

What made them believe she could do this? Had they even considered that she might fail? And then, throwing Ethan into the mix—they must've been out of their minds. It would never work between them. He irritated her, and to him she was nothing more than an amusement. They should've sold the entire thing to an investor rather than dividing it between her and Ethan.

Emily glanced at the clock on the wall, its quiet ticking a constant backdrop to the silence in the kitchen. It was time to poach the eggs as the guests would be down soon, and the bread would be ready as well.

By the time she had everything prepared and had carried it in silver chafing dishes to the dining room, the guests appeared at the bottom of the steps and wandered in.

"Good morning," she said.

They nodded their hellos and set about serving themselves from the small buffet she'd set up. The scent of freshly baked sourdough filled the room, along with the warmth from the fireplace. She stood beside the espresso machine and took orders from the guests, before retreating to the kitchen to clean up. As she walked away, an overwhelming feeling of satisfaction filled her heart. She'd done it, served her first breakfast at the Manor alone and so far, it seemed the guests were happy with everything. All it would take for a full house would be for her to increase the amount of food, and that wouldn't take much more effort. Maybe she could do this after all. If only she could learn to cope with having Ethan Flannigan around as well, she'd be perfectly content.

CHAPTER 10

ETHAN

*T*he words on the page weren't drawing him in like they usually did. Something was distracting him from the thriller in his hands. Ethan folded it shut and set the book on the bedside table. His hair, still damp from the shower, fell onto his forehead and he swept it back with one hand.

Something was bothering him.

Or someone.

It was her. Emily Jones. She'd gotten under his skin. He'd vowed to himself while he was out riding waves that morning, that he wouldn't let her. They had a business relationship, and he intended on owning his share of the Manor long term. Which meant he had to get along with her, at least well enough to maintain their professional relationship. He had no idea what he'd done to upset her, or perhaps she was like that with everyone—bristling, abrupt, anger bubbling beneath the surface.

He sighed and rubbed his eyes with his fingertips. Never mind, he'd managed difficult people before, and he could manage her as well. He had to dig deep for that charm he kept for the most challenging clients. It had never failed him before. Only this time, he had a hunch it might not work the way it usually did.

With a grunt he got out of bed and stretched his arms over his head. His muscles ached from the long day. His body still wasn't used to surfing on a daily basis and coupled with the physical labour he was doing at the Manor and in building the dining table in the backyard, every part of him hurt. Including the base of his spine where something seemed to be pinched and twinged with almost every step he took.

He spent a few minutes stretching his muscles and his back on the carpet. Then, wandered out to the kitchen, where the scent of Italian food beckoned. His stomach rumbled, and he licked his lips when he saw a basket of garlic bread on the bench. One look in the oven, revealed two cheesy lasagnes. He swallowed hard.

"Smells delicious mum. Are you cooking for a crowd, or for leftovers?"

Cindy grinned, as she sliced tomatoes. "I've invited a few people to dinner."

"Oh?" He reached for a piece of garlic bread, and she slapped his hand away.

"It's almost time to eat, you can wait… I've invited Athol, as well as Sarah and Mick."

"That's good, I'm looking forward to seeing Sarah. I haven't seen much of her or Mick since I've been back."

Cindy nodded. "That's what I thought. Time for a family catch up. And I invited Emily as well."

His stomach fell. "What? Emily Jones from next door? Why would you invite her?"

Cindy shot him a sharp look that only a mother can give her son. "She's on her own in a new town, she's our neighbour and your business partner. Those are three reasons why. The fourth is that she's my best friend's niece. Do you need more?"

He shook his head, pursed his lips. "Fine. But I wish you'd spoken to me first about it."

"I'm sorry," she said, looking confused. "I didn't think—"

"It's okay. I've had a long day, that's all. I'm not looking forward to making small talk over dinner."

Cindy smiled. "Oh, you poor boy."

"I guess I can manage," he grumbled as he carried the garlic bread to the dining table.

"What was that?" Cindy called after him.

"Nothing," he replied.

Athol arrived a few minutes later, let himself in and patted Petal on the head before she started barking. He shook Ethan's hand, his blue eyes crinkling as he smiled. "Good to see you again, Ethan. I hope that bed and breakfast of yours is going well—I've always loved that place. Beautiful old building and fantastic gardens. It'll be a lot of work to keep it all going."

Ethan nodded. "It's good, so far anyway. I've been fixing things here and there and keeping the garden maintained — I worked for a landscaping company during the summers in high school and helped Mum with her garden as well, so I have a pretty good idea of how to manage it. Although I'll ask Diana if I get stuck, I know how much the garden means to her. It'll be a lot more work in the warmer months, for now I'm figuring my way around the place. But I know what you mean—it's always been a bit magical over there. Something special about it, that's why I jumped at the chance to invest."

Athol sat in an armchair. "You're right about that."

Cindy carried a platter of nibbles into the room and set them on the table in front of Athol. "There you go," she said.

Athol smiled at her, she smiled back, and Ethan watched with interest as a flicker of chemistry passed between them. Was something going on between his mother and their oldest family friend? Surely not. He shook his head, dismissed the thought, and reached for an olive.

"Hello family!" called Sarah from the hallway.

Ethan stood to greet her with a hug, then shook Mick's hand.

"Hello you two. I move back to your town and have barely seen you, sis. What's going on?" he chuckled, punching her gently on the shoulder.

She grinned. "I've been busy. Sounds like you have been as well."

"Not too bad. Went for a lovely surf at the point this morning. Made me think of all those times we surfed together years ago."

She nodded. "Those were the days. Hey, let me know ahead of time and I'll join you next time."

They sat on the various couches and chairs in the living room and soon caught up on everything going on in each other's lives.

"And how's Vicky?" Ethan asked Sarah when the others retreated to the kitchen in search of drinks.

Vicky and Sarah had been friends since childhood and had rekindled their friendship when Sarah moved back to Emerald Cove.

"She's good, some kind of health issues which she assures me aren't serious. I don't know...I worry. But otherwise good. She's an amazing vet, which is still hard for me to wrap my head around considering I used to chase her with frogs and she'd squeal her head off."

Ethan laughed. "Well that's good to hear."

"My other friend, Meg is going through something difficult. Do you remember her? She married Brad Taylor?"

He nodded. "Oh yeah, I know who you mean. Red curls. Cute smile. She moved away for a while, didn't she?"

"That's right. She's been having a tough time, you know, since the accident."

"I'll bet." He rubbed a hand over his stubbled chin. "I was really sorry to hear about Brad. I've called him a few times, but he doesn't seem to want to talk."

"He's struggling with his paralysis, of course. It's hard for him to accept he'll never be the international surfing champion he was. But it's also hard on Meg—she's working long hours, trying to manage everything, including Brad's mood swings. I feel bad for her. Anyway, Vicky and I have been doing our best to support her. Vicky's been a rock, so I haven't seen as much of her lately as I'd like, but I'm glad she can be there for Meg."

"That's good," he said.

He hated to think what it must be like for Brad and Meg, going through what they were. It wasn't something anyone should have to experience at such a young age.

The doorbell rang and Petal scampered off down the hall to bark at whoever dared to stand on the doorstep. Cindy hurried after her, soon returning arm in arm with Emily. Ethan's smile tightened. She wore an emerald green slip dress that accentuated her lithe figure, her grey eyes were highlighted by a light dusting of smoky makeup and a single silver disk hung on a chain around her tanned neck.

"Everyone," began Cindy, "This is Emily Jones, she's our new neighbour."

Sarah hurried forward and embraced Emily. "Emily it's so good to see you again. It's been an absolute age."

Mick shook her hand, followed by Athol. She sat next to Ethan on the couch as everyone peppered her with questions and exclaimed over what had happened with the Manor. She glanced his way, gaze connecting with his, and nodded.

"Hello, Ethan," she said.

"Good to see you again, Emily."

Then her attention was taken up again by the rest of the family and he watched as quietly and confidently she answered some questions and dodged others. She didn't lose her cool like she had with him. She was polite, friendly, and seemed happy to talk. He studied her with a furrowed brow, his eyes narrowed. So, she wasn't rude to everyone, just him. He was right, she must hate him, or be upset with him about something. Though what that could be, was beyond him.

He could test the theory, see if he was imagining things.

"Did you walk through the gate to get here?"

She arched an eyebrow. "Of course. What should I do instead, fly over the fence?"

He cleared his throat and was about to respond, but then Sarah asked her a question about her aunt and uncle. With a warm smile Emily leaned forward and fell into conversation with his sister. Not a sign of disdain on her pretty face, no angry turning up of the lips.

He shook his head and went to hide in the kitchen. If he helped Mum with the meal, he could avoid Emily for most of the evening. Then he'd only have to deal with her when he ran into her at work. It was a shame they couldn't get along, but there wasn't much he could do about it and he wanted to keep their professional relationship in working order. It seemed the best way to do that was to stay out of her way.

* * *

AFTER DINNER WAS DONE, Ethan and Sarah helped their mum wash and dry the dishes, leaving their guests in the living room discussing whether music had taken a downward turn in creativity and quality in the last two decades, or if it was simply different. He was relieved to hear Emily standing up for his generation's creativity as he walked away. While they cleaned up, Mum and Sarah engaged in a conversation that only required the occasional nod or grunt of assent from him. So he allowed his thoughts to wander.

He considered what he'd do when the time came for him to get a job. He'd had a nest egg to back him up, but most of that had gone into securing the loan for his investment in the Manor. He had a few more weeks, but after that he'd have to find work. The idea of returning to Brisbane put a stone in his gut. He was loving being back in the Cove, but there was very little work for an engineer.

As he put away the last plate, he noticed through the back window that the thick cloud cover from earlier had broken apart and a brilliant moon shone through the partition.

It was stunning.

He set down his dish towel and wiped his hands down the front of his pants as he strode for the back door. If he stood on the porch, he'd get an even better view.

Outside, there was an eerie glow to the landscape. The moon issued a blueish light that gave the world a haunted feeling. Eyes skyward, he walked forward slowly, marvelling at the shape of the clouds as they rolled and twisted, shifting westward on the cool breeze. They covered the moon again for a moment, then it was free, light blazing towards the earth.

That was when he noticed the figure leaned against the porch railing. Emily. He slowed his pace, inhaled a deep breath, then joined her.

"Beautiful, isn't it?" he murmured.

She startled, then offered him a half smile. "Yes, amazing. I couldn't stay inside. When I saw it, I had to come—I hope they haven't missed me yet?"

He shook his head. "No, Athol and Mick are loudly debating the virtues of eighties hair bands."

She laughed and the sound lit him up from the inside. She was beautiful when she wasn't scowling. The worry that lined her face lifted and she looked young and carefree for a single moment.

He leaned against the railing, taking in the beauty of the blue-tinted garden, the bulging clouds, the black outlines of the trees. In the distance, a curlew's haunting call filled the night air.

"They sound so sad," said Emily, her voice dripping with sorrow.

"I know. When I was a kid, I always thought it was someone screaming. Of course, Mum would comfort me, tell me it was a bird. I couldn't imagine how those cartoon looking creatures with long spindly legs, that ran around in the scrub by the beach during the day were the same ones that sounded so terrifying at night." He chuckled and ran a hand through his hair.

"I know what you mean. I was scared of possums."

"What? Really?" He faced her, leaning on one of the posts that supported the porch roof.

"There were a few who lived around the Manor, so when I came to visit, I'd hear them fighting and hissing in the middle of the night. It sounded like some kind of vicious swamp creature or something. I didn't realise they were possums until I was a teenager and said something to Aunty Di about the noise." She shook her head. "I'd get so scared I'd hide under the bed with my teddy bear."

"Wow, I wish I'd known. I could've told you what it was, saved you from some of that fear."

"You would've?"

He nodded. "Of course."

"That's a nice thought, but you didn't even notice me, back then."

He frowned. "Yeah, well I was a kid too. I was very focused on surfing, skateboarding, and becoming an iron man. I wasn't exactly sure what it meant to be an iron man, but I liked the sound of it."

She laughed, her blonde hair shimmering in the moonlight. "That definitely sounds like you."

"And what about you, what were your dreams back then?"

She cocked her head to one side, thinking. "I don't know... I'm not really surprised you didn't notice me. I was kind of a mousy, timid child. I'd hang around on the edges of your group of friends, Adele was nice to me though, she included me. I didn't really have dreams of what I'd become, I only knew I wanted a family. I loved my mum, but it wasn't the same as what you guys had—mum, dad, siblings, BBQs on the weekend. The way you teased each other, but I could always tell you really loved one another...to some extent, I was jealous I guess."

His eyes widened. He hadn't expected her to open up, and her words made his heart ache for the little girl he'd known. If only he'd realised, had included her more. But he'd been too busy, too focused on his own life and friendships.

"Well, you're definitely not mousy and timid now," he replied, bumping her shoulder with his own.

She chuckled. "I suppose not, although I still feel like that little girl a lot of the time."

"Well, I'm glad you came back to the Cove. It's right that you should take over running the Manor. You belong here."

She smiled up at him, her eyes glimmering. "Thank you for saying that. Sometimes I think..." She wiped her eyes with the back of her hand. "Nothing...never mind."

"No, don't stop...tell me. I'd love to know what you think

because, honestly, most of the time I have no idea what's going through that pretty head of yours."

She turned to face him, eyes narrowed. "What does that mean?"

He stepped back, thoughts spinning. What had he said to upset her? He only meant he wanted to hear her thoughts, find out what was going on inside her brain so they could get along. So he could be there for her.

"I didn't mean anything...only, you tend to keep your thoughts to yourself. If you'd only open up occasionally, share with me what's going on, what you're thinking... I think it'd help our relationship..."

"Our relationship?" she questioned with one eyebrow arched.

He swallowed. "You know, professionally."

"What I *think* about is none of your business."

He blinked. "What?"

"Forget it," she said.

She took a step in the direction of the house, then spun on her heel to look into his eyes. "We work together Ethan, that's it. You don't have to pretend like you care, and I'll keep my thoughts to myself. Deal?"

He nodded, mute.

"Great, I'll see you tomorrow."

She strode through the back door, letting it slam shut behind her, and she was gone. He leaned against the porch rail with a loud exhale of breath. What'd happened? They were talking, having a nice time, and she'd turned back into the taciturn business partner all over again in a single moment. He shook his head. Working with Emily Jones was going to be more of a challenge than he'd thought it would be.

CHAPTER 11

DIANA

*D*iana squinted at the page, willing her mind to process the words she was reading. Her tired eyes slipped closed briefly as the book slid in her lap. She tugged it up higher, turning the page and setting a bookmark in place before shutting the book and placing it on the side table.

Next to her, Rupert snored softly in his armchair. The footrest up, his chair was leaned back and his mouth ajar, his breathing a constant rhythm that filled the silence in their new home.

She glanced around the compact living room. From where she sat, she could see their small kitchen, tiny dining room and the doors to the two bedrooms that made up the entire unit. It was strange to live in a place where her words didn't echo, and that she could traverse with a few short steps.

She missed the Manor, but at the same time it was a great

relief not to have to wake so early, serve breakfast to guests, manage cleaning and maintenance staff, and keep up with such a large building and garden. Already, after only a week of rest, she was feeling much better than she had. She was sleeping better, had taken several long walks on the beach and was onto her second novel.

The only thing bothering her was her conscience. She hated to keep anything from Rupert. Having a secret between them gave her a feeling of loneliness she hadn't felt since she was a scared teenager; ever since Rupert first kissed her and had chased that loneliness away. Now it was back, knocking on the door to her soul, pushing back the contentment that'd reigned for so long. Nothing stayed hidden forever. And the thought sent a rush of nerves through her body that set her heart pounding.

When her mobile phone rang, she jolted in a panic, then sighed with relief when she realised what it was. She pulled it from her pocket.

"Hello, Cindy, dear, what a pleasant surprise to hear from you."

"Diana, I miss you already. It's time you moved back to the Manor," quipped Cindy.

Diana could hear the pout in her voice. She laughed. "There's no going back, I'm afraid."

"Don't you miss the old place?"

"Yes, of course I do, my garden most of all. Although I've started planning out my new garden. I've done a sketch of the back yard. Rupert says I can't turn the entire thing into a garden bed, since he wants to be able to sit out there sometimes. So I'm going to put raised garden beds around the inside of the fence-line instead."

"Ah...sounds like you've got it all figured out. And I was only joking, I'm happy for you in your new, fancy, retirement community."

"Will you come for tea soon?" asked Diana.

Cindy's smile echoed through her voice. "Yes, that would be wonderful. How about tomorrow?"

"Perfect. How are Emily and Ethan going at the Manor? Emily doesn't give me any information, it's like pulling teeth to get her to talk about it," grumbled Diana.

Cindy chuckled. "They seem to be working things out. Although there's a bit of tension between them over something. I asked Ethan about it, but he claims he has no idea what's going on."

They chatted about the other members of Cindy's family, Rupert's health and caught up on the local gossip. Meanwhile, Rupert roused and wiped his eyes. Diana hung up the phone, smiled at him. "I'm sorry, my dear. Did we wake you?"

He nodded. "Yes, but I don't mind. The sound of your voice is a wonderful way to wake. Besides, I've slept long enough. I won't be able to get to sleep tonight if I keep going. This chair is too comfortable." He chuckled and used a lever to lower the footrest.

Diana had bought him the chair as a surprise gift when they moved in. He'd slept in it every day since.

"I'm glad you like it," she said.

He stood, then leaned in to kiss her forehead. "I love it. Although I can't seem to stay awake in it for more than ten minutes." He chuckled and lumbered in the direction of the kitchen. "I'm making tea, would you like some?"

"Yes, please."

Once Rupert was gone, Diana glanced in his direction, then reached into her pocket and pulled out the envelope. It was wrinkled now, had been folded in half and hidden in her pocket every day for the past week. The handwriting on the front and back was as familiar to her now as her own. She'd read it through so many times, running her finger over the slanting words as she mouthed them.

She couldn't tell Rupert about it. She hated to hurt him, after so many years. They'd had a wonderful marriage, a full life. He didn't deserve what she'd done—keeping something from him. It wasn't like her either, usually she'd share every thought she had with her husband, and he'd interject the occasional sound of support.

How would he react when he found out she'd held a secret in her heart for so many years? Would it change everything between them? Especially given the way they'd longed for a family and had never been able to have one. He'd never taken his disappointment out on her; he was a good and kind man. The love of her life without a doubt. If only she could go back in time, do things differently. But if she could—what would she change?

She shook her head. It was a mess, that was for sure. Still, even if she had a time machine, she wasn't sure she'd change a thing—except for the dishonesty, the withholding of herself, her heart. That was the one thing she'd do differently. She should've come clean back then, to everyone.

She pulled the sheets of paper from the envelope, lay them on her lap with another glance in the direction of the kitchen. Still no sign of Rupert. Hands shaking, she raised the first sheet closer to her face, read through the words.

I think I am your son.

Her heart clenched every time she read those words. She'd never expected to hear from him. So many years she'd wished, hoped he would show up. But he hadn't. And now... he'd made the connection. It was almost too much.

Are you the Diana Felder who gave up a baby boy forty-four years ago...?

"Do you want a shortbread with your tea?" asked Rupert as he carried a tray into the room. "I brought a plate of them, in case." He chuckled. "I think I'm getting used to this retirement business. Take a walk, read a book, have a nap, time for tea!"

Diana shoved the letter back into the envelope and pushed it deep into her pocket, her heart thundering against her ribcage. A cold sweat broke out across her forehead. "Wonderful! Yes, please."

* * *

SARAH

The twinkle lights that lit up the al fresco dining area attached to the Emerald Cafe could be seen far down the street. Sarah hurried towards the cafe, with another glance at her watch. She was running late to meet Meg and Vicky for dinner.

Inside, she glanced around, but before the seating hostess could help her, she spotted her friends in the back corner close to the blazing fire. With a grateful smile, she headed in their direction. She wasn't sure she could manage sitting outside, it seemed her body had acclimatised to the milder weather in Emerald Cove and even with the scattered heaters throughout the space, she'd have felt the cold coastal wind go right through her flimsy coat. Still, there were plenty of diners seated outside. Most likely tourists from down south who were used to frigid temperatures.

"There you are," she greeted her friends, throwing herself into a chair at their table.

Meg laughed. "You okay, Sarah?"

Sarah nodded. "I'm fine. What are we drinking?"

Vicky arched an eyebrow. "Mineral water..."

"Ugh, I think tonight calls for something harder. A bottle of shiraz?"

Vicky and Meg nodded. Meg's eyes narrowed. "Are you sure you're okay?"

Sarah caught their waitress's attention and placed an order for shiraz and a basket of fries.

She sighed. "I'm fine, had a rough night. I'd rather talk about you two. Sorry I'm late. How are you? What's going on? Catch me up."

Vicky eyed her a moment, then pursed her lips. "Well, I was telling Meg that I'm still not feeling well and I'm starting to get a little worried. I mean, what if it's something serious? So far, none of the tests my GP's done have found anything. They don't know what's wrong with me. I've googled so much I'm completely confused — I think I have Swine Flu or Leukaemia…"

Meg chuckled. "Stop googling! It's going to drive you crazy."

"I know," conceded Vicky, rubbing a hand over her face. "But I have to find out what's going on with my health. It's really minor things, but they add up. I'm so tired all of the time. My stomach feels bad sometimes, but not always. I get this rash on my stomach…although I don't feel feverish. I don't know. I'm starting to get a little more concerned about what's going on with me."

Sarah reached for her hand and squeezed it. "I'm so sorry, honey. Surely if you keep going to the doctor someone will be able to figure it out."

"I hope so." Vicky smiled, but her eyes were clouded with doubt. "And how about you, Meg. How's things at home?"

Meg leaned back in her chair with a sigh. "I don't want to complain… I feel like all I do is complain."

"No you don't," reassured Vicky.

"Definitely not," agreed Sarah. "You hardly ever complain, especially given how hard things are for you right now. We're your sounding board, complain away. We promise not to judge you for it." She pulled a face that made Meg laugh.

"Okay, well—I think things are okay. Not great, but not terrible either. I'm working a lot and holding everything together. I'm not sure I could manage anything else—if something new comes along, it might all fall to the ground in a heap, me along with it." She grunted. "But as things stand, I'm coping. Just. But it's hard. It's so hard."

"I hear you," replied Sarah. "That you're holding it together at all is amazing. You're amazing."

"Absolutely," agreed Vicky.

"Come on, you have to tell us why you're in such a mood, Sarah." Meg studied Sarah, her green eyes gleaming in the glow from the fire at Sarah's back.

Sarah drew a deep breath. "It's nothing really. I was on the phone to the office before I came here, that's all. It didn't go well. I can't remember what it was I used to enjoy about working there anymore. It's so pretentious, so political... ugh." She ran a hand over her hair, smoothing it out of her face. "I've lost the joy of working. I used to love it, now I dread every conference call. And it doesn't help that my nemesis undermines me at every turn—she's got her eye on my senior editor job, and she's not afraid to do whatever it takes to get there. The thing is, I've got no desire to fight her for it."

"What would you do if you could do anything in the world?" asked Vicky.

"What do you mean?" Sarah frowned.

"For work...if you could have any career of your choosing with no obstacles or limitations, what would it be?"

Sarah hesitated. She'd never thought of things that way before. There were always obstacles. Always limits to the opportunities available. It was an enticing thought—to dream of what her life could be. To some extent she'd done that. She'd moved from the city back to Emerald Cove, bought and renovated the cottage, and ended her engagement to a selfish, cheating fiancé. Now she was dating Mick, a part-time architect and full-time contractor. Her personal life was exactly what she wanted it to be, even though she'd never thought she'd end up back in the Cove, dating a local man. It'd been the furthest thing from her thoughts ten years ago, heck even one year ago. So, why was it so hard for her to imagine her dream job?

She'd always been too practical. Too sensible, responsible. Careers weren't even considered if they didn't have the prospect of a solid paycheck.

"I suppose," she began slowly, "If I could do anything, I'd be a fiction writer—a novelist."

Vicky grinned. "I knew it!"

Sarah grunted. "What? You did not. I didn't even know it until this moment."

"You've always loved books and you're a great writer."

"That was in high school," protested Sarah. "We don't know I'd be a great writer now."

"Why would it be any different now?" asked Meg. "You're talented, so add hard work, determination, and grit, and you can't lose. At least, that's what Brad always told reporters when they asked him about the secret to his success as a surfer...before the accident."

Sarah considered her words. "You think?"

"Definitely," replied Meg.

"For sure," agreed Vicky. "I think it's a great idea. You should go for it."

"What? Do you mean quit my job and become a novelist?" That was crazy. She didn't do things like that. She worked hard at a steady job; she was reliable, dependable, and she always made the smart choice.

What would she do if she failed?

A failed author…could she work as an editor? Would any publishing house have her after that?

It was a big risk to take, but there was a flutter in the bottom of her gut that suggested she might want to try.

She smiled. "Okay…I'll think about it."

CHAPTER 12

EMILY

The hum of the refrigerator was the only sound in the cavernous house, apart from the chirping of birds outside the kitchen window. Emily drummed fingers on the kitchen bench. They'd had no guests last night. None. Not a single one. Sunbeams refracted through the window and painted rainbows on the white marble bench top. She traced their outline with a fingernail, her lips pursed.

This wouldn't do. How could they run a business if they didn't have any guests to stay at their bed and breakfast? She could almost hear the money sifting from the Manor's bank account moment by moment. A place as big as this one involved a lot of upkeep. There had been taxes and suppliers to pay, as well as the cleaning, maintenance and serving staff. There was so much work to be done, things to be replaced, and supplies to restock.

To save money she'd laid off most of the part-time staff, including their servers. Ethan had replaced the handyman, so that helped. She'd begun baking the treats for the guests for their pillows on arrival and for morning and afternoon tea, ending their longstanding relationship with a local baker. Diana hadn't been happy about it, since the woman was a friend of hers from way back, but Emily had assured her that they didn't have a choice, at least until bookings increased. And besides, what was the point in Emily's expertise as a chef if she wasn't going to use it?

Still, she'd decided to continue to pay the cleaner even though there wasn't enough work to keep her going—it wasn't fair to cut off the woman's source of income because they'd hit a bit of a slump. And if there was one thing Emily hated to do more than anything else in the world, it was to clean—especially other people's messes. Things would turn around, they had to. And the last thing she'd need then would be to have to scramble to find and train good help. So, the cleaner was currently tasked with spring cleaning every room of the Manor, one per day. Emily was determined that the entire building would be sparkling from top to bottom before the slump in bookings was over.

Since there was no breakfast to make or clean up, she'd decided to get started on a stocktake. Emily padded in her slippers to the office, slid into the chair, and stared at the blank computer screen. It still felt strange to sit in Aunty Di's chair, in her office. When she was a kid, the office had been out of bounds for her. She was only allowed in it on special occasions to share tea with her aunt. Any other time she had to stay well clear of the neat, dark room.

She'd stood at the doorway many times, staring inside with longing glances at the rows of books that lined the bookshelves on one wall—thrillers, mysteries, true stories of survival, all the books her aunt loved.

She stood to her feet, wiped her palms down the fronts of her pyjama pants and walked over to stand in front of the bookshelves. They were custom built in dark timber and covered one entire end of the office. Emily plucked a book from the shelf closest to her and ran fingers over its dust jacket. The colours on the cover were faded and there was a tear in the paper, but otherwise it was in decent shape. Auntie Di hadn't wanted to take them with her when she left; she said she wouldn't have the space to keep them. Maybe Emily would get back into reading. She hadn't done much reading since Mum died; it was something they'd done together—Mum would read a book, then pass it on to Emily, and the two of them would discuss over coffee and cake when she was done. She missed that. It made it hard to pick up a book and open the pages now.

There was a quiet knock on the door and, startled, she dropped the book to the floor. It thudded softly on the carpet as she swung to see who was there, her heart in her throat.

"Hi," said Ethan.

She huffed. "You scared me!"

She pressed her hand to her chest, breathing deep to slow her heart rate. He chuckled and crossed his arms over his chest. His light brown hair was as perfectly mussed as always, and his hazel eyes glinted with a mixture of what seemed like curiosity and mischief. A twinge of longing ran through her—longing to belong, to be known, to be in Ethan Flannigan's inner circle. She'd never been part of his chosen crowd, as a kid she was always hanging around the edges. She was certain he wouldn't understand something like that.

People like Ethan were the pied pipers, the ones others flocked to. He couldn't help it, it was the way he was made —attractive, charming, strong. He knew how to talk to people, put them at ease, made them feel interesting, as though he cared. And maybe he did. She hadn't quite figured him out. Not yet. She wasn't particularly good at measuring people, if her ex-boyfriend was anything to go by, and she didn't trust her natural inclination to let herself be drawn to Ethan.

"What do you want?" She found herself slipping back into the clipped tones she often used with him.

The gleam left his eyes. She hadn't meant to speak to him that way; it happened before she realised what she was saying.

"I was checking in, wanted to see what you're up to. We don't have any guests tonight either so I thought it might be a good time to do some strategising about the future."

She picked up the book and returned it the shelf, then sat behind her desk. He lowered himself into a chair and crossed one long leg over the other.

"Great," she replied. "What were you thinking?"

"There are a few things we could improve around here…"

"Definitely. I'd love to get some painting done. The paint's a bit old fashioned and in need of an update." Emily leaned back in her chair. She had a lot of ideas, but how many of them could be done on a shoestring budget? Their first priority was getting occupancy rates up, and any small thing they could do to encourage that was a win.

"We can do that. And I'd like to build a pagoda in the garden. It's so beautiful out there in the warmer months, I think the guests would like it, and it might attract some weddings."

Emily nodded. "Good idea." She only wished she'd thought of it. Weddings were exactly the type of business they should be courting. "And I thought I might get some brochures printed, update the website, visit some local travel agencies. We have to try to increase bookings for the peak holiday season. At the moment we're looking at about a twenty percent occupancy rate and that won't get us through the year."

"I'm glad we're on the same page. I can do a lot of the work around here—"

"And I can help with painting," interrupted Emily.

Ethan dipped his head in agreement. "Sounds good." He stood to his feet. "I'll head out and get started planning the pagoda. Let me know if you have any ideas for it."

"Thanks." She waved him goodbye, then sat for a few moments staring at the empty doorway. Was she imagining things or was he acting a little frostier towards her than usual? He generally made a joke of some kind, got her laughing, but he'd been all business. She couldn't blame him, she supposed, since every interaction they had usually resulted in her snapping at him.

She flicked on the computer and jotted some marketing ideas on a sheet of paper while she waited for it to boot up. Then, she typed the web address for the Manor's website into the browser. When it loaded, she groaned and pressed her hands to her head to stare at it in dismay. It was terrible. It looked about twenty years old, was difficult to navigate and seemed to have been designed by an amateur who knew nothing about web design. Emily didn't have much in the way of technical skills, but she'd put together a web site in the past for Callum's band, and figured they only needed something simple.

The first thing they'd need would be some decent photographs of the place. She'd pull out her camera and get to work that day. Photography was a passion of hers; she loved capturing the beauty of a moment in an image and had even taken a class on it the previous year.

A few boxes of her things were still stacked against the office wall. She opened one of them and rifled through it, locating her D-SLR camera in the bottom, packed carefully in its case. She pulled it out and looked through the lens, adjusting some of the settings, and snapped a quick shot of the bookshelves, with the armchairs in front. It was a peaceful scene, reminded her of those special moments she'd shared with Aunty Di and Mum as a kid, drinking tea and feeling all grown up.

On the desk her phone buzzed. She stood and reached for it.

"Hello?"

"Hi there, honey." Callum's deep voice sent a shot of adrenaline through her veins. She hadn't looked at the screen before answering, wasn't expecting to hear from him. It'd been months since he'd left her in Coffs Harbour.

"Callum, what a nice surprise." She adopted a neutral tone. The last thing she wanted was to let him know how much he'd hurt her. It'd only end in an argument, since he'd feel the need to defend himself and somehow, he'd turn it all around to show how it was really her fault all along. It was a game he liked to play, and she had no desire to go there— things between them were finished, including his manipulative games.

"I hadn't heard from you in a while, thought I'd check in and see how you're going down south."

He paused, waiting. She sighed. The sooner she could end the call the better. "I'm fine, thanks. How are things up in Airlie Beach?"

He chuckled. "It's great. We're playing four nights a week at the resort, making good money. Can't complain. I even went snorkelling out on the reef with the rest of the band yesterday. Amazing! You should definitely do it sometime. The colours...wow."

She couldn't help smiling. His voice was warm, he was in a good mood, and his charm never failed on her. Still, she couldn't fall for it again.

"That sounds really nice. I'm glad you're enjoying yourself."

"You should come, I've got space at my place. Come on, you'll love it. You never really warmed to Coffs."

The invitation was a surprise. He'd barely looked back when he left. It'd torn her heart out to see how little he thought of her and what they shared. Now he was acting as though she'd chosen to stay behind.

"No, thanks for thinking of me though."

He hesitated. "No? Just like that? You're not going to think about it? You don't even like living in Coffs, and you can quit that crappy waitressing job...there are much better opportunities up here."

"Are you missing me, all of a sudden?" asked Emily.

"Of course. It's not the same here without you."

Emily shook her head. He never changed. "Well, I'm not in Coffs Harbour anymore. I moved."

"What? Where are you? You didn't even send me a text to let me know you moved?" His voice was laced with irritation.

She didn't want to tell him the truth, wasn't sure what he might do knowing she was part owner of a bed and breakfast. "I'm staying with my aunt for a while, until I figure out what I want to do next."

He grunted. "You could've told me."

"We're not in a relationship anymore, Callum. Why should I keep you up to date on anything I'm doing? It's not your business."

He was silent and she rubbed a hand over her face, waiting for his response. His voice was cold. "We never had that conversation."

"I know. I'm aware of that, but you left and didn't ask me to go with you—so I assumed. Anyway, it's for the best, since I really don't think we suit each other. I believed we were right together for a long time, but I was wrong about that." She'd hoped to avoid this conversation but now they were having it, she could see it was needed for both of them.

Closure was important, so they could each move on with their lives.

"Of course we suit each other, honey. We're great together…we have so much fun. Well, when you're not being a downer, we have fun. Sometimes you're a bit too uptight, but that's something we can work on. We can get you to loosen up a bit, no worries." His grin resonated through the phone.

She rolled her eyes. "I don't want to work on loosening up, Callum. This is me, it's who I am. I have no desire to be someone else. Look, it was great to hear from you, but I've got to go. I'm glad things are working out for you up north."

Emily hung up the phone and pressed her fingertips to her eyes with a groan. Hearing his voice had her heart thundering in her chest, sweat beading on her face and beneath her arms. She hated confronting him, arguing. Throughout their relationship, he'd been the one to get his way. He'd charm, convince, and manipulate her, and because she didn't want to lose him, she'd moved away from her friends and support network to follow him. She'd found herself accepting things she never would've in the past, and falling for his words when she knew they didn't make sense.

Well, he didn't have that hold over her anymore. No one did. She was living her own life, her way. Her aunt and uncle had given her an opportunity, not only to build the kind of career she could love and be proud of, but also to be her own person. She wanted to be someone her mother could've been proud of, even the father she'd never known played in her thoughts—perhaps if she made something of the chance she'd been given, he might've been proud too. With a sigh, she pushed to her feet and headed out the door. It was time to take some photographs of the Manor to use on the website and in brochures. It was a beautiful day, the sun was shining, and the *Seaside Manor Bed and Breakfast* looked every bit the quaint, historical, and luxurious holiday destination it was. She smiled as she worked. Callum was her past. The Manor was her future.

* * *

ETHAN

The waves rose and fell in a steady rhythm, soothing, comforting, and bringing back so many memories that Ethan couldn't help smiling where he sat on his surfboard. He tented a hand over his eyes to cut the glare and studied the shoreline of Emerald Beach. The town was waking up, coming to life. Children played along the edge of the water, running with pails and shovels, or splashing in the white-wash of the waves' last gasp.

A cyclist sailed along the footpath beyond the beach, passing two women walking, arms pumping in time, heads bent together. He loved being home. There was nowhere else like it in the world.

As much as he enjoyed his work as an engineer—crafting, designing, and bringing projects together was satisfying work—he was excited about what they were planning for the *Seaside Manor Bed and Breakfast*. It was an opportunity to build something solid with his hands, rather than only using his head. A chance to see a dream come to reality and to build an investment for himself and his future family.

He thought about that sometimes—the family he didn't yet have. He wondered if he'd ever have them and hoped that he would. In the meantime, the work itself was fun to him. He'd catch one more wave, then head back to the Manor to do some painting. He was looking forward to seeing how a coat of paint would transform some of the rooms from staid to modern.

A wave rose up behind him and he lay on the board, paddled forward with a glance over his shoulder, then stood up when the wave grabbed a hold of his board. The water propelled him towards the beach, and he turned the board back into the wave, then pushed in the other direction to ride it as far as it would take him.

Finally, it petered out and he fell into the curl of it, diving beneath it and feeling the tug of the leg rope as his board bobbed overhead.

He jogged up the beach, shook the water from his hair, then stood next to his surfboard, watching the waves in their relentless journey to shore and back again. He'd left his towel, mobile, clothes and keys there in a pile. As he dried off, his thoughts wandered to the Manor and Emily. As much fun as he was having with the Manor, he sometimes wondered if he'd made the right choice in investing in it. Emily didn't seem to want him there. She'd opened up a few times and he'd caught glimpses of the girl that'd followed him and his friends around when they were teenagers, then she pushed him away again.

He shook his head as he wiped the droplets of water from his face and neck. What had he done? Or was it her? If something was bothering her, he wished she'd speak up about it. He couldn't do anything to make it better if he didn't even know what was wrong.

His mobile phone rang, the sound muffled by the t-shirt he'd wrapped it in. He pulled it free.

"Hello, this is Ethan Flannigan."

"Ethan, I'm Colin Hill with the *Gold Coast Times*. Would you like to give a response to the charges of fraud that, rumour has it, will be laid against you by the Queensland Crown Prosecutor any day now?"

Ethan's eyes widened. "What? Fraud?"

"Mammoth Engineering has been under scrutiny for

months and you're one of its key players. Do you care to comment on what the company has done, or do you think the charges are in error?"

Ethan hung up the phone, dropped it on his shirt in the sand and pressed both hands to his face, scrubbing them over his hair with a grunt. What was going on? They couldn't charge him with fraud, he hadn't known anything about what the company was up to. As far as he was concerned, it was a legitimate engineering company and he'd done his best, worked hard, to become a partner believing it was all above board.

On the way back to his truck, he called his former boss, Chester. The phone rang and rang, finally voicemail picked up.

"Yeah, hi Chester, it's Ethan Flannigan here. I want to talk to you about what's going on with these fraud charges—I had a journalist call me on my mobile, telling me I'm going to be charged. I don't even know what this is about, you've got to call me back, tell me what's going on."

As he hung up the phone, he swore beneath his breath. He had a feeling he wouldn't hear from Chester, at least not anytime soon. No doubt he was lying low. If he really was going to be charged with something, Ethan would need help. He'd never needed a solicitor before for anything other than real estate conveyancing, but one of his old university friends was a solicitor now.

He did a quick search to see if he could find his friend's number, located an old email address, and penned an enquiry. Perhaps Marc could help, or at least point him in the right direction. Then he gathered his things together and headed for the truck, his stomach in a knot. He'd always been the guy who'd done the right thing. Sure, he'd gotten into some mischief in high school, but nothing serious, nothing illegal. And ever since, he'd followed the rules. It didn't make sense that he was to be charged with fraud, but if they charged him surely that meant they had some kind of evidence against him. If that was true, what was it? He had no idea, but one thing he did know—he hadn't done anything wrong, so if it looked to crown prosecutors as if he had, someone was setting him up.

CHAPTER 13

DIANA

*T*he tea in the cup beside her had grown cold about ten minutes earlier. Still, Diana put it to her lips, sipped and then grimaced as she returned it to the table beside her. She rocked her chair gently beneath her, and she watched as some of her neighbours strode around the cul-de-sac, hand-weights in each hand. They waved at her, smiled, and called out something about the weather. She nodded, waved back then took up her knitting needles again. The spool of yarn reached down into the basket at her feet, a dark pink that she thought would be perfect for Cindy. Her friend didn't need a scarf, that was true enough, the weather in Emerald Cove barely got past chilly and certainly didn't require the wearing of knitted scarves or caps. Still, she wanted to do something with her hands, hating to sit idle, and she thought the colour would complement her friend's complexion well.

In the two weeks since they'd moved into their new

home, she and Rupert had met most of their new neighbours and had even been invited to one couple's house to play a game of Mahjong. It wasn't until that moment that Diana realised how much her life had changed. The couple told them they'd played the game with friends every week for the past forty years. They'd laughed as they said it, but she'd met Rupert's gaze with a feeling of shock. He seemed to have experienced the same realisation as she had, his eyes wide.

They hadn't done anything for the past forty years but work.

Well, that wasn't entirely true, but it felt that way. They'd had downtime, of course they had, but it wasn't regular or scheduled, and in the early days of building up the Manor as a must-visit destination, they'd worked almost around the clock.

Saturdays and Sundays were some of their busiest times. They certainly couldn't go out to dinner with friends on a Friday night, or invite them over for a game of cards on a Thursday night—there were guests to take care of, food to prepare, broken things to fix, supplies to order and marketing to be done. Running the Manor had taken almost every moment of their lives. Even her friendships were built around her business—her best friend, Cindy, lived next door which made maintaining the friendship highly convenient. Cindy often popped in for a cup of tea most mornings after the breakfast rush was done.

Diana's heart fell. If Cindy hadn't made the effort, would their friendship have survived all these years? If she were honest with herself, she didn't think it would've.

She swallowed another mouthful of cold tea before she knew what she was doing, then pushed it as far away on the table as she could with a grunt. There was nothing worse than cold tea.

A car pulled up to the curb outside their house and she

eyed it with interest. They didn't get much traffic in their street, only visitors. Who was this person visiting, and why was he parked in front of their house? He pulled the car slowly up onto the verge, to get it out of the way of any traffic that might want to pass.

The driver's side door of the black sedan opened, and a man stepped out. He was tall, with dark hair and wore jeans. He glanced around at the houses on their street. Her breath caught in her throat and her heart skipped a beat. It was him. She knew it was as soon as she saw him. His eyes found hers and he raised a hand in a hesitant wave.

"Hi," he called.

She forced a smile onto her face, then leaned to put the scarf and her knitting needles into the basket while she collected herself. What was he doing here? Obviously, she knew he had her address, since he'd written to her and she'd written back. Still, she hadn't expected him to show up out of the blue. There were protocols to follow in a situation like this, steps involved. The next step might have been a phone call, although she wasn't entirely certain she was ready for that—perhaps after a few more letters. But a visit? That was definitely something you'd talk about first. Rupert was inside, he could finish his nap and come out to the porch at any moment. What then? She hadn't discussed any of this with him yet. It would all be a complete surprise, and what about his weak heart?

She didn't have time to dwell on the subject any longer, because the subject was walking directly towards her with a hesitant smile on his narrow face.

"Diana Jones?" he asked.

She reached out a hand to shake his, then didn't let go as tears pricked and a lump formed in her throat. She squeezed his hand, unable to look away from the brown eyes, like her own, that stared back at her. It was uncanny. Almost like looking at a picture of herself, but in the form of a man. He was so familiar.

"Yes, I'm Diana. You must be Ben."

He nodded, ducked his head. "I'm sorry, I should've called first. It's just that…I lost my job, and I was out driving, thinking about everything and then I turned in this direction. I didn't think much about it, but now I'm here."

"You drove from Townsville?" she asked, her eyes wide.

"Yes. I did. I don't even have a place to stay…I didn't think it through. I wanted to see you, that's all."

She released his hand and waved at one of the pair of rocking chairs on the porch. "Come and sit down. I'd get you some tea, but my husband is inside sleeping, and I don't want to wake him. As you can imagine, this is something of a delicate subject…" Her voice trailed away. She didn't want him to think she was minimising or resented him being there. Only…she needed time. This wasn't the way she'd wanted Rupert to discover the truth. Her heart pounded against her ribcage and her head felt light.

He sat, and she lowered herself into the chair next to him, reached for her knitting without thinking and began to knit.

"I'm sorry," he said. "I guess I didn't think about that. He's not my…"

"Your father?" she asked.

He dipped his head.

"No, he's not."

These were conversations she'd never thought she'd have. The past had been left behind, so she'd believed, and she'd moved on. Still, few days had passed over the last forty-four years when she hadn't wondered about him. Where he was, what he was doing…was he happy? Did someone love him? And then her heart would ache, and the pain would travel to her gut until her entire body was full of that bitter, achy feeling and tears would clog her throat.

"Ah…right. Okay." He stared out across the road, cleared his throat. "So, I hope it's all right that I came."

She nodded and patted his hand where it rested on the arm of the rocking chair. "I'm so glad to see you. If you want to stay a while…and I hope you do…you can stay at the Manor. It's my bed and breakfast, or at least it was until a couple of weeks ago."

"Okay, I'll see if they have a room available. I'd like to stay…" He smiled, his lower lip trembling a little.

"All these years…I've thought about you every day," she said.

He glanced at her in surprise. "Really?"

"Yes, of course. I never got over giving you up, not really." She swallowed around the lump in her throat. "I couldn't have children, you see."

"I didn't know…"

"No children, only you. And I gave you away. It was a complicated situation, that's true, but I always thought I'd have more kids. I've regretted it every day of my life. I could've made it work…even if it was just the two of us." Her eyes filled with tears and she met his gaze. "I've wanted to say that for a long time. I'm sorry. I shouldn't have done it. At the time, I was so scared. I thought it would mean…well, I didn't know what it would mean. But hindsight being what it is, I know now that I could've dealt with whatever came. I didn't know it then. I was only fifteen when I found out I was pregnant. Fifteen years old, and a good girl—you know? I was always a good girl, I followed the rules, I did the right thing. Except for this…this one time."

She inhaled a slow breath to dampen the flow of tears that trickled down her cheeks unbidden. "One time…and it hurt to walk away but I thought it was for the best. And now…" She sobbed silently, letting the tears fall without doing anything to mop them up.

He knelt in front of her, took her hands into his. His earnest eyes sought hers. "It's okay, you did what you thought was best. And I'm sure it was...best, I mean. I love my parents, they've been great. They loved me and raised me to be a strong, independent man. I wish I'd known you... wish we could've been together, but don't blame yourself. I don't blame you; I only want to get to know you now, so we don't waste any more years without one another."

Diana couldn't speak. She wrapped her arms around Ben and pulled him into an embrace, then sobbed against his hair.

They talked for a few minutes once both of them had calmed down. They strolled out to his car, and stood in the street, discussing life, careers, family, and friendships, the tea she'd offered forgotten. The conversation brought a bubble of joy into Diana's soul and she couldn't stop smiling as she waved goodbye to Ben through the back window of his car.

She stood there a few moments, looking after him, one hand pressed to her lips. Then she wandered back to the house, collected her basket, and went inside. She jumped when she almost ran into Rupert, standing silently by the front door. He'd been watching her through the glass that bordered the door, his hands pushed into his pockets.

"Who was that?" he asked.

She must've looked a fright, with red-rimmed eyes, wet cheeks and who knew what else. She smoothed her hair back with one hand, her heart pounding like a jack hammer.

"Oh, uh...he was lost. Needed directions to get to the highway. Can you believe it?" She laughed, a little trill that she reserved for when she needed to distract someone long enough to buy her some time. The problem was, she was fairly certain Rupert knew exactly why she laughed that way, since they'd been married for almost forty years. And if he'd seen their embrace there was no way he'd accept her explanation.

"Okay," he said, his face a mask.

She nodded. "I'm going to make a cup of tea. Want one?"

"Yes please."

As she walked away, she released the breath she'd been holding and bit down on her lip. He didn't believe her, she could see that in the look on his face, but he hadn't questioned her further. Not yet anyway. No doubt that time would come.

CHAPTER 14

EMILY

*S*he stood with her hands on her hips and surveyed her work. Emily tugged the mask from her face and set the sander on the floor by her feet. The timber trim around the bedroom was half done, she had to sand the rest of it before she could prep and paint.

The bell at the reception counter dinged and she wiped her hands down the front of her pants before heading out to see who it was. She wasn't expecting any guests until later in the day.

She found a tall man with brown hair and dark eyes standing by the counter, a backpack slung over one shoulder.

He smiled. "Hi, I was hoping you might have a room available for a few nights."

She grinned. "We certainly do, let's see…she checked the computer to see which rooms were free. "You could have room five, it's available for the next week."

She didn't want to tell him it was empty for the foreseeable future, had no desire to scare off a potential guest. They needed every customer they could find.

"Perfect," he said, handing over a credit card.

While she entered his information in the computer, they chatted about the weather, the town, and the best places to eat.

"Have you been to Emerald Cove before?" she asked.

He shook his head. "No, never. It's really pretty, I like it here. Peaceful, I guess you could say."

"It is very quiet. Do you have friends or family in the area?" What she wanted to know was how he found out about the Manor. The marketing methods her aunt and uncle used to promote their business were still something of a mystery to her.

"Actually, yes. I'm here to visit my mother."

"Oh, that's nice. I'll bet she's happy to see you."

He shrugged. "I think so...I hope so. Anyway, thanks a lot."

He grabbed his room key and headed for the stairs.

"Second floor," she called after him. "Breakfast starts at six."

He waved a hand over his shoulder and climbed the stairs. She watched him go, eyes narrowed. That was strange. The moment she asked him about his mother it seemed he couldn't get away from her fast enough.

She shook her head. It was none of her business and she had work to do. She hurried back to the empty room on the first floor and set her mask back in place. The walls were a dark mauve colour and she intended to replace it with a light grey, with white trim. If she could lighten the place up by repainting, it would give the rooms a more spacious feel and bring the Manor into the current century. At least she hoped so. She wasn't exactly an experienced decorator, but she'd bought a few home and lifestyle magazines the previous week and thumbed through them, marking the looks she preferred with Post-Its.

By the time she was done, she was breathing hard. She set the sander down, slumped to the floor, knees bent, elbows resting on her knees, then plucked the mask away from her mouth and set it on her head.

She had no idea how hard physical labour was. She'd have to remember to make Ethan a nice breakfast the next day; after a few hours of sanding she realised how grateful she should be for all the work he'd been doing around the Manor these last weeks.

With a grunt, she stood to her feet and padded to the bathroom. She washed up, then fixed an afternoon tea of petite lemon meringue pies she'd baked that morning, tea, and coffee. She set it out in the dining room, then returned to the kitchen to make herself a cup of coffee. She stared at the steaming mug for a few moments, reached for another and poured Ethan one as well. With a shake of her head, she carried it along with a plate of pies up to the second floor where she could hear him hammering in the walk-in wardrobe he was installing.

She set the tray on a chair that'd been covered with a drop cloth, then knocked on the door frame leading into the wardrobe. He stopped hammering and glanced over his shoulder. "Hi, Emily," he said, breaking into a smile. "How's it going?"

He wore a pair of jeans and work boots. His bare chest gleamed with sweat. Muscles flexed and she swallowed hard before answering.

"So far so good. I sanded the entire skirting and wain-scoting in the room downstairs."

He set down the hammer and faced her. "Great. Now it needs a coat of paint and you'll be done."

"This is looking good," she said, rubbing a hand over the

timber frame of a shoe rack, heat travelling across her neck and face.

He shrugged. "I think it'll improve the room. There was plenty of space for it, and even room to add an ensuite."

"Thanks for working so hard on it." Her cheeks blazed. The words were easier to say than she'd thought they'd be.

His brow furrowed in surprise. "Uh…yeah, you're welcome. Of course, I'm loving it actually. It's good to get away from the computer for a while. I hate having to stare at a screen all day every day. I didn't realise how much of that I'd be doing when I became an engineer… I love working with my hands as well."

"And you look good doing it." She'd meant it as a joke, something to lighten the moment, but as soon as the words left her mouth, she wanted to clamp her hand over it. What was she thinking? They were professionals, colleagues. She had no desire to complicate their relationship. Besides, he thought she hated him, and he was going to end up thinking she wasn't in control of her faculties if she kept this up.

"Thanks," he said with a grin, his eyes flashing. "So, what's that delicious smell?"

She rubbed her sweating palms down her jeans. "Um, I brought you some afternoon tea. Thought it might be time for smoko."

"Perfect, I'm starving," he said. He strode out of the wardrobe and found the pies. "This looks amazing. Seriously, I'm going to go up a pant-size if you keep cooking for me. I'll have to start running ten kilometres instead of five each morning."

"You run five kilometres every morning?" she asked.

He nodded as he took a bite of the dessert. "Yeah, wow this is so good. Thanks."

She hardly ever ran anywhere. She wasn't really the running type. If she exercised, she preferred a gentle bike ride or a slow lap in the pool. Lately she hadn't done much of anything, spending most of her time working at the Manor.

She sat on the end of the drop-cloth draped bed and crossed her legs. "You think it'll make a difference—all this work we're doing?"

He chewed and swallowed. "Definitely. It's going to look great."

"Are you planning on staying in the Cove long term?" she asked.

He shrugged. "I guess not. I mean, I'd love to, but I have to get a job sometime. Unless, of course, this place suddenly becomes super profitable." He sighed. "But I'll have to get back into engineering sometime...if I can." He shook his head. "My old company has...a few issues that seem to be following me. Not sure anyone will hire me again, but I'll wait a while and give it another try."

He seemed upset. She didn't want to pry but wondered what kind of issues he was talking about.

She stood, collected the empty plate. "Well, let me know I guess."

He stepped closer, reaching for another pie. His arm brushed against hers. A thrill ran through her and she clutched the plate harder to keep it from crashing to the ground.

"Uh...so...keep up the good work," she said.

He arched an eyebrow. "Thanks, I will."

"I mean...I don't mean it as though I'm your boss telling you what to do or anything. Because clearly, I'm not." She was blathering like a fool now. What would she do next, trip over her own feet? His expression only made her anxiety grow—he thought she was nuts. "I'm trying to be encouraging... I'm not very good at it, I'm afraid." She grunted. Better to keep her mouth shut in the future.

What was it about this guy? He had her acting like a teenager, and not a very stable one.

"That's okay, I get it." He laughed. "And thanks for the encouragement."

His hand reached for her arm and squeezed it gently. "You're doing a great job too. I probably should tell you that more often. I'm glad we're in this together, you're a hard worker, and you have good instincts."

Her heart leapt into her throat at his touch, his words. She couldn't think clearly. He moved closer, and for a moment she thought he would kiss her but instead he plucked another pie from the plate and held it in front of her face.

"For later," he said with a wink.

She swallowed, nodded. "Oh yeah, great. I'm glad you like them. They've got to be eaten anyway, won't last long."

As she stumbled from the room, her face blazing with heat, she couldn't help wondering if the next time she saw him she should simply pick up a foot and put it directly into her mouth to save time. She groaned and slapped a hand to her face. It made no sense, this was Ethan—she didn't even like him. He'd embarrassed her once before, so she didn't need to make it so easy for him to do again. She should keep her distance, be professional, cool. That was it. She'd email him if she needed anything, or send a text, at least that way she wouldn't have to happen upon him sweat-covered and shirtless again.

CHAPTER 15

ETHAN

A magpie hopped about the garden nearby, head tipping from one side to the other as it watched Ethan with beady, black eyes.

He laughed. "I don't have any food, buddy. Sorry."

The pagoda was almost complete, at least the frame was. He liked the way it was turning out. It brought new character to the garden. Perhaps in summer they could plant a climbing vine beside it. He could imagine how it'd look in a few years' time—stained timber or maybe painted white, flowering vine, with a couple standing together hand-in-hand saying their vows.

He smiled at the thought. It would be a good draw card for the Manor.

Already, since Emily had begun spreading the word to travel agents that the pagoda was coming and would be available for spring weddings, they'd seen an uptick in bookings for those months.

If only the rest of his life looked as promising as the bed and breakfast.

He'd spoken to Marc about his legal issues and his friend had looked into it for him. It seemed the charges hadn't been filed yet, but they were still being considered. At least that was something—maybe it wouldn't happen. But he had to prepare as if it was going to happen, at least that was what Marc had cautioned him. Ethan planned on travelling to Brisbane the next day to meet Marc face-to-face.

He measured the length of a piece of timber, marked it with a pencil and shoved the pencil behind his ear. The back door to the Manor swung open, and Emily stepped out, a basket swinging on one arm.

He waved a hand over his head and she strode in his direction.

"Wow, it's looking great," she said, eyes wide.

He smiled. He was proud of what he'd achieved. It was a simple structure, but with an artistic flair. "Thanks, it's going well."

"The guests are going to love it."

"I think so too…"

She smiled. He marvelled at how pretty she was when she pushed her usual pout aside for a smile. She had a beautiful smile, and a contagious laugh.

"How's your day going so far?"

She shrugged. "I'm taking a break from sanding and painting…going to try out a new frittata recipe that I'm planning on making for breakfast tomorrow. I need some fresh herbs…" She patted the basket.

He nodded. "Sounds delicious. Count me in."

She laughed. "Of course. You can try it this afternoon, tell me if I need to change anything."

"Would you listen if I did?"

She grunted. "No."

"That's what I thought." He chuckled. "But still, I'd love to try it, and I'll keep my opinion to myself."

"Unless you love it."

"Right…unless I love it."

He shook his head and set the timber between two sawhorses, then reached for the circular saw. He sliced the timber in half and set the saw back on the ground.

"Where'd you get the idea for the frittata?" he asked.

"I found an old recipe book in Aunty Di's office."

He laughed. "It's your office now."

She shrugged. "I guess so. It doesn't feel that way. I think, for me, this place will always be theirs. The office will always be hers."

"I get it," he said. "I feel the same way, really."

He tried to focus his attention back on the work at hand but couldn't. Emily's presence had disrupted his thoughts. He couldn't find the thread. He wanted to be able to ignore her, push her aside, but he couldn't. He was still befuddled by the way she treated him when she seemed perfectly capable of being kind to other people, and even sometimes to him as well. He was confused by his feelings for her—why was he attracted to a woman who quite obviously disliked him? Usually…

But today she'd come outside with a basket on her arm, and her hair piled in messy waves on top of her head, looking cute and giving him that smile. It was confounding.

"Are you okay?" she asked.

He sighed. "I've got a lot on my mind."

"Like?"

"Like…" He sighed. How much should he say? He didn't want Emily to know she was one of the things on his mind. But so far, he'd only told Mum about the legal issues he was facing. "You know how I lost my job?"

She nodded.

"Well, the reason for that is my boss, and some of the other executives are facing charges of fraud. I don't even know what else. But whatever happened, it brought the whole company down, and me with it."

Her eyes widened. "I'm sorry, that sounds horrible."

"Yeah it is, and it hasn't finished yet. That's what's bothering me—the government's considering filing charges of fraud against me as well."

"What? Why?" Emily's stormy grey eyes narrowed.

He shrugged. "I don't know…I'm not sure what they've got. All I know is, I didn't do what they're saying I did. I didn't even realise anything was going on behind the scenes. I wish I'd paid better attention, but honestly, I was working, doing my job, and keeping my head down. I wanted to be a partner, and was on track to achieve that…now, I'm grateful that never happened. I'm pretty certain all of the partners have been charged already."

"Wow," she replied.

"Yeah. I'm going to do everything I can to prevent it from having an impact here, on the Manor, the business. But, if it ends up in court, I may have to sell my half of the business. I don't want it to come to that, but I think you should know it's a possibility."

"Okay, well thanks for telling me." She chewed on a fingernail; her gaze fixed on the ground at her feet. She glanced his way. "I'm going to get started on that frittata. I'll let you know when it's done, and you can come and taste test it for me."

He nodded, waved goodbye, and watched her leave. She'd barely reacted to what he'd said. Didn't seem bothered by the idea of him having to give up his half of the business. He shouldn't be surprised by that, he supposed, she'd never been happy about sharing the business with him. But it hurt a little, to be so easily dismissed. He loved being a part-owner of the Seaside Manor. As difficult as she was, he'd grown fond of sharing that with Emily. He found it difficult to swallow the idea that she didn't feel the same.

With a shake of his head, he returned to the task at hand —if he had to sell his share of the Manor, he'd go back to Brisbane to look for work. And if he still couldn't find anyone who'd take a risk on a former Mammoth employee, he might have to move even further away. The idea made his heart sink. Emerald Cove was home now, he didn't want to leave, but he may not have a choice.

CHAPTER 16

SARAH

"What are you reading?"

Meg glanced up, shielding her eyes from the glare of the setting sun with her hand, and grinned. "Hi Sarah. How's things?"

Sarah settled onto a beach towel on the sand beside Meg, her lips pulled into a wide smile. "Good. What are you reading?"

"Uh...I'm reading a mystery...it's good so far, but the scenery keeps distracting me."

Sarah nodded, taking in the waves, the sand, the families making sandcastles nearby. "I know what you mean, it's a pretty great view."

"I love sitting on the beach, just enjoying the sights, sounds, smells...it's very relaxing. Although, lately I haven't gotten out so much..." In truth, she hadn't been to the beach more than a couple of times in the past two months, even though they lived directly across the road from it. Brad didn't want to see the beach, much less get close to it. She'd asked him a few times if they could BBQ or picnic in the parklands beside the beach, but he wouldn't even do that. Didn't want to hear the waves, no doubt. He hadn't said as much, but she assumed. And honestly, she couldn't blame him. He'd been more passionate about the ocean than anyone she'd ever known, and now felt as though it was off limits for him. She only hoped he'd come around someday. No doubt much of his bad temper resulted from the fact that his happy place, the place that filled his soul with joy, was now forbidden to him — at least in his mind it was. One day she hoped to encourage him back onto the sand — they'd find a way to make it work. But for now, she had to honour his wishes and bite her tongue.

"Thanks for meeting me here," said Meg.

"No worries. I was glad you called. I've been worried about you."

Meg wore workout gear, her red curls pulled into a ponytail that hung down her back.

"So, what's up?" asked Sarah. "You sounded a little down on the phone."

"Nothing really...just Brad. He's having one of those days where he doesn't want to leave the unit, keeps the curtains drawn over the windows, and snaps at me for everything. I had to get out of there."

"I'm sorry," replied Sarah. "I know that's hard."

"Yeah... I mean things are a lot better than they were. Most of the time he seems happy, or at least happier than he was. I shouldn't complain..."

"You can always complain to me. I don't mind." Sarah smiled. "They say marriage is the most difficult thing you'll ever face. I guess they're right about that. I know it was pretty hard on Mum."

They talked for a few more minutes, then Meg stood and

dusted the sand from her legs. "I've got to go. It's getting dark and I want to cook Brad something special for dinner, maybe cheer him up."

Sarah waved goodbye as Meg strode away through the warm sand. Then she took a book out of her woven shoulder bag and lay on her back to read a while. She was in no rush to get home, although she hadn't gotten out any meat to defrost for dinner. Perhaps she'd have baked beans on toast. After all, she hadn't spoken to Mick, wasn't sure if she'd see him that night or if she'd be eating alone.

"Good book?" Mick's voice startled Sarah.

She sat up, scattering sand, and dropping the book in her lap. "Oh, hi, Mick, I wasn't expecting to see you out here."

Mick pushed one end of his surfboard into the sand and sat beside her, flipping his hair back from his face and spraying saltwater all over her.

She giggled. "Thanks."

"No worries." He leaned over to kiss her. His lips tasted like salt, and they were cold against hers.

"Did you have a good surf?"

He nodded, grinned. "It's beautiful out there. Perfect weather. The waves are pretty small, but the water is so nice. I even saw a few dolphins."

"Really? Oh man, I knew I should've brought my board."

"Yes, you should've." He dug an elbow gently into her side.

She laughed. "You're getting water all over me."

He winked. "That's kind of the point. Come on, it's a beautiful afternoon, the waves are great and you're missing out… I'll come back in with you."

She looked at the water. It rose and fell in a slow, soothing rhythm. The waves curled lazily towards the shore, then lapped at the sand. The sun hung low behind them, giving the entire beach a golden glow.

"I don't have a board."

"I've got a spare," he said.

She grinned. "Okay, let's do it."

She wore a red one-piece bathing suit and had pulled her hair back into a ponytail. She stood, brushed the sand from her rear end and watched with thudding heart as he ran back to the truck to get the other board from the roof racks. He really was very attractive, especially with a surfboard tucked beneath his arm. The fact that he cared about her as much as he did only made her passion for him that much more intense.

Mick splashed her as they walked through the water, then pushed her off her board after their first wave. She sputtered to the surface, laughing, and pushed him off his board right as the next wave slammed down on top of them. Then, she duck-dived through it, turned and paddled. She sailed towards shore, a grin on her face. The next wave she caught, she tried a cut-back and ending up diving headfirst into the lip of the wave. It pummelled her, spinning her like a washing machine. When she popped up again and gasped for breath, Mick gave her a thumbs up.

She paddled back out to him. "That was graceful…"

He laughed. "Yeah, but for a second I was very impressed."

"Really?" She pursed her lips. She'd gotten rusty during her years living in the city, but gradually the techniques and skills she'd learned in childhood were coming back to her.

He laughed at the look on her face and leaned over to kiss her. His strong brown arms closed around her. His face hung over hers and heat travelled up her body, burning in her cheeks. She swallowed hard. Then he pushed her forward and she was moving, carried forward by the wave. She stood to her feet in one movement, tried another cut-back, this time nailing it.

She hooted in celebration, then leapt from the board before the wave petered out.

When she stood and waved to Mick, he pumped a fist in the air. Sarah paddled back out to meet him and they surfed together that way for another hour, enjoying the togetherness, the flirting, the fun. She'd never been so relaxed with anyone before—she could be herself around Mick and he accepted her, every part of her, without question. It was invigorating.

Finally, when she was exhausted, she paddled to shore and waved to Mick, then left his board in the sand as she gathered her things together. Mick reached her soon after, and ran up the beach, panting and soaking wet.

"Hey, don't you want to keep going? I'm loving this…it's so great to share this with you." He looped his arms around her wet waist and smiled down at her, his eyes sparkling as droplets of water fell from his hair onto her.

She shook her head with a smile. "That was amazing. Thank you. I really enjoyed it, but I've got to get home. Oscar will wonder where I am."

"So…what are you doing for dinner tonight?" he asked.

She shrugged. "I was thinking baked beans on toast."

He laughed. "I think I can do better than that. How about I come over and cook us something. We can sit in front of the fire or watch a movie…"

She reached up to kiss his soft lips, happiness filling her soul. "That sounds perfect."

"I'll see you then," he said, caressing her cheek.

"See you!"

She ran up the beach, her towel wrapped around her waist, shoulder bag bumping her leg with each step. When she reached the footpath, she leaned down to slip on a pair of sandals, glanced back over her shoulder at Mick who was still watching her, then hurried to the car with a bounce in her step.

CHAPTER 17

EMILY

"*D*id you get the mini apple pies in the oven?" asked Emily.

Sondra, her new hire nodded. "They're warming now. They'll be ready for morning tea. I've got some chai tea brewing as well, thought it might go nicely with the cinnamon in the pies."

"That sounds great. Thank you."

Emily rinsed off a breakfast plate, scrubbing the egg that'd stuck to the white china like cement. She'd hired Sondra to help manage the Manor since they were pushing to grow their bookings and Diana had laid off the previous assistant manager when their vacancy rates rose. She'd argued back and forth with herself over the decision, finally realising that if she wanted to grow the business, she'd need more hands on board. And since business was picking up and she'd laid off the majority of the part-timers when she first started managing the place, she needed the extra help.

"I can do the dishes if you'd like," offered Sondra.

Emily took a step back, wiped her hands on her apron. "Thank you. I have to do some admin, so that would really help me out."

"No worries."

Emily set her apron back on its peg and headed for the front door. She skipped down the path to the mailbox, revelling in the feel of the sun on her face. She'd barely stepped outside for more than a few minutes each day in the past week. In fact, she hadn't had a day off since she'd started working at the Manor. Not that she was complaining. For the first time, they'd have a full house that night. Bookings were up. The pagoda was complete, and she'd managed to paint two rooms. Things were going well, better than she could've hoped. Still, she was exhausted.

She stopped at the mailbox, pulled open the metal door and retrieved a handful of envelopes and junk mail. With a quick glance at each, she flicked through the pile. Nothing but bills and advertisements.

With a yawn, she tucked them under her arm and was about to return to the Manor when she saw a figure in the distance, running towards her. It was Ethan—out for another run. He went every day. Surfed each morning too, if the wet hair when he arrived at the Manor around eight a.m. was anything to go by. She'd been up preparing and serving breakfast since five a.m., but he dropped by the kitchen to eat before work, all tanned and smiling. Sometimes she wanted to slap him, only he was always too nice, offering words of encouragement about the meal or her latest outfit.

He stopped at the mailbox, barely puffing. "Hi Emily. How's your day going so far?"

"I thought you were working on the upstairs bathroom," she replied.

"It's Saturday."

She pushed a strained smile onto her face. "I know it's Saturday. We're fully booked, and it would've been really great if that room was ready since I had to turn people away."

"Sorry...don't worry, it'll be done before you know it."

She spun on her heel and headed for the door.

He called out. "You know, you should take the day off as well."

She stopped. "I can't take the day off. Someone has to be responsible around here. There's a business to run."

He chuckled. "I know, that's why you hired Sondra. Come on, let me take you fishing. I'm going anyway, and you can finally have some downtime. You've got a mobile phone if anything goes wrong."

Emily's nostrils flared, but she didn't react. He had a point. Why bother hiring staff if she wasn't going to let them run the place so she could have a break? But, fishing with Ethan? She wasn't sure that was what she wanted to do with any precious time off she had. Still, what else was there to do in Emerald Cove? She was too exhausted to be creative, and she hadn't really made any new friends since she'd been so busy.

"Fishing? Beach or freshwater?"

"Beach," he replied.

She squinted into the morning sunlight. "Okay, let's go fishing."

* * *

ETHAN

It felt like a date. It wasn't a date, he was showing a colleague around town, taking her fishing, that was all. So, why did it feel like a date?

Sweat cooled Ethan's palms and he rubbed them down

the front of his pants before walking into the Manor. The back door was unlocked, and the kitchen empty. He scanned the living room—there were a few guests sitting around in front of the roaring fire, reading books, chatting. But no sign of Emily.

He found her in the office, finishing up some paperwork. She'd changed clothes since he last saw her, and she was dressed more casually now in jeans and a long-sleeved flannel shirt. Her hair was pulled into a cute ponytail that made her look younger and more carefree, and sunglasses perched on her forehead. He knocked on the open door as he peered through it with a smile.

"Ready to go?"

She sighed, pursed her lips. "I don't know. Maybe I shouldn't leave Sondra on her own yet. We haven't had so many guests in a long time…"

He shook his head. "Come on, she can handle it. She doesn't have to do much except answer questions and make sure the cleaner does her job—which she always does. It's not rocket science."

"Okay, fine. You have a point. I guess I should get out and see the Cove a little bit. I've hardly stepped foot outside the Manor since I got here. If I'm not careful, I'll become a recluse."

He chuckled. "Well, we can't have that."

She stood, pulled a small bag from the floor, and slipped the strap over her shoulder. "Okay, I'm ready. Lead the way. I've packed us a few things to eat."

She patted the side of the bag.

"Sounds perfect."

He walked with her to his ute and opened the door for her. It was strange how natural it felt, being with her. They talked about the weather, his surf that morning, how her aunt and uncle were settling into their retirement community. It was easy, relaxed, and he found himself wondering why there'd ever been tension between them.

When they reached the secluded southern end of Emerald Cove, Ethan led Emily down a winding path from the top of the cliffs to the beach below. They clambered over black rocks, around squat bushes, and finally reached the sand. Ethan kicked off his thongs and picked them up with one hand, the fishing rods in the other, the bait bucket swinging from his forearm.

"Wow, it's so beautiful here. And peaceful too." Emily removed her sandals and followed him with wide eyes.

"Most people stick to the northern end of the Cove. This place is hidden by that rocky outcropping. I find it tends to keep the tourists away. The path we followed is the best way to get down here, and it's not easy to find unless you know exactly what you're looking for."

There was one last rock to hurdle. Ethan set the rods and bait on the sand next to his thongs and reached for Emily's hand to help her over it.

She crouched low to climb on the rock's hard surface, then sighed when her feet hit the sand again. "The sand feels good between my toes. I should come down here more often."

"You live at the beach now; it's time to embrace the lifestyle."

She chuckled. "You're right. I've been so caught up in making sure I don't let down Auntie Di and Uncle Rupert...I haven't taken the time to enjoy being here."

"They'd want you to love the Cove as much as they do. Besides, you can hardly recommend outings to the guests if you don't know the place and haven't been out yourself." He arched an eyebrow. "It's only good business to make sure you relax and experience everything the Cove has to offer."

She laughed. It was a contagious sound that came from

the gut. She threw her head back, eyes squeezed shut. Her blonde ponytail lifted on the breeze and the sun glowed on her upturned face. His heart skipped a beat.

He turned away from her, anxious to hide his reaction from her. He couldn't let her see how he felt, what she made him feel. She wouldn't like it—she'd made it very clear that things between them were professional. Nothing more. And sometimes barely even that. But he couldn't seem to help the attraction he felt for her. There was something different about her, it reminded him of childhood summers, of bare feet and bicycles, the scent of heat and salt spray, of home. She wasn't like the women he'd dated in Brisbane; she was coastal, like him. And the connection they shared was like a siren's call.

Instead of showing her his reddened cheeks, he focused on the task at hand. He set up each of the fishing rods, checked the reels, made sure the lines would throw cleanly and weren't tangled, then he attached hooks and baited them with the squid he'd bought on the way to the beach from his favourite bait and tackle shop.

While he worked, he sensed Emily had gone for a stroll along the beach, although he had his back to her. He had to pull himself together. The most he could hope for was that they'd be friends. If he could manage that today, he'd be happy. He wanted her to see him as a business partner, a friend, someone she could count on. To put down the jousting stick and give him a chance—that was his goal in taking her fishing—not romance. That wasn't an option. She didn't see him that way, and even if she did, it would complicate their business relationship.

Finally, when everything was ready, he called Emily over and handed her one of the fishing rods. She studied it, took a look at the squid on the hook, and smiled. "Thanks."

Then, she walked to the water's edge and waded into the waves. "Oh...cold."

He laughed. "Yeah, it's a bit nippy this time of year, but I don't have any waders. Sorry."

"No worries, it's nowhere near as cold as the water down south."

He followed her, pushed one end of his fishing rod into the sand and stepped closer. "So, this is an Alvey sidecast reel —it's pretty simple to cast. There aren't any buttons or anything." He reached for the fishing rod, his arms closing around her. He pulled back the rod, her back pressed to him. She was warm and smelled faintly of vanilla and chocolate.

"Now, you pull it back like this...and then flick forward." He did the move slowly, demonstrating the correct motion without casting the line. Her hair tickled his nose. She didn't resist, moving with him instead. He released the fishing rod and stepped back.

She grinned. "Thanks. I think I've got it."

With a nod, he collected his own pole, and carried it a few metres away. He watched as she deftly stepped forward and flicked the line overhead—it sailed far out over the breakers, the bait landing softly in the water and sinking fast.

Ethan gaped. "Uh...yeah, just like that."

"I've been fishing my whole life, but thanks for the lesson," she quipped with a wink.

His face flushed with heat. "Oh...right. Sorry..."

"No, it's fine. It was...nice." Her smile was warm, genuine. Then she focused her attention on the line.

His cheeks flamed. "Good to know."

He cast his own line and reeled it in slowly, his thoughts whirling. Was she flirting with him?

It was nice.

What did that mean? Was she only teasing him? That was a far more likely alternative.

He noticed she was reeling her line in more quickly. "Have you got something?'

"I think so." She reeled faster, and soon a fish skipped through the shallow water. It was small, silver, the afternoon sun blinking off its side as it turned over. Water bubbled and frothed around it, then she was holding it off the ground, studying it as it turned slowly on the hook.

"It's a tiny little flathead," she said.

He nodded.

She tugged it gently from the hook, held it in the water and let it go.

"Hey, that could've been dinner," he objected.

She shook her head. "Too small. Besides, I only do kiss and release."

"What?" He chuckled. "Don't you mean, catch and release?"

She giggled. "That's what my mum always called it, kiss and release. Of course, I gave up kissing the fish when I was about thirteen years old."

Her smile faded, and she fell silent.

His lips pursed. "It sounds like she was a good mother."

She nodded. "She was."

Sadness rolled off her like the waves that lapped at his feet. He inhaled a slow breath. He couldn't imagine what it would be like to grow up with only one parent, and then to lose her while Emily was still so young. He loved having a big, raucous family. Even his parents' separation had shaken him to the core, and yet he still had both of them. His family had changed, but at least they were still around.

"I know I should've gotten over it by now. It's been three years…but I don't think I've ever grieved properly. It's a hard thing to face. I've felt so alone since she died."

She hesitated and swallowed.

He didn't know what to say. There wasn't anything he

could say that would help. So, he simply threw out his line again.

"I know Auntie Di misses her too, but I haven't spoken to her much about it. Mum was her sister, they were close, but I hate talking about her because it hurts too much. Does that make sense? I'll bet I sound ridiculous—I'm an adult, I should be able to face my grief and deal with it. I don't know why I'm telling you this..." She forced a laugh.

He shook his head. "It makes complete sense. I don't know if I'd be able to talk about it either if it happened to me. Your parents are...well, they're always there. To lose them unexpectedly like that...it would be so hard."

She nodded. "Thanks for understanding."

"Of course."

She caught his gaze, squinting into the sunlight with a half-smile. "You're not so bad, Ethan Flannigan."

He chuckled. "Thanks, that's quite a compliment coming from you, Em."

Her cheeks suddenly looked pinker, but it might've been the wind on her skin or the heat from the sun overhead.

CHAPTER 18

DIANA

A pair of hooded plovers circled above as Diana pulled her car into the parking lot at the Emerald Cafe. She should've told Ben to meet her somewhere else when he called, only he'd sounded so excited to have found a great place for them to meet for lunch that she didn't have the heart.

Her only hope was that Cindy wasn't there. She hadn't told anyone yet about Ben, about his looking for her, the letters or that he'd shown up at her door unannounced. Even Rupert didn't know her secret yet. She knew it was only a matter of time before she'd be forced to spill the beans, but she hoped to wait a little longer. Keep him to herself for a few more days at least. It was such an adjustment. A life lived without the children she'd always believed and hoped would come. And now, here he was—the child she'd given up so many years ago, believed she'd never see again. It was almost too much. And yet, the joy she felt was tinged with fear over what might come when the truth about who he was found its way into the open.

The air was light, the sunshine warm as she made her way into the cafe. She glanced about, her heart in her throat.

"Is Cindy in today?" she asked the young waitress who sang most evenings. She couldn't remember the girl's name. Something exotic.

The girl shook her head, smiled. "No, not today. Can I seat you outside?"

Diana nodded. "I'm meeting someone…oh, there he is."

She waved to Ben, who waved back, then made her way over to where he was sitting, at a small, square table near the back of the cafe under the twinkle lights that now lay dull in the hot sun. They came to life at night and turned the cafe into a wonderland that made Diana feel as though anything could happen—that there was some kind of magic in the air. She'd loved that about the Emerald Cafe for as long as she could remember. Was proud of her friend for what she'd built.

A lump lodged in her throat. She didn't know what she'd do without Cindy in her life. She was the only person who'd always been there for Diana…except for Rupert, of course. He'd been her rock over the years, but Cindy had understood the grief she'd endured through the years of infertility. She'd been the shoulder Diana had cried on, she'd been the one who'd let Diana be part of every single one of her own children's special days, celebrations, and milestones. It was something Diana had been forever grateful for. But now what would happen?

She pushed the fears from her mind and forced a smile to her face as she stood across from Ben. He was so handsome, the picture of her own father from what she'd seen of photos of him in his younger years. Her own memories of those years were as faded as the photographs themselves.

He stood as well, embraced her a little awkwardly, then they sat.

"I hope this is okay," he said. "It looks really good, and when I asked at the Manor about somewhere to eat, this is what Emily suggested."

Diana gave a brief nod. "Yes, it is very nice. My friend Cindy owns it." Then she swallowed down the rest of what she wanted to say, afraid more would tumble out of her mouth than she was ready to reveal.

"Oh really? Wow, that's great. So, what's good here?" He reached for a menu and flipped it open.

"I love the grilled fish and Greek salad...it's very fresh."

He nodded. "That sounds delicious, but I think I'm going to go with the steak pie with chips."

She chuckled. "It's lovely too. The exact meal that Rupert goes for every time we come here."

He closed the menu with a grin. "It's too hard to pass up."

The waitress took their orders while they chatted about the weather, the Manor, and how Emily was coping with running the place.

"She seems very nice. So, you said that you used to own it?" He leaned forward on his elbows, fists cupped together.

"Yes, until only a few weeks ago actually. We've owned the Seaside Manor forever..." She sighed. "But it was time to move on. Rupert's health hasn't been great, and it was getting too much for me to manage on my own. We should've given it up years ago, really. But we didn't want to sell it. Then, I had the idea of calling Emily to see if she wanted it."

"Is she a friend of yours?"

Diana held her breath. She hadn't told him yet. There were so many things he didn't know. "She's my niece."

His eyes widened. "Emily is? So, that makes her my..."

"Cousin," finished Diana.

He leaned back in his chair, pressed both hands to his head. "I have a new cousin. Wow. Does she know about me?"

Diana shook her head.

His eyes narrowed. "Are you planning on telling her?"

"Yes, of course I am. But I haven't told anyone yet. I'm sorry...I know I should've but it's all so new. I'm not very good at shifting course all of a sudden. I need time..."

"I understand. Although, I hope you don't wait too long. I can't stay indefinitely."

She dipped her head in agreement.

"You haven't told your husband yet?"

"No, not yet. It's hard...we've spent forty years together. He thinks he knows everything there is to know about me. It'll be a shock..."

Ben rubbed a hand over his face, then smiled. "I understand. I can't imagine what that would be like. I never got married."

"You're still young," she replied.

He laughed. "Not so very young, forty-four in August."

"That's young enough to find love."

"I suppose you're right. I'd like to get married, maybe even have a family someday."

"I hope you don't mind me asking...why didn't you marry?"

His lips pursed. "I don't know. I suppose I never found *the one*. If there is such a thing. I had a few serious relationships that ended, and before I knew it, I was forty years old and single." He chuckled. "But it's not so bad. I like it some days. Other days, I wish I had someone to share my life with."

"Tell me about your parents...were they good to you?" The words that tumbled from her lips had been hiding in her heart for more than forty years. They were words she'd fallen asleep wondering, hoping, praying over. Words she'd shed tears over. Her heart clenched as they left her mouth.

He smiled, reached for her hand, and squeezed it. "They were very good to me...still are. I've got nothing to complain about when it comes to Mum and Dad. I love them, they love me, and I had a great childhood. I'm not trying to replace them by coming to see you; I only wanted to get to know you."

She nodded, swallowed. "I'm so glad to hear it. I worried...all the time over whether I'd made the right choice. It seems I did."

He sighed. "I don't know if I can answer that for you. But they were, and are, good parents to me. I couldn't have asked for better. In fact, they're very anxious about this whole trip. They worried you wouldn't want to see me, that I'd be hurt. I've told them all about you, and they'd like to meet you someday, if you're up for it. They're older than you, of course. Dad turned eighty last year, and Mum will be eighty next year."

She nodded. "It would be wonderful to meet them. I feel I have to thank them—" Tears filled her eyes and she couldn't go on.

"Thank them?" he asked.

"For...for raising my baby boy with so much love." One tear spilled onto her cheek and she didn't bother to wipe it away.

He pressed his fingers against hers again. "They'd be very happy to hear that, I'm sure."

The waitress brought their food, set it in front of them and left again. Ben had released his hold on her hand, and Diana missed the warmth of his touch.

Her son. She had a son.

She was filled with so much joy, sadness, fear...emotions whirled around inside of her. She wasn't quite sure what to do with them all. She'd avoided drama as much as possible in her adult life and had put away the sadness over never having had children many years earlier, and ever since she'd lived in a quiet contentment. But now, everything was topsy-turvy, her carefully constructed world coming apart at the seams.

She took a bite of the fish, and it flaked apart on her tongue, warm and soft. The food at the Emerald Cafe really was very good. She focused her attention on the plate in front of her as she worked to calm her emotions. The tears dried on her cheeks, she inhaled slow breaths.

Ben ate in silence for a few moments as well, the only sound the crackle of crisp pastry beneath his knife and fork. He chewed and swallowed, then watched her a moment.

"There is one other thing I wanted to ask you about... well, a lot of things really, but one important thing."

She'd known it was coming, of course he had to ask. She set down her fork and braced herself.

"I need to know who my father is. His name wasn't in any of the documentation I found... I was hoping you might tell me."

CHAPTER 19

ETHAN

*T*he sounds of the office brought back memories. Telephones ringing, hushed voices in conversation, a printer whirring. Ethan shifted in his seat, tension tightening the muscles across his shoulders. His fingers closed around the manila envelope in his lap. He didn't miss it—he much preferred working at the Manor after a morning surf in Emerald Cove.

"You can go in now, Mr Flannigan," said his solicitor's assistant.

He stood and strode into the office. The musk of polished timber and leather greeted him. He shook hands with Marc Jobs and sat across from him, crossing one long leg over the other.

"It's good to see you, mate," said Ethan. "How long has it been?"

"At least five years since that dinner party in Toowong," replied Marc with a grin. "It's good to see you too."

"Thanks for agreeing to help me with this mess. I'm not really sure where to start, or what to do. I brought the signed contract for you." Ethan handed over the envelope.

Marc took it with a smile. "Great, thanks for that." He set the envelope on the desk, then his expression turned serious as he faced the computer monitor. He clicked a few times with his mouse, eyes on the screen. "We'll start at the beginning. I know it can seem overwhelming, but you'll get through it one step at a time. Let's see…"

Ethan's fingers tapped a rhythm on the arms of his chair. He swallowed. "I've been told they're charging me with fraud, but I don't know what the charges refer to."

Marc nodded. "Okay, yes I see. I've got the paperwork here. They state the fraud was related to government contracts."

"That's crazy. I don't know anything about it."

"Were you a partner with the firm? From what I understand, they're charging all of the partners and the executive."

"No, I wasn't a partner, but I was on the partner track."

"I suppose that's why they haven't laid charges yet. So, that's a good sign."

"Do you think so?" asked Ethan.

Marc nodded. "Let's hope they won't do it. I'll ask around, see if I can talk to the prosecuting solicitor and find out what's going on, then I'll give you a call. Okay?"

Ethan inhaled a sharp breath. "Thank you, I'm not sure what I'd do without your help. I've tried calling my boss, so many times. I've left voicemails…he's not calling me back. I don't know what to think."

"I wouldn't worry about that. And it's best you don't talk to anyone at the company, clients—no one who could be called on to give evidence. I'm sure your boss has been given the same advice, that's why he's not calling you back."

Ethan pursed his lips. "Okay, that makes sense. Thanks."

"No worries."

Marc stood, held out a hand, Ethan stood as well and shook it.

"Thanks again."

"You'll get through this," said Marc with a smile. "Don't worry about it too much—I'm sure the crown prosecutor isn't after you. If they lay charges, we can talk to them about doing a deal—you tell them what you know, and maybe they'll drop the charges."

Ethan swallowed. "That sounds great, except I don't know anything."

Marc shrugged. "We'll cross that bridge when we come to it."

* * *

REBECCA

The report froze on the computer screen. Black letters, unmoving. Behind her, a phone rang, then the muffled sound of a radio crackled. Rebecca leaned back in her chair with a sigh of exasperation. She clicked the mouse, nothing happened. How was she supposed to submit a report on the shoplifting incident she'd investigated that morning at the Foodstore if her computer wouldn't even wake up? She shook her head and decided to reboot.

It was time for the staff meeting anyway, so she'd have another go at submitting it later.

She wandered to the kitchen and made herself a cup of tea, then she headed for the meeting room. She was the first one there, but slowly the rest of the group filtered in, greeting her as they took their seats.

Franklin was last. He strode to the head of the long, boardroom table and stood with hands pressed to the timber. His thick, dark hair stood up in waves as though he'd run his fingers through it. His dark eyes focused on the team seated around the table.

"Good afternoon everyone. As you know, we have a few administrative things to go through, then we'll zip around the table and give an update on open cases. Sound good?"

There were nods all around, and the meeting got underway. Rebecca half listened, her thoughts wandering. She'd gotten stronger each day and was able to push herself a little harder at boxing, although sparring was still off limits. She'd managed to run from her unit to class the evening before. Maybe she'd try that again today, see if her core muscles could manage it. Her instructor was pleased with her progress but had warned her to take her time to heal. Patience wasn't something Rebecca had a lot of when it came to working out. It'd become a driving force in her life, as if building up her strength, stamina, and reflexes could keep her safe somehow, even after the stabbing.

She knew it didn't make sense. If the perp had a knife or a gun, it wouldn't matter how strong she was. But that wasn't why she was doing it. She needed to be able to fight back, it was all she knew to do. And to fight back, her naturally slight frame meant that she needed to give herself as much of an advantage as she could manage. Strength training, running, boxing—those were the things she could control, the things she could do to make sure no one was able to get the upper hand on her again.

"...Mair? Come on we haven't got all day." Franklin's voice broke through her reverie and she glanced around to see all eyes fixed on her.

Rebecca's cheeks flamed. "Uh...sorry. What did you say?"

Franklin rolled his eyes and sighed. "Which part did you miss?"

"Um...all of it. Sorry, I was thinking about something else."

"Clearly. Do you think you could manage to pay attention during staff meetings, Mair? We do this for a reason—everyone updates the team on open cases so we can determine if there's any overlap, or something being missed, maybe a clue that one person has could help resolve a case someone else is managing. Does that make sense to you Proby?"

Her face grew hotter still. "Yes, sir. Of course. I'm sorry."

"Wonderful. Glad to be of service. Now...can you give us an update on the status of your shoplifting report from the Foodstore?"

"I'm almost finished."

His lips pursed. "What's holding you up, Proby?"

"Nothing, I've got everything I need. I haven't submitted it yet, that's all."

"Get on with it then. All right everyone, meeting over," he replied. Under his breath, she could've sworn she heard him mutter. "Ian would've had it filed and solved by now."

Her eyes widened. Had he really said that? She glanced around the room, but no one else seemed to be paying attention. They'd broken off into small groups to chat about weekend plans.

Rebecca stood slowly, collected her teacup, and carried it back to her desk. She sat and stared at the black computer screen for a few moments before flicking it on. That was the problem between her and Franklin—he was always comparing her with his old partner, Ian, the man who never got anything wrong, according to Franklin.

Still, he'd never said it out loud before. Not like that.

She shook her head. She couldn't be Ian, of course she couldn't. She was a completely different person. And from what she'd heard on the grapevine, which meant of course via Steph, the station's receptionist, Franklin and Ian had been best friends since childhood, as well as partners.

That he missed his friend was understandable. She could forgive him for being irritated that Ian had been replaced by a proby officer he didn't know. But when would he stop comparing her with his dead, best friend? It wasn't fair. She'd never be able to live up to a memory.

She gulped down the last of her tea, then strode to the reception desk. Steph glanced up in surprise, and a book about managing strong willed children thudded to the floor. Steph reached for it, then set it back on her desk with a smile. She patted an empty chair beside her.

"You look like you need to talk about something. Take a load off."

Rebecca's nostrils flared as she sat. "That man…"

"You mean, Franklin?"

"Yes. Of course." Rebecca pressed both hands to her face and groaned. "He's never going to accept that I'm his partner. I thought after the stabbing…well, he softened. It seemed like he was coming around, that maybe he liked me a little bit after all."

"He likes you plenty." Steph patted her arm with one hand. "He's not great at expressing it, that's all."

"Do you know what he muttered in the staff meeting, just now?"

Steph shook her head.

"He said that Ian would've had my shoplifting case solved and filed by now. He said it soft, so that no one else heard him. But I heard." She bit the inside of her cheek. "He's always comparing me. I'm never going to be able to live up to that kind of expectation."

Steph sighed. "Did anyone ever tell you what happened?"

Rebecca hesitated. "No, not really. The articles I found only said that he was killed on the job."

"It was bad...Franklin blamed himself for a long time. They were friends, you know. Hung out together after work, did everything together really. They were more than partners. It'd been that way since they were kids. Franklin said at the time that he'd gotten careless. Nothing much ever happened in Emerald Cove: some shoplifting, the occasional domestic. Other than that, it was a sleepy seaside town, and he let his guard down. I think that's why he's so hard on you."

Rebecca leaned back in her chair. "I guess that makes sense."

"They got a call about a gunshot...a neighbour heard something. Anyway, Franklin and Ian assumed it was probably a car backfiring, or someone setting off fireworks, since no one around here ever heard gunfire. They were laughing and joking about something or other when they got there. Franklin said they weren't paying attention; he honestly didn't think they'd even find the source of the noise. But the house the person directed them to across the street was a meth lab. They didn't know it, no one did. It was relatively new to the area, at least we think so."

"Wow," replied Rebecca. "It must've been horrible."

"Yeah, well—Ian always took the front door and Franklin went around the back of the house. He said that he heard the front door open, then there was a shot. By the time he got to the front steps, Ian was bleeding out on the lawn. The perp got away and Ian died in Franklin's arms while they were waiting for the ambulance."

Rebecca inhaled a sharp breath. "That's why he always takes the front door now."

"Yeah, I guess so. If you want my opinion, he doesn't like

you in Ian's place because he's scared of losing another partner. But maybe I'm wrong, maybe he's just being a jerk."

Rebecca stood to her feet, her thoughts whirling. "No, I think you're right. I shouldn't be so sensitive. He lost his best friend and partner... Hey, thanks for telling me. It helps."

Steph shrugged. "Yeah, don't let him know I said anything. He likes *me*, and I want to keep it that way." She winked.

Rebecca chuckled. "Okay, crawler. I won't say a word, I promise."

Back at her desk, Rebecca went through the motions of filling out the shoplifting report and submitting it. This time it processed without any issues. She opened her emails and leaned forward in her chair to skim through them.

It all made so much sense. The way Franklin pushed her to do better, the way he always went to the front door whenever they had a call out. He was doing everything he could to keep from losing another partner.

She couldn't help feeling sympathy for him—for the loss he'd suffered, and how much that must've changed him. She wondered what he'd been like before. She could ask Steph about it the next time they had a chance to chat.

An email caught her eye. It was from a sender with a name made up of random letters and symbols. Probably junk mail. She was about to mark it as spam when she caught a few of the words in the body of the mail from the preview pane.

I found you. It wasn't so hard. You'll have to do better than that if you want to lose me.

Her breath caught in her throat.

It was him. No, it couldn't be. She'd done everything she could—she'd started a new life, hidden herself away somewhere no one would be able to find her.

She clicked to open the email.

It was signed *Jake xo.*

Panic welled in her gut, and her head felt light as she sucked in quick breaths. No, he'd found her. How was that possible? If he had her email address, that meant he knew where she worked. But perhaps he didn't know where she was stationed?

She scanned the email, noticed that a reply had been sent. With quick movements she clicked on the reply, opened the message. It was her out of office assistant, with her new name and her work address and phone number. It'd gone out automatically the day before when she hadn't been scheduled to work. They all did it, set automatic out of office messages for the days they wouldn't be in the office. Franklin insisted on it. Said it was good customer service for their community, he didn't want people thinking they were being ignored by their police department.

That meant Jake not only had her new name, but he knew where she worked. He had her email address, her phone number, the station address. He knew everything.

She pressed both hands to her forehead and stared at the screen, taking in the brief email message over and over, looking for some clue as to what he might do.

She'd made the same mistake as Franklin—she'd grown complacent in the Cove. Gotten used to the sun, the sand, and the warm, curling waves. She'd grown to love her job, her dingy little unit above the fish and chip shop. She'd built a life for herself that'd seductively drawn her into its web, and now he'd found her. How? How had he tracked her down?

No matter, whatever he'd done—he knew where she was, and it was only a matter of time before he visited. He always did.

CHAPTER 20

DIANA

*D*iana pressed her lips into a long, thin line. What could she say? Of course, Ben wanted to know about his father. It was only logical. But the truth wasn't something she was ready to spill. Her thoughts raced over the dominoes of revelation balanced in a line—if this one toppled how many others would it take down with it?

"I...uh...well, it makes sense you'd want to know about that."

She took another bite of the grilled fish, along with a forkful of Greek salad and chewed slowly. He watched her all the while. Waiting, patient.

Diana glanced up and saw Cindy walk into the Emerald Cafe. In the same moment, her friend looked her way and caught her eye. Cindy's lips broadened into a smile, and she strode in their direction.

"Oh wonderful, Cindy is here—the cafe owner." Diana's heart thundered against her ribcage. Her thoughts whirled.

Overwhelmed, she pushed a smile to her face and relied on her well-honed manners to get her through this moment.

"Di, I didn't know you were coming here for lunch." Cindy kissed her cheek and slumped into a chair beside her. "Oh wow, I went for a walk around the point this morning and my feet are aching beyond belief."

Cindy faced Ben. "Oh, I'm so sorry, you have a guest for lunch…"

Diana inhaled a sharp breath. "No, it's fine…this is Ben. Ben, this is Cindy Flannigan, she owns the Emerald Cafe and is a dear friend of mine."

"Your best friend," corrected Cindy as she reached for Ben's hand. "At least that's what we used to tell people when we were teenagers, and we've never really given it up."

Ben shook Cindy's hand. "It's a pleasure to meet you Cindy. You knew Diana when she was a teenager?"

Interest sparked in his eyes. Diana could see Cindy's curiosity as well. It wouldn't be long before the truth surfaced, she felt as though she couldn't stop it. Her breath caught in her throat.

"Yes, I certainly did and let me tell you, she was very different back then to what she is now. She was wild. I know, it's hard to imagine, she's so prim and proper these days, but Di wasn't always like this."

Cindy chuckled, her gaze flitting back and forth between Diana and Ben, trying to put together who he was and why Diana was having lunch alone with him.

"So, are you one of the suppliers for the Seaside Manor…?" asked Cindy.

Ben shook his head. "No, actually I'm—"

Diana grabbed Cindy by the arm and pulled as she leapt to her feet. "Cindy, honey come with me. There's something I need to show you in the kitchen. Ben, we'll only be a minute. Keep eating, I'll be right back."

Diana dragged Cindy by the arm in the direction of the kitchen.

"Ouch! What on earth? Diana Jones, let go of my arm."

They reached the kitchen and Diana pushed through the two-way door, then released Cindy's arm. Cindy massaged the place where Diana's fingers had gripped her flesh. She scowled. "What has gotten into you? Was it because I called you a wild teenager in front of your friend? Come on, what's the big deal? You were wild, it's nothing to be ashamed of. For heaven's sakes, Di, you're sixty years old, it's time to give up on shame—shame isn't your friend."

Diana shook her head. "No, it isn't that. I'm sorry if I hurt your arm."

"Never mind, I'll recover. Tell me what's going on." Cindy folded her arms across her chest.

"Can we sit?"

"Yes, of course."

Cindy lead Diana to her small, cramped office behind the kitchen. She sat at her desk, and Diana sat across from her. She noted the certificates on the walls, the family portraits hanging beside them.

She swallowed. "I have to tell you something about Ben."

"Okay." Cindy eyed her warily.

"He's my son."

"What?" Cindy gaped. "I thought maybe you were having an affair..."

Diana sniffed. "No! Oh for heaven's sakes, he's my son. I had him when I was sixteen years old. You remember the spring and summer I spent with my aunt and uncle? You knew I was pregnant, but no one else did."

"I remember the time you went away to your aunt and uncle's and had a miscarriage..." Cindy's voice hardened. "You mean to tell me you didn't have a miscarriage at all?"

"That's right." Diana gave a curt nod. "I had a baby boy

and gave him up for adoption. Ben found me a few months ago, he wrote some letters and I responded. Then, he showed up at my door and wants to get to know me."

"Wow."

"Yes, it's been a little overwhelming...but in a good way. I'm...well, I don't know what I'm feeling entirely, but happy is one word I could use. I guess. And scared, of course. I haven't told Rupert yet, you're the first person I've said anything to."

Cindy walked around the desk, sat on it, and embraced Diana. "It's wonderful news, love. I'm so happy for you. You always wanted a child of your own, and you've got one. I only wish you'd told me. I wouldn't have said anything, you know that."

Diana's eyes pricked with tears and a lump built in her throat. "I know. I know. Only, my parents said I shouldn't tell anyone. They were adamant about it. I wish I hadn't listened...sometimes I wish I'd kept him. But he tells me he had a happy childhood, so I suppose I couldn't ask for more than that. My parents wouldn't let me keep him at the time, they refused, and I was only sixteen..."

"Of course, it sounds to me like you did the best thing you could do at that time. Don't beat yourself up over it, what's done is done. But now you have a second chance to get to know your son—I think it's marvellous."

Diana reached for friend's hands and held them in her own. "Thank you, Cindy. That means a lot to me. You've been the best friend I could've asked for over the years. I don't know what I would've done without you, to be honest."

Cindy smiled. "Right back at you." She frowned. "But what about the father...you hadn't started dating Rupert yet, if I remember rightly. And you wouldn't tell me who it was at the time. We even had a big fight about it. Couldn't he have helped you with the baby?"

Diana drew a deep breath. "No, he was only two years older than me and finishing his last year of high school."

"So, I knew him?"

Diana nodded. "Yes."

It was the same thing Ben wanted to know. Exactly what Rupert would ask when he discovered the truth about Ben. She couldn't escape it; the truth would have to come out. She couldn't keep dodging the question. And it was so long ago. She'd held onto her secret, hidden it in a hurting heart for so many years. It would be a relief to have it out in the open. Cindy eyed her, waiting for more.

"It was Andy."

"My Andrew?" Cindy's eyes widened.

"Yes. I'm so sorry."

"But Andy and I were dating then. We were in love…"

"I know. I'm sorry. It was a weak moment. He told me… well he told me things I wanted to hear. And you remember how cute and charming he was. It happened that time you had tonsillitis, and a group of us went to a party on the beach without you—do you remember? There was a bonfire. It was very romantic."

"My Andy is the father of your baby? You and Andy…?"

Diana bit down on her lip. It was always going to be bad news. She hated having to hurt Cindy. But Andrew and Cindy were separated now, and Cindy had been charmed by Andrew into believing his lies, into accepting his selfishness, so many times. Surely, she understood the way he was, that Diana hadn't been able to resist him.

"Yes, I know how it sounds…it's terrible. I felt horrible about it at the time, and I still do. Of course, after it happened, I told him it could never happen again. That you were my friend, and I wouldn't do that to you. He was fine with that…said he understood. I was in love with him for a while, until I met Rupert really. I never told him about the pregnancy, and he doesn't know about Ben."

Cindy's nostrils flared. "You and Andy cheated on me, together. You had a baby with him, and in all our years of friendship you never thought to tell me about it?"

"I wanted to tell you, of course, so many times. But it was over…in my mind…it was over. Ben was gone, you and Andy got married, I married Rupert…life went on. And the secrets my parents made me keep became normal to me. But I never really got over it, any of it."

"I can't believe it—no matter what Andy did, he never deserved for you to keep something like that from him. He deserved to know he had a son. And I deserved to have a friend who…" She sobbed. "That's a level of cruel…well, I didn't think you were capable of it, Di. Truly I didn't." With a flash of anger in her eyes, Cindy stood, strode to the door, and flung it open. "I'm flabbergasted you could do that to me, to Rupert, and to Andy; to all of us really. You're not the friend I thought you were. Stay away from me!" She sobbed again, pressing both hands to her face, and ran.

Diana watched her go, tears spilling from her eyes. She reached for a tissue from the box on Cindy's desk and dabbed at her face. It wouldn't do for Ben to see she'd been crying. Then he'd want to know why, and she'd have to tell him everything. It didn't make sense to tell him the entire truth yet, not before Rupert. Now that Cindy knew about Ben, she'd have to hurry home and tell Rupert. The last thing she wanted was for him to hear about it all from someone else—not that Cindy was a gossip, mind, but she wouldn't put it past her friend to give Rupert a call herself when she was this angry. Diana tossed the wadded-up tissue into a wastepaper basket, and walked from the office, her head high.

* * *

THE HOUSE WAS quiet when Diana parked the car and tiptoed in through the garage door. Rupert could be sleeping, or perhaps watching the television in the den with his headphones on. He couldn't turn it up loud enough to hear without bothering the neighbours, so she'd bought him some wireless headphones and he loved them. Said it was like watching a movie in a cinema with surround sound.

She left her purse on the kitchen bench and went looking for him. He was seated in the den, headphones on, head back, a light snore emitting from his open mouth. She watched him for a few moments, her heart warm. Why did the truth have to come back now and hurt so many of the people she loved? And yet Ben…she'd do it all again for him. He was the one good thing to come from all of it, and he was certainly worth every moment of pain she'd endured.

She sat beside Rupert and rested a hand on his arm. He woke with a start, then smiled at her as he removed his headphones.

"There you are," he said. "I was wondering when you'd get home. I ate a sandwich without you, I hope you don't mind."

"That's fine, I ate in town. I should've called to let you know."

He waved her off. "No worries. Were you with Cindy?" He stood, stretching both arms over his head with a yawn. "I'm going to get a cup of tea to wake up me. Do you want one?"

She followed him to the kitchen and sat at the kitchen table. She felt suddenly exhausted, too tired to stand.

"I'd love a cuppa, thank you."

He busied himself, filling the kettle and putting it on to boil. She watched him with her heart full of love.

"I wasn't with Cindy," she said.

"Huh? Oh, right...what were you doing then?" He set some biscuits on a plate.

"I met with Ben."

"Ben?"

"Do you remember the young man who came to our door? I told you he asked for directions to the highway?"

Rupert stopped what he was doing, fixed his attention on her. "Yes."

"That was Ben."

"Why didn't you tell me?" His eyes narrowed. "That's not like you, Di. What's going on?"

She sighed. "He's my son."

Rupert came to the table and sat across from her, eyebrows arched high. "What do you mean, he's your son?"

She smiled, exhaustion tinging her words with sadness. "I had him when I was very young. Before you and I started dating. I gave him up for adoption, but he found me. That day, he came to the house—I didn't know he was coming. It was a surprise...a shock really. I didn't know what to do, what to say. It was all very surreal for me. I'm sorry, I should've told you everything right then, but I didn't have the strength."

He shook his head. "I can't believe this. You're telling me you had a baby as a teenager, and never said a word to me about it?"

She nodded. "Yes, that's right. I wish I'd told you, but the years passed by and it seemed as though it was almost a dream at times. Did it really happen? When we couldn't have children, I grieved for so many years over the child I gave up. I thought it would be too cruel to tell you I had a son, but I didn't know where he was, and I'd given him to strangers to raise. It was almost more than I could bear..." Her throat closed over and she tried to swallow around it, but it continued to grow until the pain was overwhelming.

Rupert shook his head. "A son...you had a son...we wanted...I wanted a son so badly. And he was out there..."

Another nod.

Tears blurred her vision. Rupert's eyes filled too. When his cheeks were wet, she thought she couldn't take anymore.

"Oh honey, I'm so sorry." She reached a hand to his cheek to cup it, but he stood and brushed her hand away.

"We shared everything...or at least, I thought we did. I don't know what to say. That you'd keep something like this from me... Are there are more secrets? Things you haven't told me?"

He whirled to face her, his eyes wide.

She shook her head. "Only this."

"Only this. As if it's not big enough." He pressed his hands to his face and wiped his cheeks as sobs wracked his body. "It's not right, not fair. We couldn't have children..."

He strode from the room in his awkward, lop-sided gate. He had a bad hip, they'd talked about getting it replaced soon, but his doctor had said he wasn't strong enough for the surgery. Not yet. Maybe next year if they could get his blood sugar to stabilise.

The front door slammed, the echo reverberating throughout the house. Diana hurried to the window to watch Rupert shuffle down the front path, then across the street. He stopped beneath a poinciana tree, pressed both hands to his face again, shook his head. Diana cupped her hands to her mouth, eyes wide as tears streamed down her cheeks.

He was right. She'd betrayed him by keeping this secret. They'd shared everything, it'd always been that way between them. But not this. This had been hers, and hers alone. It'd kept a small part of her heart out of his reach for all this time. He'd often asked her why he felt as though a part of her would never be his. She'd brushed off his concerns, knowing all the while that it was this part of her—the piece of her heart that Ben had taken with him when he was carried out of the hospital by strangers.

While she watched, Rupert drew a deep breath, let his hands fall to his sides. Then he walked back across the street and up the path. The front door closed behind him, quieter this time.

When he found her in the kitchen, he held out both hands. "Come on, Di. Let's have a hug, love."

She ran into his arms, nestled against his chest as the tears fell. "I'm so sorry," she whispered, her voice muffled by his woollen jumper.

He stroked her hair. "There, there. I understand. It was so long ago, and you were only a child yourself. It's not your fault. Not entirely, anyway. I'm only disappointed you didn't think you could share something so important with me."

She sniffled against his jumper, her hands creeping around his neck. "I wanted to, but honestly I pushed it out of my mind most of the time and then when I thought about it, I couldn't say the words. I couldn't talk about it because it was the hardest thing I'd ever been through." He was so kind and gentle. She didn't deserve it, but that's how he'd treated her since their first kiss. It's who he was, and she was more grateful for him than she'd ever been before.

"And the father? Who is he? I would've known him, I assume..."

She squeezed her eyes shut. "Andrew Flannigan."

There was silence as Rupert processed her words. His grip on her loosened, and his breathing slowed. "I find that hard to believe...you've always despised the man."

"I know, but I was very young at the time, and he was handsome, charismatic—you know how he is." She'd had a crush, harmless at first, but it'd developed into something more. If she'd known then what she knew now... but only hindsight had such disturbing clarity.

"I suppose it makes sense now. I've always been curious about why you hated him so much; he could never do anything right in your eyes. I thought it was only because of how he treated your friend."

"It was both—he didn't know about the baby though. So, at least I can't lay the blame for what happened entirely at his door."

Rupert didn't respond, just held her. Her tears slowed, and she quietened in his embrace. He'd always had that effect on her. He was the one to quiet her tears, the calm in her storm. Relief coursed through her veins, exhausting her in a moment—he knew. Finally, he knew her secret. All those years of keeping it inside had been like a wall between them, now there was nothing there—only love.

"Have you thought about him much? Ben, I mean."

Diana sighed. "All of the time. I couldn't help wondering, of course…where was he? What was he doing? Was he happy?"

He released her from their embrace, wiped her cheeks with his sleeve. "And did you get answers to any of those questions, my love?"

She nodded, sniffled again. "Yes, he says his parents were very kind, loving and that he had a happy childhood."

"There you go, that's wonderful. Isn't it?"

She nodded, her throat tightening again. "Yes, it is wonderful. But still…"

"I know," he agreed, pulling her close again. "If only we'd been able to raise him ourselves."

CHAPTER 21

SARAH

*T*hrough the window, Sarah watched as a curlew strode across the backyard, long legs bending with slow movements, head bobbing. Another bird, its mate, stepped out of the brush to follow. They were curious birds with large heads, oversized eyes and long, spindly legs.

"...and if we follow the money, we'll sign Angela again, for another three books...that's all I'm saying." Pauline's shrill voice echoed down the phone line and throughout Sarah's office.

The telephone was on speaker, and Sarah sat in a high-backed leather chair, staring blankly out the window at the landscape beyond—waving grey and brown grasses, billowing clouds clipping across the sky, strutting birds.

"Or..." she interrupted. "We could look at someone new."

"We know Angela brings in the sales," objected Pauline, raising her voice. "We have to think about the bottom line."

"I've got a new prospect." Sarah ignored Pauline and

continued. "She's written a beautiful piece of contemporary fiction. It's literary, poetic, unexpected…"

"But it's not commercial," replied Pauline.

Sarah shook her head in frustration. Since when did Pauline get to make the call on who was published and who wasn't? Why didn't Beverly intervene?

"I think you'll be pleasantly surprised. I believe it would be popular with book clubs, even if it is a little more artsy than the usual book-club fare."

"Artsy? Isn't that code for pretentious?" Pauline laughed and the rest of the group back in the Sydney office tittered along with her.

Sarah's head began to throb with the beginnings of a headache. These phone calls were becoming frustrating at best, impossible on the worst days. And today was fast becoming one of those days.

"Beverly…what do you think? Would you at least take a look at it?" asked Sarah.

"Bev's popped out of the meeting to grab a coffee, hon," replied a condescending Pauline. "I'll make sure to ask her about it for you if you like."

"Thanks," replied Sarah, hoping her sarcasm could be heard through the phone.

"That's it for today folks…"

The phone line went dead before Sarah had a chance to say goodbye. Pauline must've hung up mid-sentence. Sarah ran both hands through her hair with a groan. Working for Greenmount Publishing in Sydney, while living in Emerald Cove, was becoming almost unbearable. Especially now that Beverly, her boss, seemed to be pulling away from the business, and Pauline had all but taken over.

In fact, she couldn't remember what it was about publishing she'd liked in the first place. She'd found herself lying in bed in the morning, staring at the ceiling, dreading getting up since she'd have to face another day at Greenmount Publishing. And worse yet, she wasn't even there, so she'd have to do it all over a telephone and with spotty internet service.

It was too much. She'd had enough. She only had one life to live, and she wasn't going to spend her days angry, bitter, and despairing because of a job. Outside her back door was the most beautiful scenery she'd ever witnessed. She lived in a stunning, renovated cottage at the top of a cliff overlooking an untouched beach that stretched almost as far as she could see. She had a wonderful boyfriend, a happy life. All except for the job that made her gut clench every time she thought about it.

She picked up the phone and dialled Beverly's number.

"Hello?" trilled Beverly.

"Bev, it's Sarah. How are you?"

"Oh, Sarah—nice to hear from you. Is the meeting finished already?"

Sarah sighed. "Yes, it's finished. I was surprised you left before it ended."

"Oh yes well Pauline is fully capable of carrying it on without me."

Sarah shook her head. Was Beverly ready to hand everything over to Pauline? Why wasn't she fighting to keep her job as editor-in-chief at Greenmount? This wasn't the Beverly she knew.

"You shouldn't give her so much leeway, Bev. She's pushing her way in, taking over. She doesn't have your impeccable taste when it comes to literature, all she's interested in is what will sell."

"I know, I know," replied Beverly. "But that's what they want, you know. The executive has been asking for more commercial contracts, so Pauline can deliver them that."

"What are you saying, Bev?" Sarah stood and paced the length of her office.

"I'm moving on, that's what I'm saying. It's time...I've been with Greenmount for ten years, and I've had an offer from a not-for-profit to be their CEO. I've taken the job, and I think it'll be much better suited to me and the stage of life I'm at. I don't want to work the kind of hours I've been doing at Greenmount anymore. I've got my horses...and I've met someone." Bev's voice softened.

"I'm happy for you," replied Sarah, frustration and panic building inside her. "But you can't leave us! You can't hand us over to Pauline like that. We won't cope...I won't cope. I can't work for her."

"The job was meant to be yours, Sarah. But you left..."

"I didn't leave! I moved...big difference." Sarah slapped a palm to her forehead. How many times did she have to say the words? She lived in another location, but she still worked for the publishing company. She never left.

"You know what I mean. You can't be the editor-in-chief from a beach somewhere in the north of the state, it wouldn't work. You haven't even met our new hires...they don't know who you are."

Sarah shook her head in silence. Beverly had a point. How could she manage staff if she wasn't in the office? Her internet access wasn't even good enough to manage a video call most of the time.

"I understand..." she said, her bravado fading. "I get it, but I'm sorry you're leaving. I'll miss you."

"Thank you, Sarah. I appreciate that. I hope I won't be entirely forgotten, at least not right away. I've dedicated the best years of my life to this career, I was so driven in the early years. I didn't get married like all my friends, I didn't have children, I was all about the job. And I was good at it, I got promoted, then promoted again. I was the youngest editor-in-chief in Sydney for a while...but then the years passed and there was no more climbing to be done. I was at the top, so where to go from there? Lately, it hasn't held the same appeal for me... I won't say I have regrets, but I do wonder how life may have gone if I'd realised then what I know now—balancing on the career ladder is a lonely and empty way to spend your days."

Sarah's brow furrowed. She'd never heard Beverly speak this way before. Usually her boss was all smiles, hurrying footsteps, and designer clothes. But she understood, it was exactly why she'd given up the corporate climb and moved back to Emerald Cove, that and the fact that her mother had needed her.

"I know what you mean, it's why I left Sydney," she said.

Beverly sighed. "Then you're smarter than I was at your age. I'm beginning to realise that when I leave this place, within a few months no one will even remember I was here. Why did I give them my life? It doesn't matter to them, not one jot."

Sarah's throat tightened. Why was she giving them her sanity, her peace?

"You're right, Bev. That's true about the company, it hasn't got feelings or a memory, but we do. I won't forget you. You've had an impact on my life that will last forever. You believed in me, gave me opportunities, helped me to grow. I consider you a friend, I hope you'll stay in touch."

"Thank you, Sarah. That's what I needed to hear." Beverly cleared her throat. "And of course, I'll stay in touch."

"Before you go, Bev, there's something else I need to talk to you about." Sarah's stomach twisted into a knot as she drew a deep breath.

* * *

SARAH LAY on her back in the middle of the living room floor and stared at the ceiling. Her head spun and lights flashed before her eyes with each rapid breath that filled her lungs. She inhaled a slow breath, squeezed her eyes shut.

There was no point dwelling on it. What was done, was done.

She couldn't change it now.

Another slow breath and the spinning in her head cleared.

There was a knock at the front door.

"Come in!" she called.

The door opened and footsteps crossed the floor to where she lay. "What on earth are you doing?" asked Mick.

She turned her head to catch him in her line of sight. "I was hyperventilating, dizzy. I had to lie down."

He squatted beside her and cupped a hand to her cheek, his eyes full of concern. "What's going on? What's wrong?"

She pulled herself into a sitting position, and her head spun for a moment. She steadied herself with one hand on Mick's arm. "I quit my job."

Mick arched an eyebrow. "What? Why?"

She stood slowly, using Mick as support. Her head felt light, but the dizziness had passed. "Because I hated it, you know that."

He dipped his head. "True, you did seem to hate it. I wondered why you kept doing it."

She faced him, eyes narrowed. "You never said anything."

He shrugged. "I didn't want to push."

"But you didn't think I should be doing it?"

"I think you should do something that fulfils you, gives you a sense of joy or at least some satisfaction."

She considered his words. It'd never occurred to her that a job or a career should do that. In her twenties, she'd worked to grow a career, to pay the bills. Now, she wasn't sure what she'd do with herself.

"I can't lie about on the beach all day, though; I have to work...I have no idea what I'll do. What if I can't find another job?" Panic began to weave ropes around her heart again, and her breathing sped up.

Mick stopped her with one hand on each arm. "Whoa, calm down. You'll be fine."

"How do you know that?"

"Because, I know you. You'll be fine. But it wouldn't hurt you to take a little time off before you dive into something new. You need a break. Have you ever taken time for yourself before?"

"Do you mean other than a two-week holiday once a year?"

He nodded. "Yes, other than that."

"Then, no. I haven't. I wouldn't know what to do with myself...I haven't had more than a couple of weeks off work since I was at university, and even then, I was studying and working part-time."

"Sounds to me like you could do with an extended holiday."

"Should I go somewhere?" she asked.

"It's up to you."

She wandered to the window, pressed her hands to the window frame, and looked out at the wild landscape beyond. "No, I think I'll stay here. What could be better than this?"

"True," he admitted.

"I could sleep in..."

"Yep."

"And watch movies, take long walks on the beach, maybe even get back into running again."

He nodded, pressed his hands to his hips. "And you could also spend more time with your amazing boyfriend."

She laughed. "That too, of course. Wow, I'm liking the sound of this more and more. You're right, maybe I shouldn't dive directly into worrying about what comes next. Perhaps I should take some time to relax first; worry later."

"I think that'd be a great idea."

She strode to the kitchen. "I'm making tea, would you like some?"

"Yes, please." He followed her and sat on one of the bar stools by the bench.

"This is a great idea. Thanks, Mick."

"You're welcome."

The more she thought about it, the more it appealed to her. Time to do nothing at all sounded impossibly luxurious. She'd never considered it before. Sure, she'd seen other people do it—take months off to laze around the house, or to backpack around Europe. But she'd never considered doing it herself. Her career had been too important to her. But now that career was over. There was no way she could continue to live in Emerald Cove and land an editing job at another publishing house.

Panic began to wind its way around her chest.

No, she couldn't think that way, it'd only make her crazy.

She didn't know what the future might hold, but she wasn't even going to think about it for at least a week, maybe even a month. Even after buying and renovating the cottage, she'd saved enough over the years to live off for at least six months, maybe twelve if she scrimped. She smiled as she filled the kettle with water from the tap. The future was completely open, she could do anything at all.

As she poured boiling water into the teapot, Mick's mobile phone rang. He pulled it out, looked at the screen.

"Besides," he said. "Didn't you want to write a book? Now you'll have the time."

He answered the phone and walked into the living room to talk.

Sarah held the kettle in the air, unmoving as his words washed over her. She had always wanted to write a book but had never seriously tried. She'd been too busy with work. At least, that was the excuse she'd used. If she were honest with herself, she was afraid to write. What if the book wasn't any good? She'd been a professional editor for years, critiquing the work of writers, telling them how to improve their craft, what to change, how to manipulate their words to tell a better story. But what if she couldn't do it herself? The fear of failure had gripped her every time she sat at the keyboard to write, so she'd busied herself doing other things. There was always plenty to do, plenty of things to occupy her time. But now...

She swallowed and set the kettle back in place, then pulled two mugs from the cupboard overhead and set a strainer on top of one. As she poured the tea into the mugs, her mind raced. If she did write a book, what type of book should she write? She loved so many different genres. There wasn't one particular genre that stood out to her. Of course, she'd had a specialty at Greenwood, they all did. Hers was historical literary fiction. She'd enjoyed every single book she worked on at the publishing house in that genre, but did that mean she should write her own?

Her heart thudded in her chest as nerves warmed her cheeks. Perhaps she should consider writing something completely different, like science fiction?

Mick strode into the kitchen as she finished pouring milk into the two mugs. She held one out to him and he took it with a smile.

"Who was that?"

"Work...I'll have to get back to it soon. The carpenter

over at the new reno place is insisting I didn't order the right timber. It's fine, I'll sort it out when I get there."

She nodded. "I thought about what you said—that I should write. It's a great idea. In fact, I've been pondering over it lately...I don't know, I never really considered doing it before because it wasn't practical. But now..."

He laughed, moved around the bench to kiss her lightly on the lips. Then he wrapped his arms around her waist and pulled her close. "Ponder away, and take some time to rest as well, okay?"

They chatted together, nestled in each other's arms on the back porch while they finished their tea. Then, Mick kissed her goodbye.

"What are you going to do for the rest of the day?" he asked.

Her eyes widened. "I have no idea. I've got work to do, there are projects I have to tie up or hand over before I finish with Greenmount... but I don't feel like doing it. Suddenly, I'm completely exhausted."

"Quitting is tiring," he said with a laugh. "Let's go out for dinner tonight to celebrate."

"Celebrate?"

"Of course," he replied. "New beginnings."

She waved goodbye, then returned to the porch to sit in a rocking chair and think. New beginnings. It was exciting and scary all at the same time. She felt a little lost, without defined activities to fill the rest of her day. Perhaps she'd find Oscar and see if her wayward dog wanted to take a walk. No doubt he was asleep in a hole he'd dug on the other side of the cottage in the sun. It was his favourite place to sleep, other than at her feet. A walk along the beach with Oscar, then dinner with Mick. The perfect way to spend an afternoon.

CHAPTER 22

DIANA

*I*t was unusual for the big, hardwood door to be shut at this time of day. Cindy usually kept it open, with only the screen to keep out the insects. Diana raised her fist, hesitated a moment, bit down on her lip, then knocked.

The sound reverberated throughout the quiet neighbourhood. Diana glanced around. Someone cycled past along the street. The sound of bees in the garden filled the air. She could see the side of the Manor from where she stood, a feeling of nostalgia and loss swallowed her before she pushed it away and faced the closed door again. Another knock, this time louder.

Surely Cindy couldn't ignore her forever. She understood that her friend was angry, she had every right to be, but they were friends. That hadn't changed. Cindy had to see that.

There was no sound from within the house. Maybe Cindy was at the cafe, although Diana knew her schedule well enough to know that Cindy rarely went to the cafe before ten o'clock in the morning. And she'd purposely come to Cindy's house to see her at seven a.m. in the hopes that she'd catch her at home, and they could talk.

She wanted to explain, to talk to her friend about what'd happened and why she hadn't been able to bring herself to discuss any of it over the years. It'd been too much for her to bear thinking about, let alone discuss with other people, even her best friend. The loss of her son had left her heart empty and broken. She couldn't bear to lose Cindy as well.

Diana walked around to the garage but couldn't see inside. Perhaps Cindy was out, but if she wasn't, she was definitely ignoring Diana.

Pain welled in her throat. With a toss of her head, Diana swallowed the pain and strode back to her car. Cindy was being unreasonable. Her affair with Andrew had happened so many years ago Diana could barely remember it. She'd been young, insecure, looking for love and attention—she'd made the wrong choice and she'd suffered for it ever since. Wasn't that enough punishment? Having to give up a son, the only child she ever birthed, to strangers to raise? It was more than enough, in her opinion.

By the time she reached home, she had talked herself into a spitting rage at Cindy. How dare her friend act as though she'd never made a mistake, never done anything wrong? It wasn't as though she and Andrew were still married, either. She knew what kind of man Andrew was. Some of the blame for what'd happened rested squarely on his shoulders, not that he'd ever admit to it. Of course, she hadn't told him about Ben and that was her fault, he didn't deserve that, but still…he was no saint.

Diana marched into the house with her lips pulled into a tight line.

Rupert glanced up from his armchair, the newspaper

open in his lap and a pair of half spectacles perched on the end of his nose. "Hello, my dear, where have you been?"

She slumped into the chair beside him. "I went to see Cindy. I wanted to talk to her about everything, get it out in the open, resolve things…but she wouldn't even open the door."

His lips pursed. "Perhaps she needs a little more time."

Diana's head swirled with anger. "She's being impossible! It was so long ago; she can't hold it against me forever."

"She's only just found out about it though…"

"I know, but it's caused me enough pain to last a lifetime…surely she can see that I've suffered enough."

Rupert set the newspaper aside and reached for Diana's hand. "Come on, my dear. Let's have a cup of tea and talk about something else. You can't resolve anything now. When Cindy is ready to talk, you'll talk. Until then, you have to be patient."

All the wind in Diana's sails died away and she slouched in her seat. "You're right. I'm sorry. I'm so sorry for everything."

"No need for any more of that. We can't change what's been done, but we can face tomorrow with our heads high. Okay?"

She always marvelled at the way Rupert was able to change her attitude, to help her see things from a positive perspective. She inhaled a slow breath and nodded. "You're right, of course. Thank you, my love."

She patted his hand and rose. "I'll put the kettle on."

* * *

REBECCA

The song on the radio grated on Rebecca's nerves. Although, everything was doing that lately. She was on edge, of course she was. Jake had sent her an email, and she was tense, waiting to see what he'd do next. She'd gone through it often enough to know he'd wait until she'd let her guard down before he made his next move. He was sick. He always had to have the upper hand, and it gave him some kind of thrill to keep her in a constant state of fear.

Well, not this time. Her brow furrowed. She wasn't going to live in fear. He couldn't have that hold over her anymore. She was sick of it, done with that way of living. She should really leave the Cove, change her name, and not look back. But the problem was, she liked it there. She hadn't meant to fall in love with the place, and at first, she'd felt strange there. It was so different to the bustle of city life that she was used to. But now, she couldn't imagine living anywhere else. And the thought of giving up her job, friendships, the boxing gym...all of the things she'd built into her life over recent months, was too much.

She didn't want to leave it all behind to start over. Again.

She crossed her arms and stared out the front windscreen of the cruiser with her eyes narrowed behind dark sunglasses. No, she wasn't going to run again. Not this time. That was what he would expect her to do, and he'd be waiting when she did. He always held the upper hand, always had the control. But this time, she wouldn't run, she'd keep living her life, and if he came for her, she'd be ready.

"Are you okay over there, Proby?" asked Franklin, with a concerned glance in her direction.

"Fine," she snapped.

From the corner of her eye she could see his eyebrow arch. "Really? You don't sound fine, and there's a definite rage-vibe coming from your vicinity."

She huffed, stared out the passenger window. "Since when do you care?"

He didn't respond to that, simply drove in silence. Then

he pulled the car over to the side of the road, set it in park and faced her. "Okay, what's going on?"

She pushed her sunglasses on top of her head with a sneer. "Nothing's going on. Why? I can't be angry? Can't experience an emotion?"

He shook his head. "No, not usually. This isn't like you, so spill."

She sighed. "It's nothing, let's keep driving."

He studied her a moment. "If there was something wrong, you'd tell me. Right?"

Rebecca didn't respond. Could she trust him? What if she told him the truth about who she was, why they'd sent her here? What would he do? From what she'd learned of Franklin since she started in her job in the Cove, he was a good man, an honourable man. But she'd been wrong about men before.

"Just something from my past...someone, actually. He's gotten in contact with me, and I'm not happy about it."

"Anything I can do to help?"

She shrugged. "No, not really."

"Okay, well you let me know if there is."

"I will."

He pulled the car back onto the road and headed towards the centre of town. They weren't going anywhere in particular, doing their normal trip around Emerald Cove. They did it several times a day, whenever there were no cases to manage—looped around the town, over the hill, through the small suburban neighbourhoods and back to the station. Most of the time she enjoyed it, the feel of the car beneath her, the music on the radio, the wind on her face through the open window.

But not today. Today, her nerves were rolled like a ball, tense and ready to spring.

Franklin's phone rang and he handed it to her to answer.

"Hello, this is Rebecca," she said.

"Bec, it's Steph. Can I speak to the boss please?"

"He's driving," replied Rebecca.

"Get him to pull over, hon. This is important."

Rebecca waved a hand, signalling to Franklin to pull the car to the side of the road. He set the handbrake in place and took the phone.

"This is Franklin. Oh, hey Steph, what's going on?"

Rebecca watched his face fall in the silence that followed. He pressed a hand to his forehead, then shook his head slowly. "Okay, thanks Steph."

When he hung up the phone, Franklin stared straight ahead in silence, his face ashen.

"What's wrong?" asked Rebecca.

He didn't respond. So, she waited, watching for some signal, an indication of what he'd heard. Finally, he sighed.

"It's my dad. He had a stroke."

"Oh no." Rebecca's heart leapt into her throat. Franklin had moved in with his dad to take care of him. He loved his dad, that much she knew. She also knew his father had dementia, and that he'd been a challenge to care for, but other than that, Franklin kept much of his private life to himself. "I'm so sorry. Is he okay?"

"The ambulance came, apparently he was in the backyard, so the neighbour saw him fall. He's at the hospital. I have to get over there."

Rebecca nodded. "Hop out, I'll drive."

He didn't object, instead, climbed out of the car and wandered around to the passenger seat, before folding his long limbs back into the vehicle.

"I'm so sorry, Franklin," she said. She never called him that, it was always sir, or boss, or Sarge. Never Franklin. It felt strange to say his name, but in a good way.

He didn't respond, stared straight ahead. She set the car

in drive and pulled out onto the road, turning in the direction of Tweed Heads.

"I wasn't there..." said Franklin all of a sudden. "I wasn't with him."

"You couldn't be there all of the time. He knows you love him."

"Does he?" Franklin faced her, his eyes welling with grief.

"Of course he does," she said. "You're a good son. The way you talk about him - the two of you...I've never heard a son talk that way about his father before. You're close, I can tell."

Tears glinted in his eyes. "Thanks, Proby."

They were silent for the rest of the trip to the hospital. Franklin stared straight ahead. Rebecca's throat was so tight it ached. When they reached the hospital, she pulled through the emergency drop off and Franklin climbed out, ran inside. She watched him go, then eased the car into the parking lot to find a space to park.

By the time she'd made it inside, Franklin was nowhere in sight. She settled into a chair in the waiting room and stared without seeing at a television set mounted in one corner of the ceiling. Waiting was something she could do; she'd had plenty of practice. Waiting in hospitals, in emergency rooms like this one—with cream walls and metal chairs, people dotted about, heads in hands or staring at the walls. Although, usually she was the one waiting to be seen by a doctor.

She inhaled a long slow breath, let her mind wander over everything that'd happened that morning. What should she do? How could she help Franklin? She felt helpless, powerless to do anything that might bring him relief from the pain he was no doubt feeling. There wasn't anything she could do except wait. She scrubbed both hands over her face with a sigh.

An hour later, Franklin emerged through a pair of automatic glass doors. His hair was mussed, the top buttons of his shirt were undone, and his collar hung open. He drifted into the waiting room with glassy eyes, red-rimmed and vacant.

Rebecca jumped to her feet, hurried to meet him. "Hey boss, how is he?"

His gaze focused on her. "Oh hi, Proby. You didn't have to wait."

"Of course I did. Besides, we came in your car."

He grunted. "Oh, right. He's unconscious. They don't know if he'll recover."

"What do you want to do now? Can I take you somewhere? Maybe we could head to your house and pack you a bag or something?"

He combed fingers through his hair, his face blank. "Huh? Oh, um…I don't know. I guess I should get back to work. They said it isn't likely he'll wake up today…"

"No, definitely not," replied Rebecca with a shake of her head. "Come on, I'll take you home."

Franklin didn't object, so Rebecca drove him back to his house. She'd never been inside before but had waited outside for him plenty of times over the past few months. It was a small, red brick house in a neighbourhood of small, single-story brick homes. It perched on top of a rolling hill with a million-dollar view of the ocean but with the front door angled away from the view as though it didn't understand the big deal.

Franklin sat in the car, unmoving. So, Rebecca climbed out, jogged around to his door, and opened it. Then she helped him out, and with one hand on his arm led him into the house. He didn't say a word, and the side door wasn't locked. She could see where the paramedics had been. There were wheel marks on the lawn, and grooves in the mud by the side door where they'd wheeled his father to the ambulance.

She led Franklin to an armchair in the living room, and he sat down with a whoosh of released breath. She studied him a moment, then walked to the kitchen, and set the kettle to boil. While she made them each a cup of tea and searched the kitchen cupboards for something to eat, she could hear Franklin talking on the phone in the other room. His voice fell quiet, then the phone rang again. She understood how these things went, for the next few days he'd be talking to people on the phone sharing the news with loved ones. He wouldn't have time to think about his own fears, not for a while. Not until later, when everything was still and quiet.

Memories of her own brought back a rush of grief that she squashed with a swallow as she poured hot water over tea bags into two cups.

She carried the tea and a packet of chocolate biscuits into the living room and set them on the coffee table. Franklin hung up the phone with a grimace and tossed it onto the table as well.

"Have a drink and something to eat," she offered.

"No thanks, I'm not really hungry."

"I'm sorry, Franklin. I know how hard this is..."

His gaze found hers, connected. She felt it like a jolt down her spine. "You know?"

She nodded, inhaled. "I lost my dad when I was sixteen. It's not something you can ever really be ready for. But I'm sure your dad will get through this...he'll be okay."

His eyes softened. "I'm sorry, Bec. I didn't know—you don't share much about your past."

"I know, I don't like to talk about it. I miss him still, we were close."

Franklin leaned forward, elbows on his thighs. "What do I do if he dies? What should I do now? I don't know..." His voice drifted away. "I knew this day would come, of course. I mean, he hasn't been well, and there was the dementia. But not yet, not so soon. This place is so quiet without him. He might not come home...that's what they said...he might not come home ever again." He glanced around, his voice breaking. He cleared his throat.

"What you do now is call the relatives, call his friends, let people know. Then, you eat something, pack a bag with things you'll need, and we head back to the hospital."

He nodded. "Thanks, Bec. I'm glad you're here."

"It's really not a problem, I'm happy to help. I'll drive if you like."

He nodded. "Okay, I'll make us something to eat...do you like spaghetti bolognese?"

She offered him a wry smile. "I love it."

He stood, wiped his hands down the front of his pants with a sigh. "Great, we'll eat and then go back to see Dad. And hope for the best..."

CHAPTER 23

ETHAN

"*Y*ou have to flick your wrist, like this," said Ethan with a chuckle.

He leaned forward and flicked, sending the coin into the cup after bouncing once on the table in front of him.

"That's crazy, I can't do that," objected Emily. "Mine goes flying off in another direction. I don't know how you do it."

Ethan shrugged. "I had a lot of spare time when I was at university. The dorm rooms were full of boys with nothing to do, so we learned a few tricks to pass the time. Of course, we could've been studying, I suppose. But where's the fun in that?"

He offered her a wink as he retrieved the coins from the cup to start all over again.

"Well, all of the guests are tucked in their rooms, every-thing's done for the night, so I'm going to grab a drink. Do you want one?" asked Emily, pushing up from her chair and heading into the kitchen.

The Manor was quiet, only the sound of cicadas and an occasional muffled bump from an upstairs guest room interrupted the silence. In the background, there was a constant shush of waves, but Ethan couldn't hear it unless he sat perfectly still and listened. It was one of his favourite things about living in the Cove, that the waves were always there, rhythmic and comforting, as a backdrop to his life.

"Yeah, what are you having?"

She glanced back over her shoulder. "Hot chocolate?"

He grinned. "How about a wine?"

Her lips broadened into a smile. "Red?"

"Perfect."

It was hard for him to believe they hadn't gotten along at first. Lately, there'd been none of the awkwardness, or terse comments from before. Emily's attitude towards him had softened, and even though sometimes he caught her looking at him as though he'd done something wrong, with that crease between her eyebrows, most of the time she seemed relaxed.

She soon returned to the den with two glasses of red wine and set his on the table beside his armchair. In front of them on a coffee table was a game of checkers one of the guests had left out. Ethan loved this room. They hadn't made any changes to it since Diana and Rupert left, and had no plans to either. It was perfect the way it was with a filigree patterned wallpaper in green, above white wall panelling and dark, heavy furniture, it was the picture of old-fashioned elegance. The guests seemed to love it as much as he did, often gravitating to the den to read, play board games or talk.

Emily sat across from him, sipping her wine. She studied him, her stormy eyes dark.

"Do you remember the summer when you were seventeen?" she asked.

He nodded. "Yeah, of course."

"I followed you around all summer long…you were pretty frustrated with me."

He laughed. "I remember. All I wanted to do was surf, and you kept showing up. My friends were teasing me about you, relentlessly."

Her eyebrows arched. "Is that why you told me to go away?"

His cheeks flushed with warmth. He hated that he'd said anything like that to her. "Did I say that? I'm sorry…that would be why, yes. They were constantly heckling me about you having a crush on me. It was a bit much for my seventeen-year-old ego to take."

She took another sip of wine. "I didn't realise that. I thought you didn't like me, hated me actually."

He leaned forward, held her gaze. "I'm sorry, Em. I didn't hate you, I was embarrassed, that's all. It's hard being a teenager."

Was that what she'd thought? He hated her? No wonder she'd been so standoffish when he bought half of the business.

"Is that why you…acted so strange towards me?" he asked.

She blinked. "Did I? When?"

"You know you did."

She chuckled. "Yes…no, partly. It's not the whole reason."

"What is the whole reason?" he asked.

She sighed. "There was a time when I didn't realise I was sensitive to some types of suncream. I used to wear it all the time when I was a kid, and it caused this red dermatitis on my face. So, other kids called me pimple face, things like that."

"Oh yeah, that's right," he said. "I forgot all about that."

She grimaced. "I wish I could."

Ethan swigged a mouthful of wine.

"Anyway, a couple of times I got a nosebleed as well, probably from the suncream, maybe the heat. I don't know for sure. But it happened that same summer when I was staying here at the Manor with my aunt and uncle. I was out with you and your friends, when I got a nosebleed and I didn't realise it at first. It gushed all down my red, pimply face, and over my clothes. That happened twice. The first time, everyone acted grossed out, but the second time, you called me a name."

Ethan's eyes widened. "I did?"

"You said I looked like a zombie, so from that moment on, for the rest of the summer, every kid in the Cove called me Zombie. It was my nickname for months. You graduated from high school a few months later, and I didn't come back to the Cove for another summer…so that was the last time I saw you…until now."

Ethan shook his head slowly. "Wow, I'm sorry. I don't remember that. I'm really sorry though. I'm sure that must've stung."

She grunted. "It did. I mean, I was the city kid who didn't really fit in with the kids from the coast. I didn't surf, I wasn't cool, and I had this dermatitis thing on my face all of the time. So, to be called a Zombie on top of it…well, it was hard. I cried a lot."

Ethan swallowed, reached for Emily's hand. "I feel horrible about that."

He squeezed her hand, felt its warmth on his palm. He hated that he'd caused her any pain. Hated that she'd held this thing against him for so long. Without thinking, he threaded his fingers through hers, staring at their entwined hands. When he glanced up at her face, it was pinker than it'd been.

"It's okay. I realise now that you didn't mean it, but for a long time I thought you'd done it intentionally. That you didn't like me and meant to humiliate me."

He shook his head. "I'm glad we were able to clear things up."

"Me too." She laughed. "Wow, I feel like a weight has lifted from my shoulders."

He grinned. "I'm glad. Anything else you need to get off your chest? Because honestly, I'm fairly certain most of the things I said as a teenager weren't well thought through…"

"Nope, that's it."

"Great." Now they could get back to thinking about the future. Their future together. He hadn't broached the subject with her yet, had been nervous to do it, but the fact that she wasn't pulling her hand out of his, wasn't shrinking away from his touch, was a good sign. His heart rate accelerated as each moment passed, and he met her gaze. His skin fairly hummed with electricity where her hand touched his.

Ethan's phone buzzed in his jeans pocket. He tried to ignore it. Then with a sigh, released Emily's hand and reached for it.

"Hi, Marc," said Ethan when he saw who was calling.

"Ethan, how are you mate?"

He would've been better if Marc hadn't called at that exact moment. "Great thanks, how about you?"

"I'm good. Listen, I won't keep you, but there's been a development in your case I thought you'd want to know about."

Ethan straightened in his chair, his breath caught in his throat. "Okay."

"I've had several long conversations with the crown prosecutor, and she says that if you come in and give the police a statement, tell them everything you know about what was going on over at Mammoth, they'll drop their plan to file charges against you."

Ethan scrubbed a hand over his face. "That's great, but I don't know anything."

"Then, tell them that. I think they realised that they don't have any evidence that you're involved, so they want to get whatever they can from you. The charges will go away as soon as you cooperate."

"Wow, Marc—thank you so much. I don't know what to say...that's amazing. I couldn't have done this without you, mate. I owe you."

Relief coursed through his body, and his breathing returned to a normal pace. The charges would be dropped. As the tension dissipated from his shoulders and neck, he realised how much strain the threat of prosecution had put on him. He'd thought he was coping fine with it all, but as he hung up the phone emotions welled within him. He squeezed his eyes shut and sighed.

"What is it? What's wrong?" asked Emily.

He opened his eyes, met her gaze. "Nothing. Nothing's wrong. They're not going to press charges against me over the Mammoth fraud, as long as I go up to Brisbane and give the police a statement."

Emily's eyes widened. "That's great news. Congratulations, Ethan. I'm so happy for you."

He stood to his feet, pumped his hands in the air. "Yes! Oh wow, that's a load off."

Emily stood too, smiling so that her eyes gleamed.

She was close to him, close enough that he couldn't look away. Her eyes were the kind of grey that reminded him of the ocean during a summer storm. Wide and grey they fixed on his, and he was caught up in their depths. His pulse hammered, heat travelled up his body and made his head spin.

"Emily... I..." He reached for her, pulling her close.

When their lips met, his breath caught in his throat. His heart thundered in his chest so loud that every other sound faded away. His eyes drifted shut as she stood to curl her arms around his neck, moaning softly as she fell against him.

She tasted like chocolate and wine and smelled of vanilla. Her body against his was lithe, soft, and shivered against him like summer waves curling to shore.

* * *

SARAH

Oscar sat on her foot and Sarah sighed. "No, Oscar honey, you're supposed to go forward when I say 'forward'. We practiced sitting. Ugh. He's never gonna get this."

She shook her head and Vicky laughed. "I don't think Oscar's really the rule-following type. I think he knows exactly what you want him to do, but he's making a point."

"Can't he make a point while the dog whisperer isn't watching us?" she groaned in a pained voice. "Come on, Oscar, Ruben's looking over here in complete disgust at my dog whispering skills. I'm going to fail puppy training, dude, and it's all your fault."

"I don't know if you can put all of the blame on Oscar for this one, Sar, he isn't exactly a puppy, so this might not be the right class for him."

Sarah's shoulders slumped. "Fine, let's do some more sitting then."

She glanced up to see Meg and her new puppy, Walton, acing the test by walking in a straight line around a red cone and heading back to where they'd begun.

"Sit, Walton," said Meg. The tiny cavalier sat, held his head high and let out a sniff—or at least it seemed that way to Sarah. Walton was showing off.

Sarah groaned. "You're being humiliated, Oscar. Don't you even care?"

"I don't think he cares," replied Vicky, scrolling on her phone.

"Don't feel too badly," said Meg with a chuckle. "Ruben says that Walton is a prodigy."

"Can you have dog prodigies?" asked Sarah, her brow furrowed.

Vicky laughed without looking up from her phone. "I'm staying out of this one."

"But you're the vet!" objected Sarah.

Vicky shook her head. "I'm not getting involved in who is, or is not, a puppy prodigy."

"Always the peacemaker," complained Sarah. "Up, Oscar, up. Stand up boy."

Oscar ignored her and continued sitting and staring at the horizon without so much as a glance in her direction.

The class soon ended and the trio, along with the two dogs, headed for the cafe on the edge of the park. Gum trees lined the footpath, throwing dappled shade over them, and a kookaburra set up a call from one of the trees.

"See, even the birds are laughing at you, Oscar," grumbled Sarah.

"Don't be too hard on him. He's probably past the training age," said Vicky.

"You're right, I'm putting too much pressure on the old boy." Sarah shook her head. "I just wanted him to do well."

They found a table outside and sat beneath the shade of a black umbrella. Sarah ordered a chai latte, Vicky and Meg ordered tea. Both dogs lolled beside the table, puffing gently after their workout.

"So, how are things with you, Vicky?" asked Meg as she stirred sugar and milk into her tea.

Vicky glanced up with a half-smile. "I found out what's wrong with me. Even though it's not great news, it's not terrible either. I mean, I'm not dying or anything."

"Well, that *is* good," Sarah said. "Although I didn't think you were."

Vicky shrugged. "It sure felt like it some days. Anyway, my natural therapist tells me I have a dairy allergy."

"Dairy? Well, at least it's nothing serious, although… ice cream, yoghurt, cheese…" replied Meg, concern on her face.

"I know, you don't have to remind me. But thankfully there are plenty of substitutes these days, so it's not so bad."

"Well, I think it's good news," said Sarah. "I was getting a little worried."

"I know, me too. I'm relieved to know what it is, although I'll miss my daily feast of cheese and biscuits."

"Is there anything you can do about it?" asked Meg.

"There are some natural treatments I can try, but it's not curable. I don't really know much yet, I only found out a few days ago, so I'm still looking into it all." Vicky cocked her head to one side.

"It's definitely good to know what's going on," said Sarah, resting one hand on Vicky's arm with a smile. "Next time we have a movie night I'll bring dairy-free chocolate."

Vicky nodded. "Thanks. Actually, I feel better already since I've stopped eating dairy. It's really taken a load off my mind to know what's going on with my body."

"How about you Meg?" Sarah sipped her chai. "What's new in your world?"

Meg grinned. "I'm pregnant!"

"What? Congratulations!" exclaimed Sarah, pushing out of her seat to embrace her friend.

"That's amazing! I'm so happy for you." Vicky joined in

and soon the three of them were locked in an off-balance hug.

When Sarah sat again, she couldn't wipe the smile from her face. "Wow, how far along are you?"

"We're fourteen weeks, and we told the family yesterday. I've been dying to tell you both." Meg grinned. "It's so hard to keep it a secret when you're sick all the time, but I managed it, and the doctor says everything's going along as it should."

"That's so great." Sarah beamed. "How does Brad feel about it all?"

"He's excited, of course. We weren't sure…well, we didn't know if it could happen for us. Of course, he still has his moments when he gets down, thinking about all the things he won't be able to do with his son or daughter, but he's getting better. It'll take some time, I think."

"Definitely. He'll be a great dad," said Vicky.

"For sure," added Sarah.

"How are you guys going to cope when you take maternity leave?" asked Vicky.

Meg shook her head. "It's amazing really…everything's finally coming together. We got the insurance payout for Brad's injury last week. It's enough to buy a house and plenty to live off for a long while. Also, the paperwork went through for disability, so if we need it, those payments will be available to us. We figure I'll stop work soon, and Brad can finish up his degree while I'm at home with the baby, then he'll get a job and can support us. It's what we always wanted to do… before everything happened. And now, it seems like we can. That's the plan, anyway."

Sarah's throat tightened as tears filled her eyes. "That's fantastic news, Meg. I'm so happy for the two of you. You both deserve a break after everything you've been through."

CHAPTER 24

EMILY

*T*he scent of poached eggs, freshly baked cranberry nut bread, and bacon drifted through the air, tickling Emily's nose and eliciting a groan from her empty stomach. She carried the last platter of food into the dining room, checked that each guest had everything they needed, left Sondra in charge, and hurried back to the kitchen to begin the clean-up.

"It smells amazing in here," said Ethan, coming in through the back door with a grin.

He walked over to her, laced his arms around her waist and kissed her soft on the lips. A shiver ran through her body, delicious and bursting with anticipation.

She wasn't used to it yet, this closeness with him. It was new, unexpected and she'd woken that morning with a smile on her lips even before her alarm had broken the quiet.

"Good morning," she said, with a shyness she hadn't felt in years.

"Great morning," he replied with another kiss, this one lingering and sending goosebumps up her arms and down her legs.

"Hungry?" she asked.

He nodded. "I don't know what you made, but I can't wait to try it. My stomach is almost inside out after my surf this morning; I'm so hungry."

She laughed. "Surfing seems to do that to you."

He followed her around the kitchen as she piled food onto two plates, then set them on the table. He sat next to her and reached for a fork.

After a mouthful of the cranberry bread, she decided that she'd have to add it to the regular breakfast schedule. With a thick layer of butter on one side, it melted in her mouth, bursting with savoury flavours and a hint of sourness from the berries.

When her phone rang, she shook her head. Of course someone would want to talk to her when her mouth was full and her stomach empty.

She answered around a mouthful of bread. "Hello?"

"Emily, how are you babe?"

Callum. She hadn't seen him in so long she'd almost forgotten about the way he'd left her, the pain he'd caused. But for some reason, hearing his voice didn't bring back that same sting it once had.

"Hi Callum, I'm great, thanks. And you?"

"Good... I'm glad to hear you're going well. Have you thought about when you'll come up to Airlie beach? I miss you, babe."

She shook her head. "I'm not coming. I told you that, but I don't think you were listening. As usual."

"What?" his voice morphed into a snarl. "What's going on with you? You've changed or something? This isn't like you."

"This is exactly like me, Callum. I don't want to come up there; we're finished. That's all."

"At least tell me where you are so I can come and talk to you about this. I hate doing it over the phone." He huffed and for a moment she felt bad for him.

"I'm in Emerald Cove, but don't come here. It won't change anything."

"Isn't that where your family lives?" he asked.

She smiled. He'd remembered something she'd told him about herself at least. "Yes, that's right."

"So…why are you staying there? What about us, about me?"

She sighed. "Callum, I'm sorry—things between us aren't going to work out. We don't suit each other, we're too different."

"It didn't seem that way when we were together," he complained. "I don't understand…"

"I saw the drugs, Callum. I found them in your jeans pocket right before you left. You told me you didn't do drugs, that the others were involved but it wasn't for you. You knew how I felt about it, how much I hated it. And you lied to me."

He didn't answer right away, she knew he'd be considering his words carefully. That was how he responded whenever he was cornered—carefully, slowly.

"They weren't mine…"

"Don't try that with me. I asked around. Turns out you were not only doing them, you were dealing as well."

He laughed. "Well, I guess I couldn't keep it from you forever, although it took you long enough to open your eyes. You were so clueless."

Emily shook her head. How had she ever fallen for someone with so much disdain for her, someone who'd treat her that way? But he was right, she'd been naive for far too long. Perhaps she hadn't wanted to see the man he was because she had no one else.

"You were my family for a long time, Callum. I loved you...or at least I thought I did. But it's time to put that all behind us. I wish you only the best."

He grunted. "Yeah, you too, babe. You too."

She hung up the phone, leaning against the kitchen bench with a sigh, her eyes squeezed shut.

"Who was that?" asked Ethan in a soft voice.

She blinked, focused on his handsome face. "My ex. He wants me to move up to Airlie Beach with him; I told him no."

"I heard," he replied.

Ethan came to her then, and she rested her head on his shoulder as he wrapped her up in his arms.

"I don't know what I was thinking...I guess I didn't think much at all when it came to Callum. I left my friends, my job, everything in Sydney to move to Coffs to be with him. But all that time he was a completely different person to who I thought he was."

Ethan stroked the hair away from her face.

"I think I did it because I was still grieving over losing Mum, and I thought I was all alone in the world. That he was the one person left who cared about me, so if I didn't have him—I didn't have anyone." She choked back a sob. "I wish... I wish I'd done everything so differently."

He kissed the tip of her nose. "Grief can make any of us do things we wouldn't otherwise do. It's the one thing we have no control over in life—we can't decide whether or not we want to grieve. It pushes through us one way or another."

She smiled through a blur of tears. "Thank you for being here."

He grinned. "You're welcome." Then he kissed her again.

* * *

SARAH

The cool wind whipped up over the jagged cliff tops. Moonlight reflected off the grassy yard and made the white walls of the cottage glow an eerie bluish colour. The moon hung overhead, low, and almost full, like a cozy night light.

Sarah lay beside Mick on the swinging bench seat, her head on his lap, a blanket nestled around her shoulders. He swung the seat slowly, thoughtfully, as he gazed out at the expanse of dark ocean that stretched away into nothing.

"What could be better than this?" he asked.

She smiled, watching him. "Nothing."

He looked at her, caught her eye, his own sparkling. "This is the life."

Below Sarah, under her seat, she heard the faint thud of a tail beating against the floorboards. Oscar liked to be close to her, as close as he could manage. She never thought she could love a dog as much as she loved him. He followed her around during the day, slept on her feet in the evenings and did his best to crawl into bed with her at night—but that was a line she hadn't let him cross yet, instead insisting he sleep on his own cushion.

"Have you ever thought about tying the knot?" asked Mick.

Sarah sat up with a start, pulling the blanket tighter as she faced him. "Well…yeah, I was engaged once. Remember?"

He nodded. "I'd forgotten you two were engaged. So, you wanted to get married?"

"I thought I did."

"And now?"

Her eyes narrowed. What was he asking? "Do you mean, do I want to get married now?"

"I'm curious," he replied.

She pursed her lips. "I don't know. I almost got married back in Sydney, and now I can see that would've been a huge mistake. I don't entirely trust myself, after that. And rushing into that kind of commitment...it's not something I'll take lightly. Especially after everything that's happened with Mum and Dad."

Mick studied her, chewed his lower lip.

Her heart thudded against her ribcage. She didn't want to upset him, to push him away. But she wasn't ready to commit her life to someone. Not yet. What if things turned out for her like they had with Mum? Realising after forty years that she didn't really know her husband the way she thought? Watching him run off with someone younger? What then? She hated to think of herself wasting away in a loveless marriage for the best part of her life.

"What about kids? Do you want kids?" he asked.

She smiled. "Yes, I definitely want kids."

He grinned in response. "Me too."

That wasn't something Sarah had to think about. It didn't scare her the way intimacy did. She knew she wanted children, as many as she could manage. She loved kids, always had. She couldn't wait until she was ready for a baby. Something about the idea of it lit her up inside.

"What about you? Would you ever remarry?" she asked.

Mick didn't hesitate. "Yes, I would. I want to."

She loved the way he knew his own mind so well. Knew his desires, what he wanted from life. She was never as certain as him, always had doubts floating around inside her head.

What if? What about? Maybe...might...possibly...could...

She couldn't stop the barrage of questions, concerns, and worries, whenever she thought about things like getting married, raising a family, changing careers, starting over. It was almost paralysing, until she was thrown into those decisions by something as impulsive as quitting her job or leaving her fiancé.

But seeing Mick's resolve, his determination, and his love —bubbles of happiness welled inside her and drifted like balloons, growing as they rose.

She smiled. "I'm glad you're so certain about it, and I love that you're willing to jump in again even after you were so badly hurt."

"Let's get married," he said, tracing a line down the side of her face with his fingertips.

The look in his eyes woke a passion inside her that built and grew with heat as its fuel.

She leaned forward, kissed his lips, revelling in their warmth, softness and the invitation that lay there.

"I want to..." she said. "But I can't make that decision yet. I'm still...it scares me. I'm sorry. I have to know I wouldn't be making the same mistake as Mum. She thought she knew... she loved dad and look what happened to them."

Mick inhaled a sharp breath, stood, and combed hands through his hair, standing the dark blond locks on end, as his gaze returned to the ocean. "Fine. I get it." He spun on his heel to face her. "But just so you know—I'm not your father. I'm not like him; I wouldn't do that to you. I thought you understood me better than that."

CHAPTER 25

DIANA

*T*he white walls of the *Seaside Manor Bed and Breakfast* rose majestic beside them. Diana lowered herself into one of the rocking chairs on the front porch and Ben sat beside her. His luggage waited near the front steps, a simple shoulder bag, nothing more. He hadn't intended to stay in the Cove so long, but they'd been enjoying spending time together and now she was sad to see him leave. She'd told Emily about him, introduced Ben to his cousin and the two of them had hit it off right away. It warmed her heart to see them laughing together. They had the same nose, Ben and Emily - it turned up slightly at the end. It was a small thing but brought a lump to her throat as she watched them.

After all these years, she had a son. They'd taken beach walks together, visited the Murwillumbah Art Gallery with Rupert and sipped coffee while discussing which local artists they loved best. The three of them had shopped for things she and Rupert needed for their new home, things that fit snug into small spaces, since they'd had to leave so much behind at the Manor. And Ben's help had been invaluable.

She finally understood what it was like to have someone so much like her to spend time with—he looked like her, but also shared so many of her personality traits. And there were glimpses of Andrew in him as well. She'd been counselling herself not to push those away, but to embrace every part of her son—Andrew had helped bring him into the world and for that she'd be forever grateful. Even if she did regret the hurt they'd caused, she couldn't regret what'd happened now. Not since it'd brought her Ben.

"Rupert wanted to come and say goodbye, but he wasn't feeling well this morning," she said.

"I hope he's not coming down with something," replied Ben.

She nodded. "It has been cold the past few nights."

"I'm glad I came," he said.

She smiled, reached for his hand, and squeezed it. "So am I. So glad."

"You're not sorry?"

"You can't possibly know how much I've longed to know you. I only wish it'd happened sooner."

He beamed. "Good, so let's stay in touch. Okay? And I'd love you to come up to Brisbane to meet my parents. They're not very mobile these days, but I know they want to see you."

She was nervous to meet them, but knew it was impor-tant to him. What would they think of her, a woman who would give up her child? But she hadn't been a woman, she'd been a girl. "Yes, I'd love to meet them. We'll do that soon, perhaps when Rupert is feeling a little better…I hate to leave him alone for long these days, and I'm not sure he's up to the trip at the moment."

"Of course," he replied, standing to his feet.

They embraced, and she waved as he carried his luggage

to the car and drove away. Her heart ached and tears lodged in her throat as his car disappeared around a curve in the road.

How empty her days would be now that he was gone. She might go inside and see if Emily had time to share a pot of tea before she went home.

Just as she was about to open the Manor's front door, she noticed Cindy watering plants in her garden next door. She could see her over the fence from where she stood. Cindy had her back to Diana. If she was quiet, she might make it over there before Cindy saw her and had time to escape. Cindy had been avoiding Diana ever since their argument.

She crept down the front steps, along the garden path that led to the street, then bent as low as she could manage to stay hidden by a hedgerow before turning into Cindy's long, wide driveway. The drive curved towards the garage, with a turning circle in front of the house. Cindy was watering the flowers that lined the circle.

Diana hurried along the driveway, careful to keep her footsteps as light as she could—something that wasn't so easy these days. She always intended to go on a diet, to lose some of the weight that'd gathered around her waist and thighs in recent years, but could never manage to stay away from sweets long enough to do it.

"Cindy Flannigan!" she called when she was close enough to do it without shouting. That was something her mother had taught her that she'd never managed to shake—a lady doesn't shout. Even now, so many years later, she found herself holding in her voice until she was near enough to someone to be ladylike. The ridiculousness of that gave Diana's cheeks a flush of heat and put vigour into her final steps before she reached Cindy.

Her friend turned, a look of surprise on her face that was quickly replaced by a stubborn anger.

"Oh, it's you. Go away, I would've thought by now you got the point—I don't want to talk to you!"

Cindy stormed towards the house, the watering can dangling from one hand and spilling water on the ground with each step she took.

"You have to talk to me, we're best friends," cried Diana, trailing after her.

"Not anymore, we're not."

Diana stopped, pressed her hands to her hips. "That's ridiculous, Cindy. We've been friends since we were girls, you can't let something that happened more than forty years ago ruin that."

Cindy whirled about, her eyes flashing. "*You* let it ruin us! You did it. I can't believe you'd do that—can't believe you'd betray me that way. Andrew...yes, of course. I'd believe it of him. He did it often enough to establish a pattern of behaviour, so we all expect it of him. But you?" Cindy's voice broke. "I don't want to talk to you right now, you really hurt me. I can't help thinking that all these years, you were hiding that from me—you didn't really love me the way I thought you did, the way I loved you. You were secretive, and betrayed me, and I don't want to see you!"

Cindy climbed the stairs in a rage and slammed the front door behind her.

Diana watched her go, mouth agape, still puffing slightly from the effort of hurrying up the long driveway. Grief welled within her, and her eyes blurred with tears.

She spun on her heel and returned the way she'd come, this time with dragging feet. She'd expected Cindy to be angry with her, but not this angry. It was so long ago, almost a lifetime. So much had happened in that time, and surely Cindy could understand that she'd been a silly, immature girl who hadn't thought it through entirely. Surely.

Well, she couldn't stay angry at Diana forever. And Diana

would simply have to think of something she could do to win her friend back. She'd start with baking, it's where she always started whenever she had a problem to ponder. And Cindy couldn't resist Diana's baking.

She wiped the tears from her eyes with the back of her hand and headed for her car, parked on the curb in front of the Manor. She climbed inside and sat in the driver's seat a moment, gathering herself. She didn't want Rupert to see her so upset, he'd want to know what'd happened and she had no desire to talk about it, to relive what her friend had said to her.

When her phone rang in the purse on the passenger seat, it startled her. Heart thudding, she dug through the black, leather bag to locate the phone and pressed it to her ear.

"Hello, this is Di."

"Diana Jones?"

"Yes, speaking…" Who was it? The screen had shown an unknown number, but the only people who ever called her on her mobile were Rupert, Emily, Ben and Cindy.

"Mrs Jones, this is Adam Brown from the Tweed Emergency Services. I'm calling to let you know that we have your husband en route to the hospital in an ambulance."

Diana's heart leapt into her throat. "What? Rupert? What's happened? Is he okay?"

Her hands shook as she held the phone to her ear.

"I'm afraid he's in cardiac arrest, Mrs Jones."

"A heart attack?" Her head spun. This couldn't be happening.

"Yes, that's all I know for now. We're expecting him to arrive at the Tweed Heads Emergency Department any minute now, if you'd like to head over there to meet him."

"Thank you, I will."

She hung up the phone and started the car, before screeching out onto the road. Usually she was acutely aware of keeping her speed to a minimum in residential neighbour-hoods, but all she could think of was getting to Rupert before it was too late.

When she pulled into the hospital parking lot, she felt numb. She hadn't allowed herself to follow her initial train of thought into the realm of what could go wrong, what might happen, what if he died? She'd pulled herself out of that spiral of thinking halfway to Tweed Heads and instead, sat in silence merely looking ahead and going through the motions of driving. She had to believe her husband would get through this, that he'd be okay. She couldn't imagine life any other way.

Diana clutched her purse to her shoulder and bustled into the emergency room, through wide, glass doors that swung open as she approached. She hurried by the rows of seats, dotted with people waiting, and approached a reception counter, shielded by glass. She peered through an opening at a woman, typing on a computer, dressed in something resembling scrubs.

"Excuse me?"

The woman nodded, smiled. "Just one moment please…"

"I'm in a hurry, my husband came in via ambulance… Rupert Jones."

The woman's lips pursed. "Okay, let me see where he is." She pressed a few keys on the keyboard and studied the monitor. "Yes, I see…he arrived about fifteen minutes ago via ambulance and is currently in one of our rooms being treated by a doctor."

"Can I see him?" asked Diana, panic rising in her throat.

"Come with me," said the woman, compassion softening her face.

She disappeared for a moment, then emerged through a nearby doorway and beckoned Diana to follow her. With her purse tight beneath one arm, Diana trundled after her with her legs tiring as the adrenaline in her system began to fade.

They reached a room, sectioned off from several others by drawn curtains. Behind the curtains, voices murmured. The nurse she'd been following, she assumed the woman was a nurse anyway, stepped behind the curtain and spoke with a man in a hushed voice. Then, the curtain drew back slightly, and he stepped out to see her.

The doctor wore green scrubs with a face mask pulled down, hanging around his neck. His matching cap covered most of his greying hair, his eyes were brown and crinkled at the edges when he saw her.

"Mrs Jones, come over here with me, let's sit down and I'll update you." He took her by the elbow and led her over to a small room with chairs and a table inside. He shut the door behind them.

She sat down and released her grip on the purse, feeling the blood drain from her face. "Where's Rupert? Is he okay?"

The doctor sat beside her. "Rupert's heart attack was a severe one. The paramedics did everything they could for him. We tried to revive him when he arrived here at the hospital. But I'm sorry to say that Rupert died in the ambulance and we weren't able to bring him back."

Diana's world crumbled around her. Her mouth opened but she couldn't speak. Instead, she heard a wail and wondered where it came from.

"I'm so sorry, Mrs Jones. It happened quickly…if it's any consolation to you, he didn't suffer for long. From what I understand, he died soon after the paramedics arrived and got him into the ambulance. As I said, they did everything they could to revive him, and we picked it up when they got here, but we were unsuccessful."

Diana dropped her head into her hands, the tears hot and wet on her cheeks. She sobbed as a swell of grief crashed over her. She raised her head, her vision blurred with tears. "Did he say anything?"

"I don't believe so. Apparently, a neighbour was visiting at the time…the good news is that they were able to call the ambulance as soon as he fell. So, he wasn't there long. The neighbour then sat with him until the ambulance arrived, from what I understand. So, he wasn't alone. Perhaps you could speak with her when you get home to find out more."

Diana nodded. A fresh wave of tears came then, and she couldn't speak any longer. The doctor patted her shoulder, then left her in the room alone with the door shut.

It wasn't fair, wasn't right—Rupert was good, he'd never done anything underhanded, or secretive. He didn't have a bone of betrayal in his entire body. She'd been the one to do those things. It didn't make sense that he should die before her. She'd always hoped she would go first, but not yet. They hadn't had a chance to go on that cruise they'd been talking about for twenty years. Hadn't visited London or seen the Eiffel Tower. They shouldn't have put off their dreams for a business…she could see that now. Now that she'd stepped away and the Manor didn't occupy her every waking moment—she understood that it'd consumed them for far too long.

Sobs wracked her body, and she slumped sideways onto the row of chairs, ignoring the pain of the plastic as it dug into her side. Rupert was gone. With a start, she sat up, wiped her cheeks dry and stared at the door.

He was gone, but his body lay beyond that door. She had to say goodbye, to give him one last kiss before he was gone. She leapt to her feet and pushed through the door.

CHAPTER 26

ETHAN

$\mathscr{T}$he Murwillumbah council was a place Ethan had never considered working before in his life. Too country, too rural…he'd always had his sights set on bigger and better, and those kinds of jobs were in the city.

But now, everything had changed. The town itself was quaint, and the council building old but in decent shape— dark brick, with a rabbit warren of offices hidden inside along narrow hallways. As many phone calls as he made, as often as he explained to prospective employers that he hadn't done anything wrong at Mammoth, hadn't known what was going on and that, in fact, he hadn't been charged with anything, they didn't hear him. Didn't care. There was a mark against his name he wasn't able to remove with a few weeks of living in Emerald Cove.

Here it was different. In Murwillumbah, only a twenty-minute drive from Emerald Cove, he was Ethan Flannigan. Nothing more, nothing less. He knew someone, who knew someone who worked for the head engineer at the council. They'd recommended him for a job opening, and that was all it took. Here he was, seated in one of a row of chairs, waiting for his chance to interview for a job as an engineer.

Nerves fluttered in the pit of his stomach. Strangely enough, he wanted the job. One look out of the window at the small, picturesque riverside town, was all it took. He'd visited the town several times throughout his childhood, had ridden there by bus regularly for inter-school sporting competitions, high school dances, camps…and even though at the time he'd wondered who in their right mind would live by a river instead of the beach, now he understood. There was a natural charm to the place.

Set by a slow-moving, wide river, the centre of town was a study in century-old architecture. Every shop front was a relic of the past, painted anew and holding modern wares, but a walk through the town was like a stroll through the past. And now, in his late twenties, he liked it. Enjoyed the feeling of history, the old-fashioned town clock sitting in the centre of the main street on an island of its own, the banks that looked as though bush rangers might emerge from their front doors at any moment, bandanas obscuring their faces, pistols held high.

He wanted to work there. And wanting made him nervous.

"Mr Flannigan, you can come in."

A woman ushered him into a dark office, then shut the door behind him. A man, seated at a dark timber desk, stood to offer him a hand. "Hi Mr Flannigan, I'm John Riordan, the head engineer here. Please, take a seat."

Ethan shook the man's hand, then sat. "Pleased to meet you."

"You as well. You have an impressive resume," continued John, flipping through a set of stapled pages in his hands.

Ethan smiled. "Thank you."

"Can I ask you something before we get started?"

"Fire away," replied Ethan.

"Talk to me about why you want to work in Murwillumbah. I can see from your resume that your last position was with Mammoth in Brisbane, that would've been an exciting opportunity...working here is a bit quieter, so I'm interested to understand your reasoning."

"I've moved back to Emerald Cove and am fairly settled there. My mother lives there, my sister as well...I'd like to stay there if I can. I have very fond memories of this town from when I was a kid, and honestly, I'd like to slow the pace a little bit."

John nodded. "Okay, that's good to know."

The rest of the interview went well. It was an informal chat, and John showed him around the offices, introduced him to people, and generally gave Ethan the impression that the job was his already. By the time they were done, Ethan shook John's hand with confidence.

"I'll give you a call when we've interviewed the rest of the candidates. It was nice to meet you," said John.

He wasn't about to give anything away, it seemed, but Ethan could tell he'd made a good impression. He grinned as he walked back to his car in the large parking lot that served the council building and the nearby public swimming pool. The swimming pool was shut for the winter, but Ethan knew that it would buzz with activity before long—children laughing, squealing, splashing. Some practicing their moves in the large diving pool, others swimming laps and still others careening down the hillside slide on blue, plastic mats.

As he climbed into the car, he wondered what Emily would think of this opportunity. Would she be happy if he got a job, or would she think he was abandoning the Manor? The truth was, they weren't making enough of a profit for both of them to draw a full-time income, and he wanted to make sure she was paid. She was the only one of them working full-time. Now that he'd fixed a few things, redone a bathroom, painted most of the rooms and built the pagoda in the garden, there wasn't enough to keep him busy for eight hours a day. Besides, after having a nice break from engineering, he was feeling refreshed and part of him itched to get back to it.

CHAPTER 27

SARAH

*W*ith a sniffle, Sarah tugged her jumper more tightly around her frame, then shivered. She peered into the darkness, the sound of rain pounding on the roof overhead. Where was Oscar?

The dog hadn't come in for his evening meal as usual. He was like clockwork. He loved to go for a wander through the bush in the afternoon, but he always came back in time for dinner. Ever since he first showed up as a stray in her yard and she'd fed him a bowl of kibble, he hadn't missed a meal. But today he hadn't come home, and she'd been concerned. Now it was pitch dark, a storm had rolled in and was drenching the cottage, and there was still no sign of him.

Where could he be? Would he have found shelter somewhere to wait out the storm before he returned? Or had something happened to him?

She squinted again, wondering if the dark shadow in the distance was him or a shrub. It didn't move. Shrub. She shook her head; it was so hard to see him at night. His fur was a dark brown, almost black, and as soon as the light dimmed, he faded into the shadows.

She strode inside and blew her nose on a tissue, then hurried to the kitchen to throw it in the rubbish bin on top of a mound of soiled tissues. Her cold was worsening. She'd had a tickle in her throat a few days ago, but since then it'd developed into a debilitating head cold, and she could barely go for five minutes without having to blow her nose.

She shook her head, sighed, and blew her nose again, even as a headache pounded in the base of her skull.

Of course, Oscar chose tonight to disappear, right when she was too sick to do anything much about it.

She pictured him crossing a road, headlights slashing across him as tyres squealed.

With a sharp intake of breath, she reached for a handful of tissues to shove into her jeans pocket. She was going out to find him.

Sarah donned her rain jacket then searched the kitchen drawers for a torch. She found one, switched it on and the light glowed dim and orange—the batteries were almost dead.

Just great.

She found some more batteries after a ten-minute search, adrenaline filtering through her veins more with each passing moment. What if he was out there somewhere, injured, alone, soaking wet? Her heart pounded, and her head spun.

On the back deck, she called his name a few times, shouting until her raw throat fairly throbbed.

There was still no sign of him. She'd brought his dinner bowl outside, hoping that if he did show up, he'd stay on the porch eating until she found him there. She couldn't believe the stray dog who hadn't let her pat him for weeks was now so important to her that she couldn't sit and relax while he was out in a storm. What'd happened to her?

With a huff of disgust at herself for giving her heart to a mangy dog, she tugged the hood of the rain jacket over her head and traipsed down the back steps and across the yard, her gum boots squelching with each step on the sodden ground.

She searched along the top of the cliffs, where a trail wound through the wild, leaning bushes that pulled away from the cliff face as though too afraid to look at the steep drop that fell over black boulders and jagged rocks to the expanse of sand below.

"Oscar!" Sarah called.

It was difficult to hear anything above the roar of the waves, whipped up by the wind, and the pelting rain against her hood.

"Oscar! Come here boy!"

She sneezed, reached for a tissue, and wiped her nose, only to discover the tissue was now wetter than her nose was. She grimaced and shoved it back into the pocket of her soaking jeans.

It was impossible. She'd get pneumonia out there, and she'd seen no sign of the dog.

She peered at the beach, hoping for a glimpse of a black shadow flitting between the rocks, but couldn't see any movement. She had to get back to the cottage and get dry before the sneezing got any worse.

When she reached the cottage, the faint glow of the kitchen light warmed her heart. She hadn't lived there long, but it was home to her. She couldn't wait to get inside and warm up by the fire.

"Oscar! Where are you?" she called, but her voice was lost in the rage of the storm.

Mick's truck was parked out front, and she quickened her

pace, anxious to see him, even as tears lodged in her tender throat.

She rushed through the front door, letting it slam it shut behind her, and peeled off the jacket, leaving it in puddle at her feet as she dripped in place.

"Mick?"

He appeared from the living room with eyes wide. "There you are. I was wondering what'd happened to you. Your car is outside, the lights are on, there's even a cold cup of tea on the kitchen bench...I was beginning to think something terrible had happened."

She sneezed, a gigantic sneeze that shook her entire body. Her eyes watered, and the cold from her sodden jeans seeped into her body so that she shivered all over.

"I'm sorry...I can't find Oscar. He didn't come home tonight for dinner, and now it's raining..."

Mick kissed her forehead. "You're sick, you shouldn't be out in this weather. Hold on, I'll get you a towel."

He returned within moments with a soft, dry towel, and helped rub her down, shivering and sniffling. He led her to the bathroom and turned on the taps over the bathtub, checking the temperature with his hand.

"Have a nice, hot bath. I'll make you some soup. Okay?"

She nodded, unable to do more than stand in one place, shaking from head to toe. Her headache had moved up and now resided in her forehead. It felt as though someone small had lodged themselves inside her skull and was hitting it hard with a baseball bat.

Mick kissed her forehead again, then left her alone in the bathroom. She undressed slowly, her fingers fumbling over buttons. The jeans were difficult to get free of, she had to stop and turn, twist and groan to remove the wet denim, but finally she stood, naked before the steaming hot bath. She climbed in, one foot at a time, grimacing as the pain of the hot water stung her frigid toes.

Finally, she slipped beneath the water's surface with a gasp, then smiled. It felt so good. Warmth filtered its way through her body, and she lay there until she was afraid, she might go to sleep if she didn't get out.

Thoughts of Oscar, stuck out in the storm, filled her mind again as she dressed in a tracksuit and slippers. Tears pricked her eyes.

She'd done everything she could. There wasn't anything else she could manage, not while she was sick.

Mick was in the kitchen, stirring something in a pot on the stovetop.

He smiled at her as she sat at the dining table. "Better?"

She nodded. "Much better. Thanks."

"You really shouldn't be out in this weather, not while you're feeling unwell. I'd hate for you to get worse."

"I know...but I'm worried about Oscar. It isn't like him to stay away for this long. He never misses a meal; he's a complete pig when it comes to his food."

Mick chuckled as he set a massive bowl of pumpkin soup in front of Sarah. Steam rose from the surface, there was a dollop of cream in the centre, and a plate holding a soft, bread roll in his other hand. She eyed it even as hunger gripped her stomach in a growl.

"Wow, this looks amazing. Thank you. I didn't have time to come up with anything since I was so worried about Oscar."

"You're most welcome. I brought it with me—it's from the Emerald Cafe. Your mother is an amazing cook; you can thank her."

Sarah sipped at a spoonful of soup, almost singeing her tongue. "Mmmm...I love Mum's pumpkin soup. It's perfect for the way I'm feeling."

"I thought it might cheer you up a bit."

She forced a smile onto her face; it was hard to be happy with Oscar still missing. "You're the best." She cupped his cheek with one hand, and he turned his head to kiss her arm.

"And don't worry about Oscar, I'm sure he's fine. We'll find him."

She nodded, hoping that he was right. Although, she'd have to wait until morning now before she could go looking again and hope that the rain stopped by that time. The sound of it pummelling the roof overhead almost drowned out their conversation.

Mick headed for the front door, pulled a raincoat from a hook on the coat rack and shrugged his muscular arms into the sleeves. He'd hung up her coat while she was in the bath. It hung limp, still dripping wet, on another one of the hooks, her gumboots neatly lined up next to the wall.

"You're leaving?" she asked, her heart falling. She'd hoped he'd stay—it was lonely in the cottage without Oscar, especially with the storm lashing the point where the cottage was perched.

"I thought I'd check a few haunts around the place to see if I can find Oscar. I won't be long." He smiled as he lifted the jacket hood over his head. "Stay warm, and I'll see you soon."

She gaped as the door shut behind him. He was going after Oscar in the worst storm they'd seen at the Cove in months—emotion welled up inside her and tears sprang into her eyes. He was the best boyfriend in the world. He'd asked her to marry him, spend the rest of her life with him, and she'd turned him down. She must've been temporarily insane. There wasn't anyone else in the entire world she could imagine growing old with. He cared as much about Oscar as she did. The dog was a stray, a mutt, old and ragged with hip bones that still protruded from his sides. And yet Mick was out in the rain looking for him.

She sobbed and reached for a tissue to blow her nose. She honked hard into the tissue, then tossed it into a nearby bin. She should be out there with him, and she would be if it wasn't for her darned cold.

By the time she finished her soup, she'd pulled back the curtains to check the yard for any sign of either of them three times. At least she was warm now, and the sneezing seemed to have stopped, or at least was in temporary hiatus.

She sniffled and nestled onto the couch, clicking on the television but leaving it on mute. The flickering image helped stave off the loneliness, but it couldn't distract her from the thought that now both Mick and Oscar were out in the torrential rain and inky black night.

The back porch was drenched, along with her banana lounge and rocking chairs, dining table set and hammock. Even the glass doors that led outside were wet with water droplets carried in on the howling wind.

Sarah tucked her legs up beneath herself and stared out into the darkness. Then, Mick ran up the back steps carrying Oscar in his arms. She gasped, leapt to her feet, and flung the back door open. Mick hurried inside, dripping a river of water in his wake.

"I found him. He's hurt his leg, I think. He was caught in a roll of barbed wire that'd come loose from a fence down the road."

Mick carried Oscar to the bathroom and set him in the tub. He was covered in mud, soaked to the bone and shivering. Sarah turned on the taps, filling the tub with warm water. She washed Oscar while Mick showered and changed in her ensuite. The bath water turned pinkish as blood seeped from the wounds on Oscar's front right leg. She bathed it gently, eliciting a yelp followed by Oscar licking her hands.

"Okay, boy. I won't hurt you, at least I'll try my best. Come on, let's get you dried off and warm."

He'd stopped shivering before she got him out of the tub as the hot water did its job. She rinsed him with clean water after flushing the muddy remnants from the tub. Then, carefully, she towelled him dry. Finally, she carried him to the lounge room where his pillow-style bed was, laid him on it and hurried to fetch the first aid kit. By the time she'd bound his leg with antiseptic and bandages, Mick had joined her, freshly showered, and dressed in a spare set of clean work clothes he'd found in his truck.

"He looks much better," said Mick, slumping onto the couch with a hot cup of soup in his hands.

Sarah nodded. "He is. Thanks to you."

She joined Mick on the couch, as Oscar nibbled at his dinner. He set the soup on the coffee table and slipped an arm around her shoulder. His face hovered over hers as his green eyes crinkled around the edges, gaze locked on Sarah's. The way his two front teeth crossed a little bit in the front was so cute she couldn't resist kissing him.

"You're welcome," he said, kissing her in return.

She grinned. "I'm so happy he's home, and you as well. I was worried about both of you. You didn't have to do that... but I'm so glad you did. Thank you."

"Of course," he replied. "I'd do anything for you Sarah... you and Oscar mean the world to me. I hope you know that."

She nodded, unable to speak around the lump in her throat.

Mick extricated himself and set about building a fire in the hearth. With everything going on, Sarah had let it die out. He had it roaring again in no time and stood with his hands outstretched, warming them. By now the sound of rain on the roof had dimmed to a patter, but the wind still screeched as it closed around the cottage whipping directly off the ocean below and up the steep cliff face.

He faced her with a smile. "I love you, Sarah Flannigan."

"I love you back, Mick McIntosh," she replied with a catch to her voice.

He knelt in front of her, took her hands in his. "It's why I want to spend the rest of my life with you—you're my family already. I want to make it official. I can't go on living somewhere else when my heart is here. Say you'll marry me."

She nodded, tears filling her eyes. "Yes, I'll marry you. I don't know why I hesitated; you're so different to my dad and to Jeremy. I love you, and I know you're the right man for me."

He laughed once, out loud, then cupped her cheeks with his hands to kiss her passionately on the lips. Sarah couldn't think of anything other than his lips on hers, the promise of their lives together stretching out ahead of them—pure, hope-filled and driven by love. She hadn't expected to find someone in the Cove, someone she could share her life with. She'd left the city and moved home to get away from Jeremy, and instead she'd run smack into Mick and had loved him before she was even aware it was happening. It was a surprising thing to find herself in love with a man she'd known since she was a child, someone she'd never have considered when she was younger but now knew was a perfect match for her in every way. She couldn't wait to get started on their new life together.

CHAPTER 28

EMILY

*T*he phone rang as soon as she put it down and Emily found herself booking a couple into a newly renovated suite for the following weekend. She smiled as she hung up the phone—bookings were up, she felt as though she was on top of most things now and everything was running like clockwork.

With a hum she jumped to her feet and skipped to the kitchen. The oven dinged as she reached it, and she pulled the cinnamon tea cake from it with floral mitts, inhaling the delightful aroma as she did.

The entire ground floor smelled of baking, upstairs guests were settling into their rooms, and the cleaner had left the place sparkling only a half hour earlier. Life was good.

No sooner had that thought entered her mind than an image of Ethan followed it.

Of course, whatever was going on between her and Ethan complicated things. She liked it, liked him—there was no question about that. But they were business partners; they worked together at the Manor every day. If things turned sour between them, it could ruin everything.

Now that she'd been living at the Manor for two and half months, she'd fallen in love with the place all over again. She'd adored it as a teenager, had looked forward to every summer her mother had allowed her to stay with her Auntie Di and Uncle Rupert.

Her heart fell and tears filled her eyes.

Uncle Rupert.

She missed him so much already. It felt wrong for her to be happy, to smile, when he was gone. It'd been three days since her aunt called to tell her the devastating news. Poor Auntie Di was beside herself. Emily had never seen her that way before. She'd always considered her aunt to be stoic, reasonably unemotional, or at least not expressive. But she hadn't been able to stop crying—on the phone call or when Emily had visited the house later with flowers.

Emily sighed, shaking her head. She was baking things now, trying them out for the wake, which they planned to hold at the Manor after the funeral. So far, she'd baked cheesecake, scones, caramel tarts, and lemon meringue pies —all of Uncle Rupert's favourites. And the Manor's guests certainly weren't complaining about her experimentation. She had the menu planned out and intended to make certain everything was done so that Auntie Di didn't have to do a thing but show up and grieve with her family and friends.

Even thinking about the funeral reminded her of her mother's. Her throat tightened at the thought of seeing the casket, Auntie Di crying, and hearing those hymns again. The memory of saying goodbye to her mother was seared in her brain, and even though it'd been years ago, she couldn't think of it without tears blurring her vision and her heart constricting in her chest.

Ethan burst through the back door, dressed in jeans, a white button-down shirt open at the collar, and blue canvas sandals. His hair was brushed to one side and his light brown eyes sparkled.

"Good morning, Em," he said, sweeping her up in his arms and kissing her full on the lips.

She blushed under his gaze as he pulled back to drink her in.

"Good morning. You seem chipper."

He grinned. "It's because I get to see you."

Emily busied herself setting the cake out to cool, her face burning. She wasn't accustomed to being adored by anyone, and certainly not the way Ethan expressed his adoration on a regular basis with no guile, nothing holding him back. It touched her heart and made her uncomfortable all at the same time. This thing that'd developed between them was so unexpected, she wasn't sure where it was going, and she hated to think that it could end — but experience told her it probably would.

"Would you like a slice of cake? Fresh out of the oven..."

He licked his lips. "Yes please. That smells amazing."

She sliced two pieces, poured them each some coffee and sat with him at the kitchen table. He ran a hand down her arm, giving her goosebumps, then dug into the cake with his fork.

"Did you hear back from your solicitor friend?" she asked, taking a sip of coffee.

He nodded, swallowed. "Yes, apparently the police were happy with my statement, so they won't be pursuing charges against me."

She laughed. "That is very good to hear. I'm so happy for you."

"Me too." He took another bite. "But that reminds me, I have to talk to you about something."

"Oh no, not more legal issues…"

He chuckled. "No, nothing like that. But I do think we need to plan for things possibly going wrong. I mean, if something happened to my finances, it could impact on the Manor, and I don't want that. So, I've applied for a job at the Murwillumbah Council."

She frowned. "Doing what?"

"Engineering," he replied. "Like I was doing before, but more low-key."

"I didn't know you'd started looking for work yet."

"I hadn't really…but then this opportunity came up and I thought, wouldn't it be great to be able to stay living in Emerald Cove, and commute to Murwillumbah for work?"

So he wouldn't be moving away—the thought buoyed her spirits. All this time she'd assumed he'd head back to the city at some point and the two of them would have to figure out how they would make things work, or if they would even try.

Emily surprised herself by leaning forward to kiss Ethan. Sparks ran through her body sending tingles down her legs and out her toes. She smiled against his lips, then leaned back in her chair.

"I think it's a great idea."

"You do?" he asked. "Because I was worried you'd think I was leaving you with the Manor to run on your own…"

She shook her head. "No, it's fine. You've done a lot around here and I can't expect you to put aside your career goals and be my handyman. We can hire someone local to do that."

He inhaled a deep breath. "I'm glad you feel that way."

Emily nestled into the crook of Ethan's neck, and listened to his heartbeat as he took another sip of coffee. She'd thought their relationship would cause her more stress, that it'd only be trouble. But in that moment, all she felt was peace. She cared about him more than she'd realised she could care about anyone. The things in their past that she'd held onto for so long in order to push him away had been misunderstandings—letting them go had been a relief. And she'd found love and affection had taken the place of the bitterness and anger that'd been lodged in her heart for so long.

CHAPTER 29

REBECCA

*T*he rabbit warren hallways, lifts, escalators, and rooms that made up the Tweed Heads hospital were familiar to Rebecca now. After three evenings of driving Franklin to see his dad, bringing him meals, visiting him with messages from the office, she knew exactly which turn to take, which stairs to climb, and which door to walk through.

She strode ahead with purpose, stopped, and knocked on the door.

Peter, his father, was awake but not responding much to anything the doctors or his friends and family did or said. The doctor had assured Franklin that it might take some time, but Rebecca could see the concern in her boss's eyes.

"Hey boss," she said.

Franklin glanced up at her from the newspaper he was reading to his father's still form. He grinned.

"Proby, there you are. I was beginning to think you'd gotten lost on your way here."

She shook her head. "Nope. And don't whinge, I'm right on time."

He stood then kissed his father's forehead. "Dad, I'm heading to work. I'll be back to see you again in the morning. Okay?"

They walked to the cruiser together. She was glad to see that Franklin had showered and was wearing a fresh change of clothes. He'd been a little more fragrant than usual that last few times she'd driven him to work. His car was parked next to the cruiser she'd brought over from the office.

"So, I'll drive you back tomorrow, then?" she asked.

He nodded. "That'd be great, thanks."

"How's he going?" she asked as she climbed into the passenger seat.

"Better I think," he replied. "Although, he's not talking or anything. But the doctor seems to think he's improving. It's hard to tell."

"Any chance he'll come home soon?"

Franklin started the car's engine, then huffed out a small breath. "Uh, I don't think so. Doc seems to believe the best we can hope for is some kind of nursing home." He swallowed. "But I know Dad would hate that idea."

They drove to the police station, chatting about the weather, Rebecca's boxing class, anything other than his father. She knew what it was like, having a sick father—she'd been through it herself and what she'd needed at the time was for people to treat her like they normally did, and to talk about something other than the grief she was experiencing. She could see Franklin's shoulders slowly loosen as he drove back into work.

He parked in the lot beside another cruiser. It was dark outside and streetlights glowed, casting shadows on the bushes and shrubbery that surrounded the police station in long, winding garden beds.

"Thanks for coming to get me, Bec," he said, gathering his things together. "And for letting me drive."

She nodded. "You're welcome."

"It feels so good to get back to work, back to normal."

"I'll bet it does." She smiled, climbing out of the vehicle.

He climbed out too, a satchel slung over one shoulder. There were dark smudges beneath his eyes.

"You should head home and try to get some sleep tonight," she said as she walked around to the driver's side.

He nodded and yawned. "I will."

"Good."

He grinned. "Oh hey, we were talking about something when I got the phone call about Dad. Something that was bothering you. Did you figure out what to do?"

Rebecca had thought about it a lot over the past three days—what would she do if her ex came calling? She'd prepped her house in case he showed up there. But if he came to the office, she'd need some support. Perhaps she should tell Franklin more than she'd hinted at earlier. Then again, he had enough to deal with in his own life.

"Yeah, I think I'm on top of it. The thing is..." she sighed; it was so hard to bring herself to say the words. She'd hidden the truth from this community, from her colleagues, for so long. Fear stabbed in her chest. "It's my ex-boyfriend...he might be coming to see me, and I don't want him to."

Franklin's eyes narrowed. He dropped the satchel to the ground and crossed his arms over his chest as he leaned against the car. "Okay, spill. What's the deal, Proby?"

She sighed. "I know you've been interested in finding out more about my past, and I haven't exactly been forthcoming..."

"That's an understatement," he said.

"There's a reason for that…a reason corporate covered for me as well."

He arched an eyebrow but didn't speak.

She swallowed. "He's violent, a criminal. They caught him a few years ago, and I testified against him, but he managed to skip out on the charges…none of the other witnesses came forward—surprise, surprise. Anyway, he's never forgiven me for that, or for leaving him. I moved here to get away from him, to start a new life under a new name…"

Franklin's eyes widened. "What? Wow. Bec, I wish you'd told me sooner."

"I couldn't, that was part of the deal. I couldn't tell anyone…haven't even been able to call my mum or my sister. They don't know where I am. Anyway, somehow he's figured it out. He sent a message to my work email a few days ago, and I know it sent him an autoresponder with my name, work address and phone number…so, there's no doubt he knows what name I'm going by and where I am…"

Franklin scrubbed both hands over his face. "Wow, Bec… I'm sorry." His eyes darkened. "What do you think he'll do?"

She shrugged. "He'll send a few more threatening letters, make me uncomfortable for a while, then probably show up and try to convince me to go back to Sydney with him."

He reached for her, placed both hands on her arms, and met her gaze with his own earnest stare. "Keep me up to date on this, and let's get the forensics team in Sydney to take a look at that email. We should be able to make a case to have him followed."

He dropped his hands to his sides, his lips pursed. "And I suppose this will mean it's time for you to move on, start over somewhere else."

Her throat ached. "I don't want to. This is my home now, I'm sick of it—sick of pretending to be someone I'm not, sick of letting him have power over my life. I'm not going anywhere."

* * *

REBECCA WATCHED Franklin climb the stairs to the station and walk inside, she slid into her car and drove home. Her thoughts flitted back and forth between fear for herself, anger at her ex, and concern for Franklin. She was exhausted by all of the emotions that'd trolled through her body over the previous days, and ready to go to bed and sleep for as long as her body would let her.

She'd had enough of being afraid. If Jake wanted to go back to playing his games, she wasn't about to join him. He could play them alone as far as she was concerned.

The town was bathed in darkness, only streetlights blinked as she rounded the corner to where she lived. She parked in the underground parking lot, switched off the car's headlights and climbed out with a yawn. Her bed was calling her name.

Rebecca's footsteps echoed throughout the garage as she strode for the staircase. She recalled the feel of Franklin's hands on her arms, the way he'd gazed into her eyes—his own full of concern, dark with empathy.

He was such a wonderful guy, even if he did give her a hard time as her boss. The fact was, he didn't know anything about her, but he'd accepted her and taught her how to be a police officer when he hadn't wanted to. She'd taken the place of his best friend, his former partner, and yet he'd been there for her when she needed him. His gruff exterior was that—a mask. Beneath the surface, he was kind, warm, and interested in his staff. He cared about people, that much was clear in the way he approached his job. The people he went out of his way to help. It was why the town loved him so much.

She knew he didn't see her as anything but an employee, but she couldn't help imagining what it might be like to kiss him, to feel those strong arms around her, holding her close.

She smiled to herself as she climbed the staircase, then fished in her purse for her keys. She was being ridiculous. He was her boss, nothing more than that—except, perhaps a friend. And she could definitely use a friend right now. She missed the people she'd left behind but was grateful for the new relationships she'd built in the Cove.

Inside, the unit was quiet and dark. The ever-present scent of fried foods permeated the carpet, the walls, the furniture. It was probably time for her to find somewhere more permanent to live, although she loved that this place was opposite Emerald Beach, even if it was situated above a fish and chip shop that stayed open late and attracted a constant stream of noisy customers.

She set her purse on the bench and switched on the fluorescent overhead light in the kitchen. It buzzed to life as she searched the fridge for something to eat. She'd made a delicious chicken alfredo dish the previous night and there were leftovers. Her stomach growled in anticipation as she pulled out the glass dish and set it in the microwave.

"Hi, Becca," said a deep voice behind her.

She spun, her heart in her throat, and found herself facing Jake. He stood on the other side of the bench; his lips pulled into a wide smile.

CHAPTER 30

REBECCA

*S*he was taken again by how handsome he was—square jaw, blue eyes, dark hair, and tanned skin. It was his good looks that made people underestimate how cruel he could be. His smile drew people in, his anger pushed them away. She hadn't realised for at least six months what his true character was. The first time he hit her, she'd thought she would die. She'd ended up in the hospital that night, vowing never to see him again. But he'd convinced her he was sorry, it wouldn't happen again, and for some reason she'd given him another chance. That was a moment she'd regretted ever since.

"Jake, what are you doing here?"

Her mind spun; she hadn't expected him so soon. Usually he liked to toy with her for a while before he pounced.

"I wanted to see what you left me for." He scanned the room with a snarl. "You didn't trade up, baby. This place is a hovel. I could give you so much more."

She swallowed—she had to keep him calm, keep the situation from escalating so that she could think, give herself a chance to escape.

"It's not so bad," she offered nervously. "It's right across from the beach."

He shook his head. "Come on, Becca, you can do better than that."

She pushed a smile onto her face. "I wanted to start over, Jake. Is there something wrong with that?"

With smooth steps he glided around the end of the bench until he was only centimetres away from her, his eyes fixed on hers. "Why did you need to start again, Becca? Was it perhaps because you betrayed me, your boyfriend, who you supposedly loved? Betrayed me to the coppers, of all things. And now…" he laughed, "You've become one yourself. I'd say that's the ultimate betrayal. Wouldn't you?"

Her hands flitted across the drawers in front of her, searching out the handle for the drawer that held the sharp knives.

Jake reached for her hands, pulled them away from the drawer and squeezed them. "Come on, sit. Let's catch up."

He led her to the living room and sat on the couch, patting the space beside him. Rebecca lowered herself slowly, keeping as far from him as she could. He pulled her closer with a quick tug.

"Now, now, don't be shy. Come on, we have a lot of things to discuss. Like, for example, how on earth you became a copper." He shook his head with a laugh. "It's amazing isn't it, life's twists and turns."

His tone was light, but his eyes were hard and dark.

She inhaled a slow breath. "I always wanted to join the police force. I guess when you and I broke up, I decided to look into it a little more."

"Don't you mean, they let you join because you ratted me

out?" He squeezed her knee, making her jump as pain shot through her leg.

"No, that wasn't it at all. They understood the situation, but I had to prove myself like any new recruit. If anything, it was harder for me; they didn't trust me because of you."

His eyes narrowed. "I don't know what you're referring to. I'm an upstanding businessman in Sydney—I think we've proven that enough times for you to finally understand it."

"Scaring off witnesses isn't proving anything," she retorted.

He grabbed her by the hair and swore, forcing her head back. Stars popped across her vision as she yelped.

"Don't be like that. I don't want to have to hurt you again. You always make me hurt you, get me so angry…I only came here for a little chat, and you're doing it again—pushing me. I hate how you do that."

Rebecca let fly with an elbow, connecting with his rib cage. He released his grasp on her hair long enough for her to duck away, out of reach.

Jake screamed in anger, his eyes flashing. "Now you've done it. It's all your fault, remember that, Becca."

"No, Jake—everything you do is on you. Your choice. Not mine."

She was caught between Jake and the sliding doors that led out to the second story balcony. With a quick glance at the glass doors, she decided to try for the unit door instead— the last thing she needed was for Jake to push her off the balcony.

"Come on Becca," he laughed. "You've got nowhere to run to, nowhere to hide."

She shrugged. "I guess you're gonna have to come and get me then."

His eyes narrowed, and his smile faded as he lunged for her. The first punch took him by surprise. She hit him with an uppercut under the chin, snapping his head back. He grunted and staggered backwards. Rebecca shook her hand as pain surged through her knuckles—it hurt a lot more without the gloves.

Jake charged her with a roar, and she fended him off with a kick to the gut followed by a punch to the nose. Blood spurted and he fell back onto the couch with a cry.

"Well now, someone's learned some new skills," he hissed as he pulled a handgun from the back of his pants. "But it's not going to help you this time, Becca."

She backed up to the wall, hands raised, tripped over a magazine rack, and then scrambled towards the kitchen. She hid behind the bench as a single shot rang out, leaving a welt in the refrigerator door. She ducked low, tugging her purse from the bench by one strap, then searched quickly for her phone.

Her gun was locked up safe and sound at the office, but she didn't need it. She could stay out of sight, keep Jake on the defensive. If only she could get to the door and out of the unit without being shot. She crept around the end of the bench.

In the purse, her phone rang. The sound was loud in the still, silent unit and she wondered where Jake had disappeared. She pulled it free and noticed the name of the caller as the phone fell silent. Franklin.

She peeked out from behind the bench. No sign of Jake.

She shoved the phone into her pocket, and reached for her spare set of handcuffs, which she snapped onto her belt. She was taking him in whether he liked it or not and this time he would pay for his crimes—there'd be no weaselling out of it.

Her heart thundered against her ribcage as sweat beaded and dripped down the sides of her face. Her breath came in short, sharp bursts as she crept around the bench. She couldn't wait for him to find her; he had the advantage. She eyed the unit door. It was shut, locked. She had to get to it somehow without being shot, unlock it, open it, and leave. The chances of her surviving it seemed slim. She turned her attention back to finding Jake.

As she rounded the bench, he lurched out of his hiding spot in her direction, gun aimed at her head. With a round-house kick, she knocked it from his grasp even as a shot rang out, echoing through the small space. The gun skittered across the tiles and bumped into the far wall.

Jake's eyes widened. She didn't wait for his smart response, instead she leapt into her boxer's stance, and hit him once, twice. The third punch sent him sprawling onto his rear end. He jumped up and ran at her, tackling her and landing on top of her, knocking the breath from her lungs as he screamed in rage.

She winced but didn't let the winding halt her assault—instead, she continued her barrage, hitting him even while they lay on the ground. It was no use, though, he was too heavy. She couldn't make any leeway. His hand reached towards the gun where it lay, his eyes gleaming at the sight of it. She raised her legs beneath her, pressed her feet to his torso and pushed with all her might, sending him sailing across the room.

He crashed into the back of the couch, groaned, and crawled back onto his feet.

"You're gonna pay for this," he snarled.

She was breathing hard now, the breath back in her lungs, adrenaline coursing through her veins. "Am I, Jake?"

Her taunting was more than he could bear. He ran at her and she caught him in a headlock, forced him onto the ground and snapped the handcuffs around his wrists.

"You're under arrest," she whispered against his ear.

There was a bang on the door, then another, followed by

the door flying open. Franklin fell through the opening, landing on the floor with a shout.

Rebecca stood, still puffing, and studied him with her hands on her hips. "You all right, boss?"

His gaze travelled from her face, to the man kneeling by her feet, and back again. He stood, brushed his hands against his pants, his brow furrowing. "Uh…yeah, I'm fine. What's going on in here, Mair? I tried to call you, wanted to check on you, then when you didn't answer I headed over here and I heard gunshots…who's this?"

He strode towards them, nudged Jake with one foot.

"This is Jake, my ex-boyfriend. He came all the way from Sydney to see me," said Rebecca with a smirk. "Jake, this is my boss, Franklin."

Jake sneered but didn't say a word.

Franklin's eyes widened. "Jake, eh? Wow, great to meet you. I'm glad to see Rebecca's shown you some of her boxing skills, got a bit of a shiner there, mate. She's gotten pretty good at it, eh?"

Rebecca grinned. "Might want to call in the night crew to pick him up, boss."

Franklin nodded, patted her arm with a smile. "Good work, Proby. Good work."

CHAPTER 31

SARAH

*B*lack rocks lined the side of the estuary, guppies ducked and dove in unison as Sarah reached out a hand to touch them. They stayed outside of her grasp, moving as a school, turning with a flick of their tiny tails. She blew a breath out through her snorkel, dislodging some of the sea water that'd splashed into the plastic tube. Then she turned and headed parallel to the rocks, her flippers moving in a slow, rhythmic motion to propel her forwards.

Ahead of her, Mick skimmed along the sandy bottom, his blue board shorts bright in the dimly lit water. She reached him and he drifted with a smile past her and back up to the surface for a breath, his black rimmed mask obscuring most of his face.

She joined him at the surface, heart beating fast as she gulped a lungful of air. "That was amazing, did you see those bream?"

He laughed. "I nearly touched one, they're so fast though."

"I know, it was amazing swimming through the middle of that school. I couldn't see anything but bream in every direction."

They swam over to the small, sandy beach on one side of the estuary where they'd left their things earlier and climbed out, dripping as they went. Sarah slumped onto the sand to catch her breath. The tide was coming in and she'd had to work hard to kick against it to get back to the beach.

Mick draped a towel around her shoulders, then sat beside her wrapped in his own towel.

"That was great," said Sarah.

He nodded. "I love snorkelling. It's not quite surfing, but it's a close second."

She laughed. "Does anything beat surfing for you?"

"Nope. There's nothing else quite like it."

A pair of pelicans soared by overhead, heads tucked into their bodies, long wings flapping slowly. Their wings sped up as they turned and settled onto the water. One of the birds shook itself from head to wing tips, then finished with a wag of its short, feathery tail. Sarah smiled at the birds—they were so patient, carefree. They had nowhere to be, nothing to do, but whatever it was they wanted to.

"Have you talked to your family about our engagement yet?" asked Mick.

Sarah's heart skipped a beat. She'd been meaning to do it, only it was harder to bring up the subject than she'd thought it would be. She'd only seen her mother once, and it'd been right after Rupert died, so it wasn't a good time. She hadn't seen her mother grieving like this before, so withdrawn, so silent. She didn't want to talk about it, she'd said. Only wanted to be left alone, so Sarah had walked out of the bedroom and pulled the door shut behind her. She'd stayed at the house for another hour, hoping her mother might come and join her in the living room for a cup of tea, but there hadn't been a sound. She'd checked on her before she left and found her curled on her side on the bed watching old movies.

"Um…no. It's not a great time for it, with everything that's going on."

Mick's lips pursed. "I understand…although, you know it's never going to be a perfect time. And I get that it's sad right now, so I'm not going to push the point, but after the funeral…we should tell them. It's happy news, they'll want to hear it. It might help everyone feel better."

Sarah swallowed around the lump that'd built in her throat. "I know…you're right. Mum will be so excited."

"Is that the only reason you haven't said anything? Because you haven't told Vicky yet, or Meg either…"

He had a point. There was no good reason why she wasn't shouting from the rooftops that she was engaged to be married. It was how she felt—she was so excited about it. But nerves turned flip-flops in her stomach.

"No, I guess it's not the only reason. I can't tell my friends until I've spoken to Mum first. It wouldn't be right. She'd be so upset if she found out through someone else…but even without the grief she's going through I'd find it hard to talk to her about."

"Why?" pressed Mick.

"I think it's because of what she went through with Dad. It feels almost like bragging or something, as though it's wrong somehow, to tell her that I'm happy and in love, that I'm getting married."

Sarah caressed Mick's cheek with one hand. "And it's true, I am happy, and I can't wait for us to get married and start our lives together. Only, I don't know how to tell Mum about it."

"You think she'll be upset?"

Sarah shook her head. "No, I think she'll be delighted. But

245

at the same time, I can't help wondering if it will bring back all those bad memories about Dad, the way he left her, the cheating...you know what I mean? A big wedding, the vows, the guests, the promises... I wonder if it will cause her pain. I mean, I'm probably being ridiculous, but you asked—now you get an inside track into my crazy mind." She tried to laugh it off, but there was a pain in her throat that wouldn't budge.

Mick looped an arm around her shoulders and pulled her close so that one side of her was pressed against him. "I get it. You're overthinking things, but I understand. You care about her and don't want to see her hurting. It makes sense. But I want you to know that I really want to marry you. I don't need a big wedding, a fuss, or anything like that. I want us to be married, that's it. I love you. I hate saying goodbye at the end of the day and going home to my empty unit. I want us to be a family."

She smiled as her heart swelled. "I do too."

He kissed her and the pain in her throat faded.

"We should do it," he said.

Her eyes narrowed. "I know, we will."

"I mean now...elope. Forget the big wedding, everyone's too sad to think about it right now anyway. Let's elope, get married—we can tell them about it later."

Sarah straightened, her mind racing. They could do that; it made sense. She wanted to get married as soon as possible but hadn't considered running off to do it alone. Would it matter to her? What about Mum, her family, her friends? What would they think? Would they be sad to miss out on her big day? Mum was so distracted at the moment, had so many other things on her mind, perhaps she'd be relieved not to have to deal with a big wedding as well. And besides, a wedding was really only about her and Mick. It felt right. She found she didn't mind missing out on the lace, tulle, and satin. It wasn't really her style anyway. She'd planned on a small, intimate, and quiet service on the beach. Maybe they could elope instead and be married by the end of the week.

She grinned. "Let's do it."

* * *

SARAH'S VISION blurred with tears. She beamed at Mick as she walked down the sandy aisle to where he stood, waiting for her, hands crossed in front of his khaki slacks.

They'd found an elopement package for couples on the Gold Coast, had booked it two days earlier and packed their bags for an impromptu trip that morning.

She hadn't told anyone where they were going, and so far, no one had missed them. Mum had agreed to look after Oscar so that Sarah could get some work done because she claimed he wouldn't leave her alone and constantly wanted to go in and out of the house with his bandaged leg held high and a forlorn look in his big, brown eyes. That much was true, which was why her mother hadn't sniffed out the lie.

It was hard not to have her father walking her down the aisle, but with he and Mum separated, no doubt he would've wanted to bring his new, much younger, girlfriend to the wedding which would've caused all kinds of tension.

So, despite wishing Adele, Ethan, and her parents could be there to celebrate this special moment with her, she figured it was probably for the best in the end that she and Mick didn't have any distractions. They could focus entirely on each other and the commitment they were making, without having to worry about all of the drama a family event would bring. That didn't even take Mick's family into account—his drug-addicted brother, his loud and often obnoxious mother. No, they were making the right decision in eloping. The more she thought about it, the more their choice was confirmed in her mind.

The sand slipped between her toes and over her feet. She'd found a pair of jewelled sandals to wear, and they glinted in the sunlight. The white silk dress swished around her calves—she'd loved it from the moment she laid eyes on it the day before in a small boutique in Byron Bay. She'd driven south to the small town to shop for clothes, jewellery, and a new swimsuit. Even though it was still winter, she figured they'd find a heated pool or jacuzzi to swim in on their brief honeymoon before returning to Emerald Cove to start their lives as newlyweds.

Newlyweds.

Her chest felt as though it might burst with joy at the thought of sharing every day with Mick. She'd been hesitant to make the commitment at first, but now that she'd taken the step, made the decision to spend her life with him, all her doubts and fears had faded and all she could think of was how it would be to grow old with him, share every adventure together, and raise children side by side.

Finally she was there, standing beside Mick and in front of a marriage celebrant, flanked by large white stands sporting floral bouquets. The elopement provider supplied everything they'd need for a quick wedding, and she hadn't had much input into the design. But it didn't matter. The flowers were beautiful, the sun danced on the ocean's surface as waves slid quietly to shore beside them, and the sand beneath her feet reminded her of so many of the best times of her life.

Mick took her hands and squeezed them gently, his eyes glistening with tears.

"You look beautiful," he whispered.

The celebrant began the service, and Sarah did her best to focus on the words. She wanted to soak in every moment of this time, didn't want to miss a thing. But it was hard to listen with the way Mick was looking at her. The adoration in his eyes brought heat to her face and neck.

"It's time for your vows," said the celebrant, an older woman in an aqua pantsuit.

Mick went first.

"I promise that I'll always be there for you. In every storm, through all of the good and bad, I'll be by your side, and I'll do everything I can to make sure you're safe, happy, and loved. When things get hard, I promise I will remember these vows I've made to share my life with you forever, regardless of what happens."

She grinned through a veil of tears, sniffling, and wishing she'd thought to bring tissues.

When it was her turn, she drew a deep breath first, willing her voice to cooperate. "I vow, that I will love you even when I don't like you much."

Mick chuckled, shook his head.

"That I'll be faithful to you, even if Brad Pitt comes knocking."

He arched an eyebrow.

"I'm joking," she grinned. "I promise to stick by your side through good and bad, fat and thin."

He grunted.

"Even when your hair is grey and my thighs are wide, I'll still love lying against your chest and listening to your heartbeat, I'll adore your lips as much as I do now, and I'll revel in the way you always put my needs ahead of your own—I'll even try to do that myself because you've taught me that it's possible to love someone that much."

By the time she was finished, tears fell onto her cheeks.

Mick slid the ring onto her finger as he recited the vows read out by the celebrant, soon it was Sarah's turn to do the same. Then, they were married, and it was time for the kiss that would begin their lives together.

Mick's lips found hers. He tasted of salt and coffee, and she melted in his embrace, giving herself up fully for the first time in her life to love, to someone else, to their future together.

CHAPTER 32

ETHAN

The rhythm of his footsteps on the dirt path beneath his feet was soothing. Sarah always said he was crazy to run so much, but Ethan found it therapeutic. It was during his runs that some of his best ideas came to mind as well, the best solutions for engineering designs, the ideas that changed the direction of his life. Running was a great way for him to think things through—if he didn't go running, he kept his mind so busy on what he was doing that he might never get the inspiration to change direction otherwise.

His thoughts now returned to Emily, as they often did these days when he was running. Lately things between them had heated up. It'd surprised him the way she'd changed after their discussion of the past. But he still held onto some reservations when it came to the way she'd been so reluctant to let go of past hurts and give him a chance. He wasn't sure if he could trust her with his heart. He wanted to let go of his concerns and dive headfirst into their relationship, but he wasn't sure she was in the same place as he was.

He startled a pair of seagulls beside the path and they flapped furiously into the air, with a flurry of wings and frantic calls. His heart skipped a beat as well, as he hadn't seen them until he was on top of them because of the dry grasses that lined the sides of the trail.

The path ducked behind a tall, green bush and along the edge of a cliff face that looked out over the ocean, then back up the grassy hill towards his neighbourhood. He slowed when he reached the Manor, turned into the front yard, and walked the last few steps before pushing his way through the front door.

The house was quiet, silent in fact. He'd taken a look at the guest register the day before and there'd only been one couple scheduled for the previous night. There'd be a full house that night, but Wednesdays were historically slow. He'd suggested that Emily take some time to herself to relax. He hoped she'd taken his advice and he wouldn't find her painting one of the rooms or sanding back a piece of furniture to restore, as she'd been doing lately.

She'd done such a good job of updating the look of the place—it'd been traditional, a little old fashioned, and dark when she arrived. Now he was greeted by white and cream paint, lighter coloured furniture, that she'd restored with a new stain, and a generally more modern, yet still classic, style that he really enjoyed.

"Emily?"

She didn't answer.

He stood in the living room with his hands on his hips, listening. There was no sound, but that didn't mean anything. She might be in the garden. Since the front door was open, it wasn't likely she'd gone out.

He searched the Manor and found her in her own room

after knocking on the closed door. She opened it tentatively with a shy smile.

"Hi," she said, standing on tiptoe to kiss his lips in a way that made him want more. "Sorry, I'm still in my PJs."

She tugged at the white t-shirt and peered down at her soft, tartan shorts. Her hair was piled in a messy bun on top of her head, her eyes looked sleepy, and there was a sheet mark on one side of her face. She looked adorable, and he fought the urge to take her in his arms right then and there. They had things to talk about, and he didn't want to put it off any longer.

He kissed her again. "That's okay. You should relax, you work so hard. What are you doing today?"

She shrugged. "I'm watching an old black and white movie right now. Then, I thought I might take a walk on the beach before I get ready for tonight's guests."

"That sounds perfect. Hey, can we talk, then I'll leave you to your relaxation?"

She nodded. "Let me get dressed and I'll be right with you."

He waited in the den for her, reading a magazine about bushwalking trails in New South Wales state parks, then looked up as she walked in. She was dressed in cut-off denim shorts and a blue t-shirt that hung off one shoulder. Her feet were bare, and she curled up beside him on the couch.

"You look very cute today," he said. Usually she was all business. It was nice to see her dressed more casually, it suited her.

She grinned. "Thanks."

"So, I wanted to talk to you about us," he began.

Her lips pursed. "Okay."

"Nothing bad, I promise. Only, I guess I'd like to know what you're thinking. I know for me, I really like you, and I can see this thing between us becoming something special. But first, I need to know if you're on the same track as me."

She inhaled a sharp breath. "Ethan...you have no idea how long I've wanted this."

His eyes widened. "What? But...you seemed to hate me not so very long ago."

"I know, but we talked about that. The reason I held onto the shame for so many years was because...well, I had a huge crush on you when I was a teenager. I've always thought you were the most sexy, fun, smart...well, amazing guy in the world. So, I'm definitely on the same track as you."

Ethan grinned. "Well, how about that? I didn't know I'd had such an impact on you."

He leaned back, crossing his arms over his chest.

She rolled her eyes. "Don't let it go to your head."

He chuckled. "Too late for that. My head is well and truly swollen; I'm not sure it will ever return to its normal size after that."

She laughed and pretended to punch him in the shoulder. "And to answer your other question, the reason I've held back is simple. The last man I dated took advantage of me, lied to me, and manipulated me in ways I'm only beginning to fully understand now. So, I've been hesitant to give my heart to someone else. I mean, I've had some really bad taste in men. Terrible. Horrifically bad taste." She shook her head. "I'm talking Olympic-sized bad taste."

He grunted. "Well, I didn't think it could happen, but my head is definitely shrinking now, and fast."

She leaned towards him, kissed his lips, and gazed into his eyes. "But I've always known you were a good one."

"I'm not him, you know. I would never do anything to hurt you like that."

"I know," she replied.

"So, you're willing to see where things might go between us?"

She nodded. "I can't wait."

He laughed. "Me either." Then he kissed her again, his head swimming with desire.

CHAPTER 33

DIANA

*E*verything was black. Everywhere she looked, black and grim.

Diana almost couldn't stand the pain in her throat. Her chest ached, and her stomach roiled around a knot that hadn't budged in days. Not since Rupert died.

Rupert was dead.

She couldn't wrap her mind around the thought. Every time the memory rose to the surface after she found her thoughts drifting onto another subject, she was hit once again with a wave of grief that almost knocked her to the floor. And the first thing she thought was that she wanted to talk to Rupert about it. But he wasn't there.

She held back a surge of tears, choked them down, as she greeted people for the funeral. It was at the local Baptist church, one she and Rupert had attended faithfully for most of their lives. She wasn't even sure where to sit without him. She was the one who talked with friends and acquaintances until the service began, then she'd find Rupert where he was seated in one of the pews and slip into place beside him.

Now, she had to find her own seat.

How could she do this? Go on with her life without him? That was no kind of life.

She greeted more guests, then waited with her breath caught in her throat for the next arrivals. Ben told her she didn't have to do it, that no one expected her to stand at the door and greet them, but she wasn't sure she could do anything else. The idea of sitting in the pew and waiting was more than she could bear, and besides, these were her friends, her community. She loved them, and they'd loved Rupert. He was the kind of man people were drawn to, everyone said so.

A car pulled into the small parking lot, a car she recognised.

She held her breath a few moments longer then exhaled as Cindy stepped from the car, followed by Sarah and Mick, then Ethan and Adele. Adele must've flown in from Darwin for the funeral. Diana found the sight of them prompted a fresh rush of grief mixed with relief.

They were there. Of course, they were; Rupert had done nothing wrong. He wasn't the one who'd betrayed them. They'd loved him. Considered him their family.

Tears blocked them from her view for a few moments, then they were there, walking up the concrete steps. Cindy stopped in front of her, studied her with a shake of her head. Her eyes were red-rimmed, and she looked thinner than the last time Diana had seen her.

"Oh, honey," she said.

Then, she drew Diana into an embrace that she felt in her very core. The tears surged free then, soaking Cindy's collar in moments.

"Thank you for coming," sobbed Diana against her friend's shoulder.

"I'm so sorry," mumbled Cindy, her voice muffled by Diana's white, lace collar.

"Me too. Me too. So sorry. For everything. I'm so glad you came because I honestly don't know how I'll get through this without you."

Cindy patted her back gently. "I know honey, I know. I can't believe he's gone."

Cindy pulled away, bit her lip. The tears in her eyes glistened as she spoke. "I forgive you for what happened. I'm only sorry I let it get between us, it was so long ago. It's in the past. Everything that's happened over the course of the past forty years is what's made our friendship so strong, and that hasn't changed. Has it?"

Diana shook her head, dabbing her cheeks with a handkerchief embroidered with wattle flowers. "No, of course not."

"Hey, Mum, I think it's nearly time to start," said Ben behind her, his voice soft as he cupped her elbow with one hand.

He'd taken to calling her Mum after his last visit to the Cove. Said his mother didn't mind him doing it, said that they were both his mother so he could call them both Mum if he wanted. Diana would be eternally grateful to the woman she'd never met who'd done such a wonderful job of raising their son.

"Thank you, dear," she replied.

Cindy's eyes widened. Diana stopped Ben from leaving with a hand on his arm. "Ben, I'd like you to re-meet my oldest friend. This is Cindy Flannigan."

"It's a pleasure to meet you, Cindy," said Ben. "I believe we met at your cafe, but not officially."

"That's right." Cindy smiled. "How lovely to meet you, Ben. Your presence here is truly a gift."

Ben smiled. "Thanks, I'm glad I could be here. Although, I wish I'd gotten a chance to get to know Rupert better." He swallowed hard. "At least I can be here for Mum."

He returned to his seat at the front of the church, and Diana watched him before meeting Cindy's gaze. Cindy shook her head. "What a wonderful thing. I could cry, although I'm not sure I have any tears left. I haven't said anything...by the way. Sarah, Ethan, Adele—none of them knows about Ben. Not yet, anyway. I thought you'd probably like to talk to Andy first..."

"Thank you, Cindy—I would like to speak with Andy first. It only seems right...after everything."

Cindy gave Diana's hand one more squeeze, then walked into the church. Diana embraced Ethan, Sarah, Mick, and Adele as they followed Cindy. She headed to her seat, beside Ben in the first row.

Ben shot her a concerned look as she sat but she couldn't bring herself to smile. She'd known this day would come, but not yet. She wasn't ready for it yet. They still had so much life to share, so much living to do. They'd been talking about a European cruise, a trip to Fiji, all the things they'd never done that they could do now they were retired.

Emily slipped into the pew beside Ben, reached across and held Diana's hand with a blink of watery eyes. "Hello Auntie Di."

Diana nodded but couldn't speak.

The service was beautiful. She and Rupert had taken the time years earlier to plan out what they wanted for their respective services. She was glad they'd done it ahead of time, since the past few days had been a blur and she'd barely had the strength to put into action the plan they'd made. She was so grateful that Ben and Emily had been there to help her. Her only regret was that Cindy hadn't. At least her friend had forgiven her now.

A wave of emotion swelled within her and she sobbed quietly into a handkerchief. Ben's hand on her back helped ease her pain.

After the service was over, Ben drove Diana to the Manor where Emily was hosting the wake. Diana was glad she didn't have to manage it all herself. Emily hadn't let her lift a finger towards the preparations, not that she'd had the strength to do it anyway.

When they arrived, some of the guests were already there, standing around in small clumps talking in hushed voices.

She greeted them, accepted their condolences, then moved onto the next cluster. It wasn't long before the entire downstairs area of the Manor was packed with people. It warmed Diana's heart to see them. Rupert had been beloved in the community, and she was grateful to see that they'd come to pay their respects. She couldn't imagine living her life anywhere other than Emerald Cove—it was her home and she felt loved as people embraced her, kissed her cheek, and cried with her over memories.

She smiled at the sight of Emily and Adele huddled together in one corner of the room. They'd been close as children, at least during the summers when Emily visited. It was nice to see them catching up as adults. She hoped they'd be able to get to know each other all over again, although with Adele working as a pilot in Darwin their time together would be limited. Her smile faded as she imagined what Rupert would say—he'd have loved to watch Emily settling into life in the Cove. She was glad things were going so well for her niece. Emily and Ben were the only bright spots in the darkness for Diana.

After chatting with people for an hour, she felt her strength waning. She stood with Ben, sipping a cup of tea, and nibbling on a tiny slice of apple pie with fresh cream. It was delicious, as was everything Emily had served that day, but she couldn't enjoy it.

When Andrew Flannigan walked through the front door her heart skipped a beat. She hadn't known he'd come. He was there alone, thank goodness. If he'd brought his girlfriend and caused a scene at Rupert's funeral, she wasn't sure she could ever forgive him.

He caught her eye and headed straight for her. Took her hand and held it gently. "Di, I'm so sorry for your loss. Rupert was a good man and we'll all miss him."

She nodded, her heart in her throat. Ben stood beside her, oblivious to who Andrew was to him. "Thank you, Andrew. I'm so glad you could make it. Rupert had hoped he would see you..." Her voice broke and she inhaled a sharp breath. "Thank you."

He smiled. "I wish I'd come to see him...but we can't change the past, unfortunately. If we could..." He shook his head. "Anyway, it's good to see you."

He turned to walk away, but Diana caught him by the arm. "Andy, wait..."

"Yes?"

"Can I speak to you outside for a moment please?"

He shrugged. "Okay."

"Please come with us, Ben."

Ben swallowed a mouthful of pie, set his plate on the table. "Uh, sure."

She strode for the back door and stood with her hands on the back of a wrought iron chair, waiting for her thoughts to clear. How would she say it? How to break the news? She could wait for another day, but it would be strange for her to pass up this opportunity for Ben to know his father.

She spun to face them. "Andy, I want you to know that I appreciate you and value you. The reason I'm talking to you today is because I care about you and think it's best for you to know the truth."

His eyes narrowed. "Um...okay."

"You're my friend..."

"And you're mine," he replied, cocking his head to one side.

"Andy...this is Ben."

Andrew turned towards Ben in surprise, shook his hand. "Pleased to meet you, Ben."

Ben nodded, glanced at Diana with a question in his expression.

"Ben is your son."

Both men gaped at the same time. Andrew's face paled.

"What? What do you mean?" asked Andrew, his gaze flitting between her and Ben.

"The affair we had as teenagers..."

Andrew's face turned from pale to sheet white. "Yes."

"I was pregnant. I didn't tell you at the time because my parents wouldn't let me tell anyone. I went away that summer...I don't know if you remember."

"Of course, I remember...I tried to call you over and over, but your parents wouldn't tell me where you'd gone."

Diana hadn't known that. A lump rose in her throat. "I didn't realise...anyway, they sent me away to have the baby, Ben, and I gave him up for adoption. I didn't see him again for more than forty years, but then he came to find me a few weeks ago."

Her breath caught in her throat as Andrew looked Ben up and down. How would he react? She had no idea. It wasn't ideal to make the introductions at a funeral, but she was finished with secrets. She'd kept this one from everyone for so long, including Rupert, she wanted to spit it out and never keep another secret for the rest of her life.

When Andrew opened his arms and Ben embraced him,

she swallowed hard to hold back the tears and left them alone to get acquainted. Inside the house, she found Cindy watching through the window by the back door. She met Diana's gaze with tears glistening in her eyes.

"You told him."

Diana nodded. "I couldn't keep it a secret any longer."

Cindy threw her arms around Diana and held her close. "I understand. It was brave of you. And for all Andy's flaws, he's a loving father. I'm sure he and Ben will have a good relationship."

"I hope so. Only, I wish Rupert had been here to see it..." Tears clogged her throat. "He would've loved it—he was a sucker for a happy ending."

Cindy chuckled, looping an arm through Diana's to walk with her towards the living room. "Absolutely, he would've loved it."

CHAPTER 34

REBECCA

"So, what's your last name again?" asked Franklin. "Your real last name?"

"De Vries," replied Rebecca with a shy smile. "Rebecca De Vries."

"At least you kept your first name the same," he retorted with a sniff. "I don't think I could refer to you as anything other than Bec. It would be too weird."

"Do you mean, besides Proby?"

He laughed. "Yeah, well besides that."

"Thanks for doing this," said Rebecca. "You know, filling out all of the paperwork for me."

She held her bandaged hand in the air.

He shook his head. "Well, it's not like we had much of a choice since you broke your hand on that scumbag's chin. How's it going, by the way?"

"Painful," she replied with a grimace.

"I'll bet. Now, what was your address...before?"

"Do you think they'll let me stay...you know, here at the station. Let me keep working here as a police officer?"

He leaned back in his chair, one eyebrow arched. "That depends. Do you want to stay? I mean you could head back to Sydney now. Jake is behind bars and he won't be getting out anytime soon thanks to our testimony against him. You could return to your old life if that's what you wanted to do."

Rebecca shook her head with a sigh. "No, I don't want to go backwards. Don't get me wrong, I miss the people who were in my life back then, but I've moved on and so have they."

"What about your family?"

She shrugged. "Mum and Beth are coming to visit next week. They're going to love it here. I know they are dying to meet you..." She swallowed. "And the rest of the crew here."

He chuckled. "I'm looking forward to meeting them as well. Got to see where you got all that spunk from, I'm guessing it was probably your mother."

She grinned. "Definitely."

They completed the rest of the paperwork with so many questions Rebecca's head throbbed with the pain of it by the time they were finally done. She knew that wouldn't be the end of it. There'd be interviews, meetings, discussions with her contact in the head office. But for now, she could forget all about it and be a cop for the rest of the day.

It was frustrating to have a broken hand—there were so many normal, everyday things she needed help with now. It was one of the reasons her mother was coming to visit next week. Her mum intended to stay the full six weeks it was likely to take her to recover from her injuries. Still, she couldn't help feeling proud every time she looked at her hand.

For years she'd endured pain, cowered at Jake's feet when he chased her down and beat her up. She'd suffered bruises, broken bones, and cuts at his hands. She'd spent time in emergency rooms, physiotherapy centres, and doctors' offices. She'd hidden away, skulked in the shadows, given up relationships with family, friends, quit jobs, and applied for new ones in other locations. There'd been so much of her life impacted by a chance encounter with a handsome and charming boy when she was seventeen years old. Things she'd never have considered, never have known about, had happened to her in the years since.

And now, she'd used her own strength, her will, her fortitude to take him down. She didn't have to be afraid again. Even if he got out of prison, she wasn't scared of him any longer. She knew she could hold her own against him, and the realisation filled her with a sense of awe, pride and joy that was hard to contain.

She'd been walking in the shadows, living a half-life for so long, happiness felt almost alien. It was difficult to process the waves of it that washed over her whenever she remembered that he was locked up, she was free, and she could now enjoy the life she'd built with no more secrets.

When Franklin set a cup of coffee on her desk later, muttering under his breath about suddenly becoming a personal assistant to a proby, she couldn't help laughing.

"Thanks, boss, you're the best."

His cheeks coloured. "Yeah...well, don't get used to it."

She wondered what it would be like to love someone like him. A man who was good, kind, gruff but gentle. How would it feel to be completely free with someone, to have no fear around them but to know that they loved every part of you?

She decided then and there she'd like to find out.

"Well, come on then. Are you coming to the team meeting or not?" he asked.

"On my way, boss."

She followed him into the boardroom and took a seat next to Steph, who offered her a wide grin.

"You look particularly nice today," she whispered as Franklin started the meeting.

"Do you think so?"

Steph nodded. "You're glowing, like you're happy or something."

"I am," replied Rebecca.

She leaned back in her chair, sipped her coffee awkwardly from her left hand, and scanned the room. Every face in there represented someone who'd become important in her life, someone who cared about her and whom she cared for in a way she'd never thought possible when she began work there not so long ago.

Jake had stolen so much from her, but he hadn't been able to destroy her. The future was hers, and she now knew she could make whatever she liked of it.

CHAPTER 35

SARAH

*M*ick's arms around her tightened as his lips found hers. He deepened the kiss, his hair falling across his eyes in a way that Sarah found irresistible. She pulled back with a laugh, fighting the urge to stay in bed.

The sheets lay rumpled and scattered around the bedroom. Clothing lined the floor. She'd dressed to go out but had a feeling that wouldn't last long if they didn't get out of the cottage soon.

"We have to go. I called a family meeting to tell everyone that we're married, so we can't be late and with all the drama lately...all of us getting a new brother and Dad a new son, I don't want our marriage to be another family secret."

Mick grumbled as he kissed the base of her neck. "Fine, but let's tell them tomorrow."

She extricated herself from his arms. "We can't do that; Adele is flying home tomorrow morning. She only came for the funeral and then stayed another week. But I really want her to be in the room when we tell them all. Which means, we have to go now, mister!"

Mick groaned. "Let's go then."

She took him by the hand and picked up her purse, then led him from the cottage to where his truck was parked. "Come on, Oscar!"

Oscar hurried after them. His leg had healed but he still ran with a little hop. He jumped into the back seat and settled with his head out the lowered window.

The drive into town was balmy. Spring had arrived in the Cove and Sarah found herself wearing shorts and a t-shirt most days now. She couldn't have imagined she'd be dressing so casually on a daily basis a year ago, but now she generally pulled her hair into a ponytail and spent her days either walking along the beach thinking through plot points for the book she was working on, or writing on her laptop on the back deck overlooking the sparkling, deep blue ocean.

She'd decided that if she was ever going to write a book, now was her chance. She could live off her savings and she owned the cottage outright. If she didn't write now, she'd never do it. And besides, Mick had encouraged her to write. She had no excuses left.

Flowers bloomed all along her childhood street. As they pulled into the driveway, she glanced next door to see that the Manor's gardens were a study in deep greens, pinks, reds, and yellows. The garden had always been spectacular, and it looked as though Ethan and Emily were keeping up with Diana's hard work in that department.

"So, how are we going to do this?" asked Mick as he parked the truck and let Oscar out to bound through the yard to the front door.

"Quick and painless, like removing a band aid," mumbled Sarah, feeling the tension building across her shoulders and up one side of her neck. "Oh, and let me do it, please."

"Of course." He looped an arm around her shoulders and squeezed. "Don't stress, they're going to be happy. It's good news."

"I know. Only, they'll be upset they couldn't be there."

"But we agreed to offer a party. Remember?"

"Yes, I'll make sure to bring that up."

Sarah opened the front door and Oscar barrelled inside, tail wagging. He and Petal found each other, the small white dog keening as she wagged herself in a circle around the much larger, darker Oscar.

Then, the two canines ran off in the direction of the back yard. Sarah watched them go with a smile. Oscar turned into a different animal when he was with Petal—younger, more vibrant, excited about every little thing.

Sarah found the rest of the family on the back deck. Mum had made a bowl of her famous punch, with passionfruit pulp—Sarah's favourite. There was also a large antipasto platter with olives, prosciutto, cheeses, crackers, and dips on a large, timber table.

Mick went straight for the food as Sarah did the rounds. She embraced her mother, and said hello to Athol, who seemed to be attending most family functions these days.

"Did you see the table Ethan built me?" asked Mum, her face glowing with pride. "Isn't it beautiful?"

Sarah's eyes widened. "He *made* that table?"

The timber slats were polished and the warmth of the wood shone beneath the plates and dishes.

"He did." Mum grinned. "And I love it."

Diana was there too, fussing around the food, making sure there was enough of everything to go around.

Sarah kissed Adele on the cheek, hugged Ben, then embraced Ethan and Emily. She hadn't realised the two of them were dating, but Ethan definitely had his arm around her waist. "Lovely table, Ethan," said Sarah.

He nodded an acknowledgement. "Thanks. I had fun making it."

"It's really great, I didn't know you were so handy."

"I'm full of surprises," he said with a chuckle.

"So it seems," replied Sarah, shooting another look at Emily. Sarah made a mental note to grill him about her later, though she couldn't help being happy for him. From what she remembered of Emily from their childhood years, she was a sweet, if somewhat earnest, child who'd always carried a flame for Ethan, though of course he'd never noticed it.

When Mick joined her, she felt her heart skip a beat as he squeezed her arm; a reminder that they were in this together. She clapped her hands. "Hi, everyone, thanks for coming. Can I get your attention over here please?"

Another clap, and the group all looked in her direction. Just then, Dad came through the door. He smiled and waved to everyone, in that charming way that only he could do—all ease and white teeth, even though they'd hardly seen him in months.

"Hi, everyone, sorry I'm late," he said.

Sarah had invited him but hadn't expected him to show up. Her gaze flitted to her mother's face as Sarah embraced her father, but Mum seemed fine with their visitor. So, she continued.

"Welcome, Dad. I'm so glad all of you could be here for this family meeting." She laced her fingers through Mick's. "Mick and I wanted to talk to you about something and even though we were brought together by sad circumstances, it's the perfect time to share some news with you."

She smiled at Mick and the depth of love in his eyes encouraged her on. "As you know, Mick and I have been seeing each other for a while now. We're in love, and we decided we wanted to spend the rest of our lives together... so we got married."

Mum's mouth fell open.

The announcement was greeted by a moment of silence, followed by shouts of congratulations as one by one the group hurried over to dole out hugs, kisses and salutations.

Tears filled Sarah's eyes as the family surrounded them. She'd been so worried what their response would be, but they were happy for her and Mick.

Finally, it was Mum's turn. "I'm sorry you couldn't be there," said Sarah as she wiped the tears from her eyes.

Mum smiled, her own eyes red-rimmed. "I understand. You wanted to get married and there was a lot going on around here."

"That's true, but it wasn't for any reason other than our own," replied Sarah. "But don't worry, we'll have a big party to celebrate."

"Good," replied Mum with a chuckle. "Because I don't think you'll be able to stop me from celebrating my first child's wedding."

"I'll even wear the dress for you," replied Sarah.

"Could you say some vows?" asked Mum, her arm around Sarah's waist.

Sarah laughed. "Of course, we could definitely do that, Mum. And thanks for understanding."

Mum kissed her cheek. "I wish I could've been there, but all I want is for you to be happy. I'm glad you found Mick and I'm so excited to welcome him into the family."

* * *

AFTER THE EXCITEMENT of their announcement had died down, Sarah watched as Ben and Diana strolled around the back garden, admiring Mum's flowers and laughing together. She smiled at the sight, her heart heavy for Diana's loss, then went inside to sit down for a few minutes. Adele, Ethan, and

Emily were seated with Mick in the living room talking politics. So Sarah sat with them, her thoughts drifting to the book she was writing, family dynamics and how many strange twists and turns her life had taken since she moved back to Emerald Cove.

When she remembered the tense, uptight, and stressed woman she'd been back in Sydney, it was hard to recognise herself. She'd changed so much since then. Looking back, she could see that deep inside something had been crying out for that change for a long time, only she'd ignored it and kept going—pushing forward with her career, an engagement that no longer made sense, and a level of busyness that wasn't good for her health long-term.

She was so grateful that Mum needing her help had prompted her to make the life adjustments that she'd so desperately needed but might not otherwise have made.

Dad squeezed her shoulder with a smile. "I'm proud of you, pumpkin."

She grinned, reached for his hand. "Thanks, Dad."

"Congratulations. I hope you two will be very happy together. Like your mum and I were…"

She'd let that slide. It was a happy day today, and she had no desire to start an argument with her father. Besides, from his perspective perhaps they had been happy. Or maybe it was only hindsight that could give some people the rose-coloured glasses that kept them moving, one foot in front of the other, into the future.

He left her there and wandered back out on the porch. Sarah rose and followed him, then stopped by the open back door. Only Mum was out there now. The sun had set, and rays of pink and orange shot through a purple sky from the horizon towards them. Long shadows hid the garden in their inky depths. In the distance a crow cawed.

"It's nice to see you here today, Andy," said Mum with a formal tone to her soft voice.

"Thanks, Cindy," replied Dad. "I was in town, and I couldn't say no to our daughter."

"No, you never could when it came to Sarah." There was a smile in Mum's voice, although Sarah couldn't see her face.

She felt bad for a moment listening in on their conversation but wasn't able to walk away. She had a horrible feeling that they'd fight, and Mum would end up crying and she couldn't stand for that to happen today. She tensed, ready to jump in if she was needed, to stand by Mum's side.

"I've missed this place," said Dad, clenching fingers around the top railing.

"I'm sure you have."

"Keisha misses the Cove too."

Mum didn't respond. Sarah's teeth clenched.

"I thought you might like to hear it from me...I mean we did talk about it a while back, but I thought you should know—Keisha and I have found a house. We're moving back to the Cove next month."

"Thank you for telling me." Mum's voice was tense, her shoulders straight.

Sarah's eyes widened. She hadn't known Dad was thinking about moving back to town, but it sounded as though he'd talked to Mum about it. Why hadn't she said anything?

It made sense though—Dad had lived here all of his life. People in Emerald Cove knew him, they respected and admired him. When he left the Cove, he'd been just another face in the crowd. Dad couldn't abide not standing out.

She wondered how he was feeling about Ben. He hadn't said much about the secret that'd remained hidden for so long, but he seemed happy. She'd seen him and Ben in deep conversation several times since the revelation—there was an uncanny resemblance between the two of them. She smiled at the thought. She never imagined she'd get another brother so late in life. But life was full of surprises.

Dad turned, walked away from his conversation with Mum. When he brushed past Sarah, he offered her a smile. "Did you hear any of that?"

She nodded. "Sorry, I didn't mean to pry…"

"No, it's fine," he said. "You should know. I'm going to go and tell the others now. You don't mind, do you?"

"Of course not, Dad. I'll be glad to see more of you."

"And Keisha?"

"Yes, and Keisha." Sarah swallowed. That would be an awkward meeting, but she was willing to try, for Dad's sake.

Athol walked by with two coffee cups in his hands, both sending steam into the cooling night air. He set them on the outside dining table, then went to Mum and put his arms around her. She turned in his embrace and kissed him on the lips.

Sarah ducked her head in embarrassment. When had that happened?

Apparently, everyone was keeping secrets in this family. She'd have to make more of an effort to catch up with people, or she'd miss out on everything that was going on in their lives. At least most of them either lived in the Cove or were moving there soon. Now they only had to work on getting Adele back into town, and they'd all be home.

With one more backward glance at Mum in Athol's arms, staring at the brilliant sunset, Sarah hurried into the living room and sat at Mick's feet. He massaged her shoulders and she warmed beneath his touch. He was her husband, and that thought filled her with such a sense of peace, satisfaction, and security that she couldn't do anything but grin.

THE END

* * *

Want to read more about your Emerald Cove favourites?

How about MEG & BRAD FALLING IN LOVE?
Find out how they fell hard and fast in an exclusive bonus scene from the first book...
TAP HERE: Give me this scene now please!

Need to catch up?...
COTTAGE ON OCEANVIEW LANE (BOOK 1)
Begin the Emerald Cove duet for more of this heartwarming series & endearing characters...

TAP HERE: I want the first book in the series

Try the USA Today bestselling Waratah Inn series
THE WARATAH INN (BOOK 1)
Wrested back to Cabarita Beach by her grandmother's sudden death, Kate Summer discovers a mystery buried in the past that changes everything.

TAP HERE: I want this book

KEEP READING for an excerpt from **The Waratah Inn**...

Sign up to my newsletter to stay informed about writing news and upcoming releases.

EXCERPT: THE WARATAH INN

CHAPTER ONE

BRISBANE

The wind clutched at Kate Summer's straight, brown hair blowing it in wild bursts around her head and into her green eyes. The ferry lurched forward. She grabbed onto a cold, metal handrail with one hand and held her flyaway hair against her neck with the other. Then she stepped through the doorway and into the City Ferry cabin. The rush of wind in her ears quieted, replaced by the dull murmur of conversation between commuters as they huddled together in clumps throughout the cabin.

The Kangaroo Point terminal faded out of sight behind them as the ferry chugged across the sluggish, brown Brisbane River toward the city centre. Kate tugged her coat tighter around her body and inhaled a steadying breath through her reddened nose. It'd once been smattered with freckles, but time had faded them to a pale remnant of their former selves.

Sighing, she sank into one of the hard chairs that were lined up like so many church pews, smoothed her hair with one hand as best she could, and set her purse on the empty seat beside her.

She had to get to work on time today. Marco was stressed out about the new menu. He'd called her at home to tell her he wasn't entirely convinced it was a good idea to take the restaurant in a new direction, what with the economic climate the way it was. She reminded him the economic climate was fine and it was the perfect time to try something new, as they'd discussed a hundred times over the past six months. That he'd named her head chef at the *Orchid* for a reason and should listen to her ideas.

He'd agreed and hung up. But she'd heard the tension in his voice. He hated change. She knew that well enough, having worked for him for five years. But five years of creating food that was expected, safe, the same as it had always been, was more than enough for her. If he didn't want to make the change, then she would. Her creative spirit itched for something different.

The ferry pulled to a stop, growling back and forth until its ramp lined up with the dock. When she stepped onto solid ground, she couldn't help one wistful glance back at the river. She missed the water. The ocean had been like a second home to her once. She'd spent so much of her teenage years diving under the waves, floating on her back, and staring up at the sky on a calm day, or surfing the break when the wind was up. But since she didn't live near the beach these days, she had to make do with the river. It wasn't the same but paddling a kayak or riding the ferry brought a measure of peace.

By the time she reached the restaurant, she'd already run over the menu again in her mind and was convinced they were doing the right thing by reinvigorating their offerings. It was fresh, unique, delicious — it would bring diners into the restaurant in droves. She was sure of it.

Or it would drive them away.

Her stomach tightened at the thought of what Marco would say if it didn't work the way she hoped it would. Reputation was everything for a chef, and in a small city like Brisbane, failures weren't something you could hide.

"'Morning chef." Her Sous Chef greeted her with a warm smile. "Ready to change the world?"

She chuckled. "Ready as I'll ever be."

Fresh groceries from the market lined one of the bench tops along the wall. She always placed her orders the day before. Fresh produce, direct from the farmers, was the best way to make delicious meals, and the write-ups she'd received so far in the local newspapers showed it. She'd sent one review to Nan.

What she really wanted to do was drive down to Cabarita and bring Nan back with her, so her grandmother could taste the food for herself. Not that she was such a big fan of Asian fusion cuisine. Nan preferred her meat and three veg, like most Australians of her generation. Still, Kate wanted her to see the restaurant, see the career she'd built for herself over the past decade. She was proud of what she'd achieved and wanted someone to share that with.

Just thinking of Nan and the inn put a twist in her gut. She hadn't been back to see Nan in months, and when she'd gone the last time she'd only visited briefly. Nan had made her promise to stay longer on the next trip, but with everything she had going on, the visit never happened.

If the new menu didn't work out, Kate would have plenty of time on her hands to visit Nan and the Waratah Inn. Maybe she'd be a permanent guest there. She shook her head, her pulse accelerating as worry over the future, her career, and personal life washed over her again. She was used to it, this anxiety. It clogged her thoughts, put knots in her gut and sent waves of adrenaline coursing through her veins.

The new menu *had* to work. It was the first time Marco had given her complete control over what they'd serve. If people didn't like it, he might never offer her the chance again.

She wasn't ready to concede defeat and move in with her grandmother yet. But a holiday, a beach holiday, was a great idea. Davis had been bugging her about getting away together, away from the city and their crazy, hectic schedules, ever since he proposed six months earlier. She'd suggest it when she saw him that night after work. They often met up late for a light meal, since she worked when most people were done for the day. He didn't like it, but what could she do? It was her career. He'd said they should take a vacation, but they hadn't spoken of it since. Perhaps it was time to raise the subject together. They could both do with some time off. And more than that, she missed Nan.

Keep reading...

ALSO BY LILLY MIRREN

THE WARATAH INN SERIES

The Waratah Inn

Wrested back to Cabarita Beach by her grandmother's sudden death, Kate Summer discovers a mystery buried in the past that changes everything.

One Summer in Italy

Reeda leaves the Waratah Inn and returns to Sydney, her husband, and her thriving interior design business, only to find her marriage in tatters. She's lost sight of what she wants in life and can't recognise the person she's become.

The Summer Sisters

Set against the golden sands and crystal clear waters of Cabarita Beach three sisters inherit an inn and discover a mystery about their grandmother's past that changes everything they thought they knew about their family...

Christmas at The Waratah Inn

Liz Cranwell is divorced and alone at Christmas. When her friends convince her to holiday at The Waratah Inn, she's dreading her first Christmas on her own. Instead she discovers that strangers can be the balm to heal the wounds of a lonely heart in this heartwarming Christmas story.

EMERALD COVE SERIES

Cottage on Oceanview Lane

When a renowned book editor returns to her roots, she rediscovers her strength & her passion in this heartwarming novel.

Seaside Manor Bed & Breakfast

The Seaside Manor Bed and Breakfast has been an institution in Emerald Cove for as long as anyone can remember. But things are changing and Diana is nervous about what the future might hold for her and her husband, not to mention the historic business.

GLOSSARY OF TERMS

Dear reader,

Since this book is set in Australia there may be some terms you're not familiar with. I've included them below to help you out! I hope they didn't trip you up too much.

Cheers, Lilly xo

Terms

Afternoon tea - afternoon snack

Bin - trash can

Biscuits - Crackers or cookies (could be either)

Boot - car trunk

Coppers - police officers

Crawler - teacher's pet

Cuppa - a cup of tea or coffee

For a lark - as a joke, or for fun

"Love" - a term of endearment for friends and lovers alike

Tea - used to describe either a hot beverage made from leaves, or the evening meal

Unit - apartment or condo
Mobile - cell phone
Morning tea - morning snack
Nippy - cold
Proby - Probationary Constable
Sarge - Sergeant
Smoko - taking a break from work
Tea - a hot drink or the evening meal
Tea towel - dish towel
Thongs - flip flops
Tying the knot - getting married
Unit - apartment

ABOUT THE AUTHOR

Lilly Mirren lives in Brisbane, Australia with her husband and three children.

Lilly always dreamed of being a writer and is now living that dream. She is a graduate of both the University of Queensland, where she studied International Relations and Griffith University, where she completed a degree in Information Technology.

When she's not writing, she's chasing her children, doing housework or spending time with friends.

Sign up for her newsletter and stay up on all the latest Lilly book news.

And follow her on:

Website: lillymirren.com
Facebook: https://www.facebook.com/authorlillymirren/
Twitter: https://twitter.com/lilly_mirren
BookBub: https://www.bookbub.com/authors/lilly-mirren

CPSIA information can be obtained
at www.ICGtesting.com
Printed in the USA
LVHW082040151120
671781LV00030B/475